BLACK LIST

HOT Heroes for Hire: Mercenaries - A Black's Bandits Novel

LYNN RAYE HARRIS

Printed in the United States of America

First Printing, 2019

For rights inquires, visit www.LynnRayeHarris.com

Black List

ISBN: 978-1-941002-43-8

Prologue

Seven years ago…

IT WAS TIME TO GO. If he stayed any longer, he wouldn't survive the night. He had to disappear before they made him disappear. He shouldered his backpack, yanked up his hood, and strode into the Moscow night. He left his apartment behind, all his belongings. He would never see them again.

Nikolai Orlov knew how to disappear, but he also knew it wouldn't be easy. They were watching him. Waiting.

They thought he didn't know it, but he did. After all he'd done for them. Two years in the army before he'd been recruited to the *Spetsnatz.* He'd spent five years as an elite soldier, doing whatever needed to be done. Following orders, working his way to better pay and more challenging assignments. He'd given them everything he had. His best.

Because Mother Russia demanded it. Because his parents demanded it. Because they'd already given everything they had, including him. He'd had no choice in the matter. No say at all. So he'd adapted, and he'd excelled.

It wasn't enough. No matter how hard he'd worked, how loyal he'd been. He knew that now. They were coming for him. Betrayal was a bitter pill to swallow.

The night was wet with rain, chilly. It was September, not quite time for the snow to start, though it would soon. Nikolai didn't look over his shoulder, but his finely honed sixth sense told him someone was there. Following him.

Well, he would lose them. Or he would battle them. Either way, he was getting out of here. North to St. Petersburg, then to the waiting ship where he would stow away and be carried to Finland. *If* his contact had come through.

He thought of the American with the intense eyes who'd approached him. He knew who Ian Black was. Everyone in the special services knew the American who seemed to be a law unto himself. When you wanted the difficult things done, you called Ian Black. For a price, he would get it done—whatever it was. The man was a precision instrument, not a sledgehammer. When you wanted a surgical strike, you called the American.

When Ian had approached him four days ago, he'd thought it was a set up. The nail in his coffin, as it were. Until Ian began to talk about Nikolai's parents. He knew things about them, and he claimed to owe them a debt. He planned to repay it by saving Nikolai.

Nikolai still wasn't sure it was real, but he'd follow the plan until he couldn't anymore.

Behind him, there was noise. In front of him, a shape stepped out of an alley and made its way toward him. Weaving as if drunk. Nikolai didn't believe it for an instant. He braced himself, prepared to act. The shape got closer, the man beginning to sing drunkenly. Behind him, the tempo of footsteps picked up. They were going to crush him between them like a pincer closing. He darted his gaze to the left and right—and then he stopped in the middle of the sidewalk. The drunk hesitated but kept moving. The man behind him kept moving too. Honestly, the fellow had the footsteps of one whose feet were made of stone.

Nikolai waited. He couldn't cross the street because there was no sidewalk on the opposite side here. And the cars zipped past too quickly to make it safe. He would have to fight. He dropped the backpack, shoved his hood down and turned sideways, adopting a fighter's stance.

The two men stopped. The one behind him pulled a weapon and pointed it at him. "You will come with us, Nikolai Alexandrovich Orlov."

"Why?"

"Because you are under arrest for treason."

Nikolai's insides froze. "Treason? What is it I have done?"

"You can discuss that with the FSB."

The FSB was the equivalent of the old KGB, and just as frightening. "I'd be happy to. But first you have to catch me."

The man with the gun snorted. "I think we have already caught you. You plan to outrun a bullet, eh?"

Nikolai threw a glance at the man who'd pretended to be drunk. He seemed familiar somehow…

And then it hit him. Nikolai nearly laughed. Instead, he took a step back. "Maybe I do," he said, his confidence flaring to life again. If he was right…

The drunk was stone cold sober now. He pulled a weapon and motioned Nikolai in his direction. Nikolai picked up his bag and went to the man's side. The other man was laughing. But he didn't laugh for long. Nikolai took the weapon from the drunk, then spun and put two bullets in the other man's chest. He dropped onto the pavement.

"Better get to St. Petersburg. That ship won't wait."

Nikolai turned the butt of the pistol toward his savior. "Thank you."

"Don't thank me," Ian Black said, shoving the pistol beneath his jacket. "Get the hell out of here. We'll talk in a couple of weeks."

"You were with him," Nikolai said, nudging his chin toward the body on the sidewalk. "What happens when his bosses figure out you betrayed him?"

Ian snorted as he started to walk backward. "Figure out I betrayed him? Not the way it works. Now get moving before that ship leaves port."

Nikolai watched Ian retreat. He shot a glance at the body on the sidewalk, wondering if Ian was going to do anything about it or leave it to be discovered.

Not your problem.

No, it wasn't. Nikolai tugged his hood into place against the cold rain. Then he disappeared into the night.

Chapter One

"Schatz, was ist los? Aufwachen, aufwachen…"

Jace Kaiser jerked awake as the German girl he'd taken back to his hotel room last night shook him from his dreams. The memory of men in dark suits, rough hands yanking him from his bed, faded as he stared wide-eyed at the ceiling. Cold sweat prickled across his skin. The girl nestled in beside him again, lips soft on his neck as she whispered words of comfort. He'd welcomed those lips earlier. Now…

Now he just wanted to escape.

It was a dream that had disturbed him. The *same* fucking dream as always. But he wasn't ten years old anymore, and the FBI hadn't burst through the door to arrest his parents and change the course of his life. He'd been a regular kid until that moment—and then everything changed. His identity, his allegiances, his entire world.

His stomach rolled at the memories of armed men in black and he sat up, gently pushing the girl away when she clung to him.

"Was ist los?" she asked again. *What's the matter?*

"Nothing," he said, his voice rusty. Goddammit, he needed to get over this shit. It was over two decades in the past, and he wasn't the same person anymore.

Jace swung his legs over the side of the bed and reached for his clothing. He dressed quickly. The girl—what was her name again? Ingrid? Inga?—flipped on the light. He glanced at her. She was lovely. Long limbs, pale gold hair, blue eyes, pink cheeks. She let the sheet fall, exposing her pretty breasts, but he wasn't tempted. Not a second time.

"I've got to go," he told her in German, grabbing the carryon he'd never unpacked. He dropped the keycard on the pillow beside her. "Stay until morning. Order room service. It's paid for."

Her expression fell. "Will I see you again, Jack?"

It wasn't his real name. Hell, he didn't even have a name. The name he'd had until the age of ten was a lie. So was every name since—which meant Jace Kaiser was as good as any and at least he'd picked that one himself.

"Probably not," he told her. "I'm not often in Berlin." And then, because her lip quivered, he bent to kiss her one last time. "You're lovely. I had a great time."

Jace strode from the room, taking his phone out

and dialing a taxi as he did so. He'd already met with his contact earlier in the day. He'd sent the information back to HQ as soon as he had it. The mission was a success and there was no reason to stay. He'd only done so because Ian Black had insisted that he needed some R & R.

Well, he was done with that shit. It didn't help and he wasn't the idle kind. Jace stopped at the desk and told them he was leaving but the girl in his room would be there until morning. They didn't argue with him. He hadn't expected they would. They were paid not to. Jace went outside and stood in the cold pre-dawn air, waiting for his taxi. He was on alert, as always, because it was his nature. But there was nothing suspicious and no one who set off any alarm bells. The taxi came and Jace climbed inside.

"Der Flughafen, bitte," he told the man.

"Ja, mein Herr."

Jace turned his head, watched the city slide by. Why was he having that dream again? He always had it, but he sometimes went for months—years at one point—without it. So why was he thinking about the FBI and the way his world had flipped upside down one dark night when his parents turned out not to be who he'd always thought they were?

But then he hadn't been who he'd thought he was either. Jace shoved a hand through his hair, yanking on the ends to cause himself pain. If he had some pain, maybe he'd stop this mental journey before he reached the end. Before he recalled all that had happened to him and his family in the years since.

He picked up his phone and sent a quick text to Ian Black, founder of Black Defense International and legendary badass in the Spec Ops community. Ian answered within seconds—as if he weren't running a multi-layered covert organization with operations around the globe that required all his time and attention.

Thought you were planning some fun before you came back?

Jace frowned. How did Ian always know when something was wrong? *Had fun. I'm done.*

All work and no play. It'll catch up with you one day.

Look who's talking, Jace fired back.

Ian didn't answer for a few moments. But then he did, and Jace nearly snorted. *Yeah, fine. Something's come up anyway. Might have a job for you.*

Relief rolled through him. He liked being busy. Needed to be busy. It kept the demons in his head from catching up with him. *I'm ready.*

Come straight to HQ when you get in. But only if you feel up to it.

If he felt up to it? Hell yes, he would feel up to it. Even if it was two in the morning and he'd been traveling for twenty-four hours straight. He didn't know any other way to be. Stillness was death. He had to keep moving, keep searching, keep acting—or he'd wither and die.

I'll be there, boss.

IT WAS late afternoon when Jace Kaiser approached Black Defense International's Washington, DC headquarters and entered the elevator. Ian Black knew that Jace had arrived because an alert popped up whenever anyone entered the premises. More than that, the system quickly identified which agent it was, informing Ian who to expect. He spun his chair around to gaze at the camera feed from the elevator, searching Jace's expression for a hint to his mood.

Jace Kaiser was one of his best men, but Ian knew that part of what made the man so good could also destroy him in time. There were days when Ian wasn't quite sure if Jace was what he seemed, but Ian had taken a chance several years ago and he hadn't regretted it yet.

Ian kicked back in his chair and waited. Presently, after Jace had cleared the handprint and eye scans necessary to enter, he strode into BDI's state-of-the-art nerve center. Ian waited, watching the man approach through the glass walls of his office. They made eye contact and Ian nodded. Jace opened the door and stood tall in the entry. "Hey, boss. How you doing?"

Ian eyed the younger man critically. Jace was under strain lately. But Ian understood the kind of strain that required more work, not less. He dropped the pen he'd been tapping on the desk. "Doing good. Thanks for the quick work in Berlin, by the way. We intercepted the shipment two hours ago."

Jace seemed to relax. "That's a relief. Last thing we need is more weapons in the hands of terrorists."

"Truth." Ian tipped his chin. "Come in and close the door."

Jace did as instructed, then strolled over and dropped into a chair opposite Ian. "So what's this potential new job?"

"It's gone beyond potential in the past few hours…" Ian hesitated. Not because he didn't trust Jace, but he was still weighing options on whether or not he could send someone else. "We might have a lead on Calypso."

As expected, Jace's eyebrows lifted. "How is that possible? We never know where she's going until it's too late."

"True… But this time there's chatter. Might be wrong, but it might be right."

If it *were* true, it was pretty damned important. Jace knew it as well as he did. Calypso was the *nom de plume* of an assassin that had caused a lot of trouble over the past couple of years. She had appeared out of seemingly nowhere, and she'd taken out targets that Ian would have preferred she did not. He could admire her skill, but he'd often wished they weren't on opposing sides. She sometimes reminded him of his former employee Victoria Royal, though without the scruples Victoria possessed. Vic had been a hell of a sniper for BDI before she'd fallen in love and gone over to the Hostile Operations Team, a Top Secret military unit that was run by the enigmatic Colonel

John Mendez. There were days when Ian still hated that he'd lost her to Mendez's crew.

"Leonid Sokolov is having a big party at his summer estate near St. Petersburg in two days. It's his fiftieth birthday and he's pulling out all the stops. It's rumored that Putin might even make an appearance. I've received credible intel that Calypso is targeting Sokolov and plans to attack at the party. I'll be honest—I'm not sure what to make of the information in spite of the credibility. But it's coming from more than one source, which tells me there's something to it."

Jace was frowning. He understood the significance as much as Ian did. "Then why is Sokolov putting himself out there? He could cancel the party."

"He could. But he won't. He doesn't think anyone can penetrate his circle. He's got heavy security—plus he's one of those macho men who doesn't want anyone to think they can threaten him and get away with it."

Jace's eye roll wasn't unexpected. "What do you need me to do?"

This was the part Ian didn't like. He usually sent Jace to Russia when nobody else could do the job as well as he could, but Ian wasn't unaware of the mental toll it took. There might be a breaking point, but Ian was fairly certain today wasn't it. He made a decision. "I need you there in case it's accurate. There's a rumor the Gemini Syndicate wants Sokolov dead. Sending in an assassin like Calypso is something they would do."

The Gemini Syndicate was the informal name for a cabal that stretched around the world, comprised of very wealthy men and their pursuit of geopolitical outcomes that favored them. Mostly, they seemed to want the world in chaos so they could control more of it. The consensus in the intelligence community was that their name came from the zodiac sign. Mercury, the ruling planet of Gemini, was the god of tricksters.

It was a nice theory, but Ian had a better one. When the United States was racing to be first on the moon in the sixties, Gemini was the name of the many missions that tested all the variables before the successful Apollo moon landing. The moon was the goal, and Gemini was the test. Ergo, the Gemini Syndicate was testing variables before the landing.

But what was the landing? He had no idea, but he intended to find out—and prevent it from happening.

"Any idea why they want him dead?" Jace asked.

"Not yet. Might have something to do with the oil fields in Siberia. Sokolov refuses to sell, but if he's dead then presumably his heirs could be negotiated with. He has a twenty year-old daughter and she seems more interested in partying in Europe than running her father's empire. Could also be the arms deal he's reportedly negotiating with Pakistan—Boris Medved is a rival for that deal, and it might be him who hired Calypso. In truth, there's no shortage of people who aren't happy with Sokolov. But he has his uses, which means I need you to stop Calypso."

Leonid Sokolov might be a bastard, but he was

also a covert asset for the United States Government. The man's loyalties were to himself, which is why he had no problem informing on issues affecting the US. Since Sokolov could be useful from time to time, Ian's directive was specific—keep the man alive.

"Capture or kill?" Jace asked, his voice devoid of emotion. Like a good operative.

"Preferably capture. It'd be nice to find out what she knows about Gemini—but if you have to kill her, then kill her." Ian reached for the folder he'd left lying closed on his desk. Inside was a photo. He handed it to Jace. "It's grainy, but this is the best visual we've ever gotten on her. It was taken at Domodedovo Airport in Moscow yesterday. Our facial recognition software says it's a match to prior photos, but there's always an element of uncertainty, especially since we've never gotten a direct view. Still, intel believes it's her."

Jace studied the picture. Ian had done the same, so he knew what Jace saw. Long, wavy hair that was either brown or black. Sunglasses perched over a small nose. A white top beneath a navy blazer, artfully ripped jeans, and high-heeled ankle boots. She carried a Louis Vuitton briefcase and pulled a wheeled carryon. Ian had tried to find who she could be, but there was some information he couldn't access no matter how he tried. Complete flight manifests into and out of Domodedovo, for instance.

"Doesn't look like the face of an assassin, does it?"

Jace mused. "More like a spoiled socialite or an A-list actress."

"That's what makes her so good." He pushed the remainder of the file toward Jace. "Study it. Memorize it. I need you on a plane in twenty-four hours."

Jace took the folder, jaw set in determination. "I'll get her, boss."

Chapter Two

Dr. Madeline Cole jerked awake as the car came to a halt. Her eyes were blurry and she wondered for a moment where she was. Then she remembered.

Today was Friday and this was Russia. Specifically, St. Petersburg. Well, not quite St. Petersburg, as she'd left that city behind once the car picked her up. Now she was somewhere along the coast, where the land met the icy waters of the Gulf of Finland. She'd been in Russia since yesterday, but her sleep was all screwed up and cat naps were a thing.

"We're here, miss," the driver said.

"Thank you," Maddy replied, sitting up and reaching for her computer case.

The driver, who was way too sunny, jumped out of the car and came around to open her door. Then he got her suitcase out of the trunk while she wobbled on the pavement in front of the very large house they'd pulled up to.

There was a lot of activity, with delivery vans and cars coming and going. She turned to take in her surroundings. There was a long drive, with a high black wrought-iron fence and secure gates they must have passed through while she was dozing. A man with a not-so-subtle assault rifle checked each vehicle that came in.

"Mr. Sokolov's birthday party is tonight, yes?" her driver said as he came to her side. "You have come at a very exciting time, miss."

Maddy smiled. "Yes, I suppose I have."

They went inside the big house. A small man with a cool stare greeted them. His gaze raked her from head to toe, as if he were looking for fault. "You are from the insurance company? The art appraiser?"

"Yes, I am," Maddy said. She gave him a smile. She was used to this song and dance with clients and their staff from time to time. She was thirty-one, but men in particular seemed to take her for someone much younger. Or maybe it was just the fact she was female. How could she possibly be an expert on art, particularly Russian religious art?

"I will show you to your quarters. Mr. Sokolov would like you to begin as soon as possible."

Maddy lifted her computer case. "That's what I'm here for."

The man, whose name was Sergey, led her to a somewhat luxurious room in one of the wings of the house. The view left her speechless. Outside the windows, the Gulf of Finland sparkled in the distance. In the garden, there were fountains and a large tent being set up for the party. It was late May, and warm enough for an outdoor event.

Besides, it would never get fully dark. The sky would stay light, like dusk, even at darkest midnight. The horizon would remain white and St. Petersburg in particular would stay alive around the clock. It was a beautiful time to be in Russia. She'd hoped to spend some time on the Nevsky Prospekt, enjoying the sites and revelry that went with the White Nights—but first she had to finish this job.

Sergey left her with a map and told her where to start and how to reach him if there were any problems. Not the most orthodox way to begin, but whatever. Working for Barrington's of New York, she'd encountered plenty of eccentric art collectors over the past six years.

The man with the collection of Oriental sex art, for instance. He'd kept it in a locked interior room and stood far too close while she catalogued his treasures for insurance purposes. Well, he *had* stood too close, until the moment she'd accidentally-on-purpose turned and elbowed him in the kidney. Personal safety training was paramount in this business if she wanted to keep doing her job and not worry what might happen with a grabby collector.

It pissed her off sometimes though. Did the male appraisers she worked with have to undergo the same treatment when they walked into a billionaire's estate to catalogue and appraise artworks? Probably not.

Maddy went into the attached bathroom to splash cold water on her face and comb her hair. When she was satisfied she looked presentable—and felt awake enough—she took her computer and camera and followed the map to the room on the first floor where Sergey had told her to start. The house was large, a mix of modern styling and eighteenth century gilded artwork and furniture. Almost like someone wasn't quite sure which style they preferred.

Not that it was up to her, but she thought it came from too much money and not enough taste to choose a style. Personally, her style these days was flea market—whatever she could get cheap and make work. Her job might seem glamorous, but with Mimi in the memory care facility, it took everything Maddy could spare to make up the difference between Mimi's social security and the exorbitant monthly fees the facility charged.

Hence the reason she accepted these assignments and endured long hours on airplanes.

Maddy took out her laptop and set it on a table, opening the lid and powering it up. The room had four large oil paintings that appeared to be sixteenth century Italian. Maddy scrolled through her files until she found the ones she was looking for. Paintings of this nature always had a paper trail, thankfully. She would verify the details and double check the documents. Provided her assessment agreed with the paperwork and prior appraisals, Barrington's would insure the collection.

She decided the order in which she would work, then went over to the first painting to study it. She'd just taken out her laser measuring device when a tall man walked into the room.

She knew immediately that he was Leonid Sokolov. She'd seen him on the news more than once, and in various journals. He was an oligarch, one of a handful of very rich men in Russia who controlled much of the resources. Sokolov's wealth had come from oil, but now he was involved in many other industries as well. There were rumors about him, including some unsavory ones about illegal weapons sales and deals with the Russian mafia.

"You are from Barrington's?"

"Yes, sir. I'm Dr. Madeline Cole."

He eyed her. "Your Russian is good. Where did you learn it?"

"*Spesiba.* I learned it in school. High school and college." Mostly. She'd also learned some of it from her dad, who'd been a linguist in the military. He hadn't been home often, but when he was, he'd taught her words and phrases. "My specialty is Russian art," she added.

Sokolov would have been told that, but she found that rich people often didn't remember those kinds of details about lowly art appraisers.

"Russian art? Then you should see my icons. They are truly spectacular. Come, I will show you."

Maddy hesitated. But if she didn't go with him, then he might take it as an insult. On the other hand, what if *I wanna show you my icons* meant what it usually meant when a man said something about showing off a collection?

"Just let me get my equipment, sir." That should at least tell him she was expecting to work, not indulge any whims he might have about her.

"Certainly."

Maddy gathered her things and followed Sokolov to what appeared to be his office. It was a large room with a huge picture window that looked out over the same view as her room. Sokolov went over to a wall paneled in wood and a small door opened beneath his hand. Then he tapped in a code and there was the pneumatic sound of pressure releasing before a full door appeared in the paneling. Sokolov pulled it open and disappeared inside. Maddy stood with her heart in her throat, wondering if he expected her to follow him.

He reappeared with a small item wrapped in black velvet. He came over and laid it down on the table in front of her before reverently peeling the velvet away. A wooden icon painted with bright golds, deepest cobalt, and red carmine gleamed up at her.

She must have gasped because he smiled. "It is truly spectacular, yes?"

"Yes," she breathed. It was a representation of the transfiguration of Christ, and probably dated to the sixteenth century. She'd know more when she studied it and did some research.

"There are more."

"I can't wait to see them."

He lifted an eyebrow. "Look around you."

Maddy blinked and looked up. There were glass cases inset into the walls, displaying a selection of icons that ranged in size. She'd been so wowed by the icon, and by the appearance of the secret door, that she'd missed the rest at first.

A phone rang and Sokolov grumbled. He reached into his pocket and pulled it out. "*Da?*" he barked. "Give me a few moments."

He pocketed the phone again. "You will need to excuse me, Dr. Cole. Business calls." He took out a key and gave it to her. "This will open the cases."

"I... You wish me to start in here, then?"

"Yes. But if you are tempted to make off with any of my icons, it would be a very bad idea. I would not take such a thing kindly."

Maddy was indignant. "I'm a professional, Mr. Sokolov. I would never do such a thing."

His expression didn't soften. "Yes, well I find that people do not always know themselves as well as they think they do. *Dosvedanya,* Dr. Cole."

Maddy shook her head as he disappeared through the door. She might be broke, but she wasn't stupid. She took out her camera, set up her computer, and got to work.

JACE ALWAYS HAD MIXED emotions about working

in Russia. When he'd left a few years ago, he'd never expected to ever return. But working for Ian Black meant that you never knew where you were going, and that you often went places you were convinced were off limits for you. He often wondered, when he operated in Russia, if he'd ever come face to face with an old acquaintance. He didn't expect they'd know him even if he did. He was no longer the man he'd once been.

Jace took a sip of the sparkling water he'd picked up at one of the open bars set up around Leonid Sokolov's vast gardens and let his gaze roam the crowd. He recognized many of the glitterati as they mingled in the evening sunlight. No sign of Putin—or of Calypso. Not that she would look precisely as she had in the airport photo, but Jace had a good eye for faces and he knew what he was looking for.

Tonight he was Andrei Shevchenko, a Ukrainian arms dealer looking to increase his business and take it to the next level. Jace didn't know how Ian had worked his magic so quickly, but that's what he always did. Passport, IDs, photos of Jace with prominent businessmen, a wife and kid back home. The dossier was so complete that all Jace had to do was slip into Shevchenko's skin like a coat and observe.

Sokolov was well-guarded, but that didn't mean Calypso wouldn't try to get to him. Everyone coming through the gates had been searched before passing through metal detectors. Supposedly, the only people with weapons were those who were authorized to have them. But since Jace had a Sig tucked into his waistband beneath his tuxedo jacket, he knew it was possible to smuggle a gun inside in spite of security checks.

Calypso might try something besides shooting Sokolov. Poison. She could deliver it with a needle jab, or sprinkle it into a drink. She could also slip into the kitchen and grab a knife, but that would be a little too obvious for an assassin like her. She wasn't on a suicide mission, which is what it would be to strike Sokolov so obviously. If she took him down from close quarters, with his guards around him, she likely wouldn't survive.

And that's not the kind of woman she was. Calypso had left a trail of bodies in her wake, from Beijing to Moscow to London and DC and LA—and everywhere in between. She wasn't going to risk her skin to get near Sokolov. Which meant she had a plan of some kind if she were really here.

Sokolov stood nearby with several fawning guests, a gaudy diamond ring glittering as the lights of the garden refracted off the facets. Though it was nearing ten p.m., it was still daylight. The sun would not sink fully below the horizon at this time of year. The party would very likely continue until dawn. That was one thing Jace had loved about St. Petersburg when he'd lived there. The White Nights, lasting from May until July, were truly spectacular, as were the parties and activities. Watching the bridges go up on the Neva while the boats passed through at two in the morning. Walking the Nevsky Prospekt with friends.

But that life was gone, and right this minute he was Andrei Shevchenko. Tomorrow he would be someone else. Jace studied the people around Sokolov. The women especially. None of them were Calypso. It was entirely possible the information had been false, even though it came from more than one trusted source. It was also possible she was biding her time.

Jace began to walk, circling the gardens and talking to various guests when they waylaid him. Women stopped him more often than men. Soft hands, soft smiles, greedy eyes. Suggestions of finding somewhere to be alone for a while.

As much as he might like to do so with some of them, he was working. He declined with regretful words and kept moving.

"Damn, kid, you've had more offers of ass than a chair."

Jace almost snorted at Ian's voice in his ear. "I'm a married man," Jace replied in Russian, knowing that Ian would understand. Ian understood everything. The man had a talent for languages beyond anyone Jace knew.

"This time," Ian said with a laugh. "I'm assuming there's no sign of our target?"

"Nope. Could have been a ruse, don't you think?"

"Yeah, I've thought that. But it was credible enough to send you."

"Well, it's not over yet. This party will go on for a

while. Our host is tossing back vodka shots like a frat boy at a kegger. I predict somebody's getting naked in the fountain in an hour or so."

Ian was still laughing. "It's hilarious to hear you talk about keg parties in Russian."

"Just because I was never a college boy in America doesn't mean I'm not acquainted with the custom." He'd never been a college boy in America because that life had been ripped away from him. He wasn't bitter anymore, but he had been for a while. Not at the college part, but at life in general. At not being who he'd thought he was and having to learn a whole new language and customs. It hadn't been easy to be the only American kid in a Russian school. An American kid who didn't even speak basic Russian. They'd taunted him, bullied him. Made him tougher, or so his father always said.

Well, yeah, he was tough all right. So tough he sometimes thought he'd forgotten how to feel anything but the harder emotions. If not for Ian, God knows what would have happened to him.

"Hey," Ian said, softer this time, "I didn't mean to touch a nerve."

"You didn't," he lied. Because Ian would never do that. Unless it served a purpose, which it didn't right now. He'd hit on that nerve hard and often when he'd first brought Jace into the fold. He'd had to because he'd needed to know if Jace would break.

Jace never broke. Never would. He'd die for Ian Black. Not for America, not for Russia, not for patriotism or apple pie or rightness. For the man who'd saved him. That was his line in the sand.

"You're my best operative," Ian said. "That's why it had to be you."

Pride bubbled inside him. "I do my best, boss."

Somebody let out a howl and Jace jerked toward the sound. It was Sokolov, standing on a pillar and performing an air guitar riff while *Sweet Home Alabama* played in the background.

Oh, the irony. Still, Jace didn't like that the man was so exposed.

"Something happening?" Ian asked.

"Yeah, Lynyrd Skynyrd is happening."

"Do I even want to know?"

"Not really. Let's just say that Sokolov sings with a heavy accent and leave it at that." The security detail got him off the pillar so he was no longer exposed. Jace shook his head at the arrogance of billionaires.

Ian snorted in his ear. "All right, buddy. Have a good time."

"You leaving me, boss?"

"Nah, I'll be here. Just gonna hand you off to one of the techs for a bit. If anything happens, I'll be back on."

"You enjoy your whiskey. I'll be here until my ears bleed," Jace grumbled.

"Sorry, man. Perks of being in charge."

"Yeah, yeah, whatever." Jace retreated into the shadows of the garden to study the terrain and guests. Sokolov shouted something at the DJ. A moment later,

Lynyrd Skynyrd spun up into *Sweet Home Alabama* again and several guests joined the oligarch in howling and playing air guitars.

Jace groaned. Man, it was gonna be a long night. Ian owed him one if this was all that went on for the next several hours…

Chapter Three

THE MUSIC FROM THE GARDEN WAS LOUD, BUT Sokolov's office had fairly good insulation. Maddy looked up every once in a while at the noise, but mostly she kept herself busy with cataloguing the icons. There were at least a hundred of them, and she'd made it through approximately half. Leonid Sokolov had good taste in art, at least where Russian icons were concerned. But he was filthy rich and could afford it.

Her dad had brought home replicas for her when she'd been a kid. It was illegal to export real icons more than a hundred years old from Russia, but the tourist trade was filled with copies and her dad bought them for her because she'd liked them so much. There was just something about the flat figures with the burnished halos and bright gold backgrounds that fascinated her. They were so beautiful, so ornate, and they were unique in that they were meant to be displayed in even the most modest of homes. Every religious home would have had an icon. Most were small and portable, though some were much larger and meant to adorn churches and altars.

Maddy finished cataloging the latest icon and set it back in the case. Then she arched her back and twisted her neck from side to side. She picked up the camera and scrolled through the photos she'd taken so far. A red light started blinking in the corner of the display and she fished around in her bag for the extra batteries.

They weren't there. Maddy growled in frustration. They must be in her suitcase. She remembered tossing the extra batteries into her carryon because her computer bag was already packed and sitting by the front door. She'd meant to transfer them at some point, but she'd been traveling and tired and she just hadn't done it.

So now she had to go up to her room and get the batteries before she could continue with the job. Maddy stood and stretched. Maybe walking up the stairs and back again wasn't such a bad thing after all. She'd been sitting for far too long anyway.

She slipped down the hallway and toward the back stairs indicated on the map. She didn't want to run into any of Mr. Sokolov's guests, though he was the one who'd told her to start working today so maybe he wasn't all that concerned with a lowly art appraiser getting mixed up with his very rowdy birthday party.

It had been going on for about two hours now. She'd peeked outside at the lavish event and marveled at the jewels several of the ladies wore. Everyone was so elegant in tuxedos and evening gowns. No one would mistake her for a guest even if she stumbled into their midst. She was wearing black pants, heels, and a silk tank with a black jacket. Her work uniform of sorts. Elegant but understated, like a restaurant hostess or an art auctioneer.

Maddy climbed the stairs and headed down the dark corridor toward her room. A woman in a maid's uniform appeared as Maddy reached her door. She had short dark hair and wore lavish eye makeup that highlighted her features. She was striking.

"Good evening, madam," she said coolly as she twisted her key in the door of the room beside Maddy's, flashing a tattoo of a black and gray mermaid on her inner arm as she did so. It went from the bend of her elbow to her wrist. Maddy wanted to see more, but the woman dropped her arm suddenly as if she was somehow ashamed of her ink, so Maddy didn't ask her about it.

"Good evening," Maddy replied as politely as possible, smiling as she did so.

"Turn down service," the woman said with a smile that didn't quite reach her eyes as she stood beside the door she'd unlocked without opening it. "Will you be staying in now?"

"No, I have work left to do in Mr. Sokolov's office."

"He won't notice if you knock off now. He's drunk."

Maddy blinked. It seemed a rather personal thing to say about one's boss. But she didn't think the maid was wrong about Sokolov. She'd seen him standing on a pillar, playing an air guitar a few minutes ago. Definitely feeling happy.

"No, I'm sure you're right. Still, I'm not tired yet so I'll probably do a little more." It wasn't true. She was tired. But she wanted to finish more of the icons before she called it a night.

"Well, have a good evening then, madam."

"Thank you. You too."

Maddy stepped into her room and went over to her case to rummage for the batteries. The light streaming in the windows was dim like sunset, but soon it would darken to dusk. She found the batteries and set them on the table by the door. Then she went over to the window and gazed out. The party seemed lively as people laughed and talked and ate hors d'oeuvres from passing trays.

She'd been invited to parties like this one, where collectors wanted her to talk at length about the uniqueness of their acquisitions to their rapt guests. She always felt a little icky doing it, but whatever paid the bills. Fortunately, Sokolov had not asked her to attend.

She stood for a while longer, and then she sucked in a breath and prepared to head back downstairs. Fireworks popped remarkably close, making her jump.

She watched for the burst of color in the sky, but nothing happened. The fireworks popped two more times—and then people started to scream. There was a ripple in the garden as people fell and others scrambled to either get to them or get away. They ran in all directions, and it took Maddy a long moment to realize that something wasn't right. There was a door connecting her room with the one beside it and she ran over and twisted the knob. Maybe the maid was still in there and knew what was going on.

But the door wouldn't open and Maddy sprinted for the hallway as the screaming in the garden didn't seem to abate. Was that a helicopter? She stopped in the hall, turning to look in both directions, uncertain if Sokolov's house was under attack or maybe it was part of the entertainment and he was down there laughing his ass off at the way people scrambled. She wouldn't put it past him. People with money did odd things, that's for sure.

A man appeared at the end of the hall. He was tall, with dark hair and a neat beard, and he was dressed in a tuxedo. He seemed to size her up for long moments though in reality it was only a split second before he burst into action, his feet covering the ground between them at lightning speed. Maddy stared at him for a second longer, her brain chattering at her to run. He was coming for her—and she didn't know who he was.

Maddy spun and took off, though she didn't stand a chance because she was wearing high heels and she didn't know the territory well. But why was he running after her anyway? Was Sokolov's house under attack?

She hadn't taken more than a half dozen steps when strong hands closed around her torso, dragging her down to the carpet. His body was hard, solid, though he seemed to take pains not to land on top of her.

"End of the road, Calypso," he growled in her ear, his hot breath sending a shiver down her spine.

What? Maddy's cheek mashed into the carpet. Her breath wheezed in her chest and her heart slammed against her ribs like a frightened bird trying to break free.

He rolled them over and jerked her to her feet while she struggled against him—ineffectually since he didn't seem to be slowed one bit. He spun her to face him while keeping her wrists imprisoned in his hands. Her heart kicked at the anger in his handsome face.

Strong jaw, strong features. Brown hair and beard, blue eyes. He held her hard and tight and her body arched against his as he dragged her in close and searched her face like he was seeking the answer to a question.

"Yes, I've got her," he said to no one. "Copy."

Maddy was confused. And angry. "I… Who are you?" She asked in Russian because that's what he'd been speaking. Too late she thought maybe she should have stuck with English and demanded to be taken to the consulate in St. Petersburg.

"Never mind who I am. Who are you? What's your real name?"

"Real name? Ma-Madeline Cole."

He let her go and she started to breathe a sigh of relief. But then he took a gun from beneath his tuxedo jacket and pointed it at her. Fear washed over her in fresh waves.

"Well, Ma-Madeline Cole, you're coming with me. I've got some people who'd like to talk to you."

Her breath was a solid thing in her throat. She couldn't breathe. Couldn't move. Her personal defense training had included what to do whenever somebody pointed a weapon at her, but for the life of her she couldn't remember. And when she did remember in the next moment, she wasn't certain it was wise. He looked far too big and mean to attack.

He lifted an eyebrow. "Go ahead and try." He'd accurately read her hesitation, which she found terrifying. "It will not go well for you."

"I heard shots," she said. "And screaming. Please tell me no one is hurt."

"Can't do that, Ma-Madeline. You know you got two of your targets."

Maddy squeaked. "What? What are you talking about?"

He took out a cell phone and snapped a picture of her. Then he tapped the screen before pocketing the phone again. He grabbed her arm and whirled her around, pushing her forward. "Move, Calypso. No more talking."

Maddy stood her ground until she couldn't anymore. She took a halting step, and then another and another as he propelled her down the hall. The party was chaos by now. She could hear a helicopter, and people shouting. This man said she'd gotten two of her targets. What did that mean?

Desperation flooded her with panic. "I don't know who you are or what you want from me, but I can't go anywhere with you. I have a job to do, a responsibility. Mr. Sokolov—"

"Sokolov is alive," he growled. "You missed."

He pushed her forward a little harder and she stumbled in her high heels. She didn't fall, but she started asking herself why the hell she'd worn the stupid things anyway. Vanity. Sheer vanity. She wanted to look taller. But height did help, at least a little bit, when she met a new client. Still, she could wish she wasn't wearing them now. She might have gotten away if she'd been able to run when she'd first seen this man.

"Please," she threw over her shoulder. "I don't know what you're talking about. You've got the wrong person!"

They reached a doorway and he shoved it open, revealing a stairwell. "Climb. Now."

Climb? She did as he told her because she had no choice. A dozen thoughts ran through her head all at once—who was he? Who was Calypso? Why did he think she'd shot someone? And where was he taking her? The roof? Was he planning to throw her off it?

She took the last step and he reached over her shoulder to slap the door open like he had at the bottom. Maddy took a deep breath and whirled, stomping down on his instep as she did so. If she could just knock him off balance for a few seconds, she could get down the stairs and maybe lose him in one of the hallways.

He shouted and swore and Maddy seized her chance. She bolted down the first set of stairs. This house had so many rooms—and she knew where the secret room was. It was still open because she'd only stepped away for a few moments, though she'd closed the door to Sokolov's office so no one would wander inside.

She was almost to the landing when the loudest bang she'd ever heard in her life split the stairwell. Her ears rang as plaster sprayed from the wall in front of her. Behind her, the man yelled for her to stop.

She froze as her heart lodged in her throat.

My God, he'd shot at her.

Shot and missed—but he wouldn't next time. She knew he wouldn't. She put her face in her hands and stood there trembling while he grabbed her arm, more gently than she expected, and turned her toward him.

"Cooperate and I won't hurt you."

She barely heard him through the underwater muffling in her ears. She'd shot guns before, but always with ear protection. Maddy nodded and started up the stairs again, her feet aching, her knees trembling. This time she went through the door. They were on the roof.

A helicopter dropped from the sky and skimmed the air in front of them. The man pushed her toward the craft. Rough hands reached out and took her arms, dragging her inside. He got in after her and the craft lifted swiftly from the roof before banking and turning toward—well, she didn't know toward where. All she knew was that she'd been kidnapped by an armed man in a tuxedo who thought she was a woman named Calypso—and that she'd killed people.

The men in the helicopter didn't look at her. Except for the one who'd tackled her. He studied her with gleaming eyes that missed nothing. He intimidated her, but she wasn't going to show it. *Never let them see you sweat* is what Mimi always said. Well, lots of people said it, but Mimi was the one who'd said it to Maddy the most. Usually it was when Maddy was about to do something that scared her, like try out for the dance team or defend her dissertation a few years ago. Back when Mimi still had her wits about her.

Maddy's throat tightened as tears pricked her eyes. Still, she swallowed them down and lifted her chin. She didn't know who this man was or what he wanted from her, but she knew who *she* was. And she wasn't going to let him—any of them—see her sweat. All they had to do was call Barrington's corporate office and they could verify her identity.

But what if they didn't want to? What if that wasn't the point at all? What if they planned to lock her up for crimes she didn't commit?

Maddy shivered and closed her eyes to escape the glare of dislike emanating from the man across from her. *It'll work out, Maddy. He'll realize you aren't who he thinks you are. He'll let you go.*

She wished she could believe it was true.

Chapter Four

There was something about her that wasn't quite right. Jace couldn't put his finger on it precisely, but something niggled at him. He'd expected Calypso to be a good actress. He'd even expected that Russian might not be her first language.

And it wasn't. He could tell because he sensed an accent here and there. An American accent by the sound of it. It was subtle as hell, but it was there—and that was shocking because they'd had no indication Calypso was American. He'd sent her photo to Ian but he hadn't heard anything yet.

It had all happened so fast. One minute he'd been circling the garden, observing the gathering, and the next he'd seen something in a second story window that drew his attention. A window opened and something glinted in the light—then the shots happened and he'd taken off, his focus solely on getting to that room before Calypso could break down and escape.

He'd caught her in the hallway instead. She hadn't been carrying her gun case, but that didn't mean anything. He wasn't there to sweep up behind her. He'd grabbed her and gotten her the hell out of there. Ian had people who would retrieve the weapon and any other evidence.

The helicopter was too noisy to question her about the hit, so he studied her instead. She was lovely, and she made things stir that he wished she didn't. When he'd tackled her, felt the litheness of her body beneath his, he'd almost had a reaction. He was principled enough not to let it happen, but the idea it was there beneath the surface had been a shocking one. This woman was a stone-cold assassin, not a potential hookup.

She was pretty though. Not supermodel gorgeous, but there was something about her that made it hard to look away. A vulnerability he hadn't expected. Calypso was an Oscar-worthy actress to be able to pull that one off. But she had. She *was*.

Her head was turned, her face in profile to him. He swore he saw the sheen of tears in the corner of her eye. Her nose was finely sculpted, like in the photo, and her cheeks flushed with color. His instep still throbbed where she'd stomped him. He'd been surprised she didn't go for his gun. Instead, she'd run—and she hadn't even kicked her shoes off first, which hadn't helped her in the least.

"We have a match," Ian said in his ear. "Facial recognition says there's a ninety-nine percent chance she's the woman from Moscow. Call when you get airborne. And good work, Jace. I never doubted you'd get it done."

"Copy," Jace said. Ian would hear that much, but he wouldn't hear a whole conversation so Jace would wait until they were on the plane and in the air.

The helicopter began to drop in the sky as they reached the private airport outside of St. Petersburg. Jace studied the airfield and the surrounding landscape as best he could in the dim light of late evening. He expected the Gemini Syndicate might anticipate this move so he needed to be prepared. He wished they'd lit the airfield, but it was safer to take off in darkness. The pilots were former military and capable of blind takeoffs and landings when necessary.

This one wasn't going to be blind, though. There was too much light in the sky. A blue and white 737 with no markings sat on the tarmac. Waiting for them to arrive.

The helicopter put down nearby and Jace jumped out. Then he turned and waited for Calypso. He held his hand out as she struggled with the seatbelt. It came free and she shot a wide-eyed look over their surroundings.

"Staying there won't do you any good," he shouted above the rotors. "They'll just toss you out when they reach altitude again."

She put her hand in his. There was a spark of feeling that zapped into him as he clamped down on her hand and pulled her from the craft. Then he hustled her toward the stairway that had been rolled up to the door of the 737. At the top, Colton Duchaine waited. Relief pulsed through Jace at the sight of his BDI brother. Of course Ian would have sent others, but they'd be on the plane now and out of sight. Ian was prepared for anything, including a battle if that's what it took to get Calypso away.

She stumbled halfway up the steep stairs. Jace caught her before she went down. Maybe he should let her fall, but he wasn't wired that way. She might be a brutal assassin, but that didn't mean he had to be brutal in return. Unless she forced it somehow.

The wind whipped her hair into her face and she dragged it away as he held her steady. Then she jerked free of his grip and continued the climb. Once they were through the aircraft door, he guided her toward the seats. The aircraft wasn't standard. It belonged to BDI and was far more plush than a commercial jet. The seats were club-style, comfortable, with entertainment centers and the ability to lie flat for long journeys.

"Pick one," he told her. "Then buckle in and kick off your shoes."

Because they needed to make sure those heels didn't conceal weapons or poison. She turned and he saw the tears streaking her cheeks for the first time. But she didn't look terrified. She looked angry. Precisely what he would expect from Calypso.

"Where are you taking me? I'm an American citizen. I demand to be taken to the embassy."

"You aren't in a position to demand anything. Sit, take off your shoes. Nobody's going to hurt you."

Her jaw worked, eyes flashing hot. And then she flung herself into a seat and tugged the belt into place, kicking off the shoes as she did so. "You'll pay for this," she gritted between her teeth.

"I don't expect so, but you're free to think I will if it helps."

He picked up the shoes and started to walk away, but she reached for him, tugged on the sleeve of his tuxedo jacket. He'd already loosened the tie and collar, but he hadn't removed the jacket yet. He gazed down at her with mild annoyance. And interest, damn him. Such pretty green eyes. Her top lip had a little dip in it and her bottom lip was full. Kissable.

Just what he needed to be thinking about a deadly assassin.

"I'm not who you think I am. I'm Dr. Madeline Cole—Maddy to friends. I work for Barrington's of New York. I was appraising Mr. Sokolov's art collection for insurance purposes. Call them and they'll tell you."

The words tumbled from her. He frowned as he considered them. She seemed so sincere. But she was an expert so of course she'd memorized the story until it was second nature.

It was an interesting cover. He'd pass the information to Ian. It was bullshit, probably, like so many of his personas. It would take time to dig through the layers of deception, but Ian would get it done.

"We will, I assure you."

"My passport—my computer with all my work, everything—it's in Mr. Sokolov's house. I was there for the next few days, working on the collection. I went up to my room to get batteries for my camera, and that's when I heard the shots and screaming." Her chin quivered and he knew she was fighting to hold in her tears. Or maybe it was anger considering the look she aimed at him just then. "When I came out, you attacked me."

"You tried to run."

"What would you do if somebody was heading straight for you and looked like he planned to kill you?" She folded her arms and thrust out her pointy little chin. "When I finally get out of here, I'm going to sue you for everything you have."

Jace couldn't help but laugh. "Sue away, sweetheart." He switched into English to see her reaction. "Dr. Cole, is it? Where were you born? Where did you grow up?"

She frowned for a second. Thinking? "My father was in the military. I was born at Landstuhl military hospital in Germany, but when he was assigned to the Pentagon, we lived in Virginia and Maryland for most of my childhood. Now I live in Annapolis. My grandmother is in a memory care facility there. The Oaks."

The plane began to move. Colt walked into the cabin. "We're cleared. Be airborne in a few."

Jace took a seat across from Calypso and began to

examine her shoes while Colt sat across the aisle from them.

"Shoe fetish?" she asked in an acid tone.

Colt snickered. Jace didn't react. He tugged on the heels, checked for any separation, and when he was satisfied they weren't hiding a weapon, he tossed them at her feet.

"Nope, not in the least."

She didn't move to put them back on, wriggling her toes instead. They were nice toes with pink polish and a silver toe ring on the second toe of her left foot.

Colt was watching those toes too. Then he lifted his head and watched her. Jace didn't blame him. First, she was pretty. And second, Calypso was a legend in their line of work. A stone-cold killer who would eliminate anyone for a price. She'd slipped through so many dragnets that there was speculation she wasn't real. That her work was actually done by a group of paid mercenaries.

But here she was. And she didn't look all that dangerous after all. Probably what made her so effective.

"Please tell me where we're going."

He didn't see any reason not to. Her reaction might give more away than she intended. "Washington. There are people who wish to talk to you."

She frowned, her sculpted brows drawing low over her smooth forehead. Creating anger lines.

Interesting.

"Well, good. Because I wish to talk to them too.

This is bullshit. You can't kidnap American citizens and do whatever you want with them. We have laws about that."

Jace leaned back against the seat as they left the taxiway and hit the airstrip. The jet picked up speed quickly. "If you're who you say you are, you'll be free to go." The wheels left the ground and the pilots aimed the jet sharply upward. He'd been expecting it. But Calypso's face blanched.

It wasn't the kind of takeoff commercial airplanes did, even though they could, and it was startling for anyone who'd never experienced it. He'd been through it many times, on more exfiltrations than he cared to remember. He would have expected her to be familiar with it as an covert operative. Clearly, she was not.

"Standard procedure," he told her. "Nothing to worry about."

She licked her lips. "I don't even have my passport. It's in my purse, which you can see I don't have. How are you possibly taking me to the States?"

"You don't need it where we're going."

She didn't say anything else. When the plane leveled out and Colt gave him a look, Jace took a pair of cuffs from the storage drawer nearby. Calypso looked up as the metal snapped open, her eyes widening as he reached for her arm. She jerked it away.

"What the hell?"

"We've got to make a phone call, sweetheart. No

way am I leaving you loose while we go into the back."

Panic flared in those pretty eyes of hers. "You can't mean to chain me. Where would I go? Look around you, jerk face. We're thirty-thousand feet in the air."

Jerk face? He would have laughed if this wasn't so serious. "Where would you go? Aircraft door? Cockpit?"

"I'm not an idiot."

He wrenched her arm free and snapped on the cuff. Then he fastened the other end to the ring on the seat that was made for such a thing. She paled, and he tried not to feel guilty about it.

"Neither am I," he growled.

"DR. MADELINE COLE is an art historian and appraiser. She works for Barrington's of New York, and she was sent to St. Petersburg two days ago in order to catalog Sokolov's artwork for insurance purposes. She flew out of BWI."

Jace sat in the command center located on the aircraft and studied a side by side comparison of the real Madeline Cole and the photos of Calypso they'd obtained. Colt lounged in the chair beside him while Ian talked to them on the satellite phone.

"They look alike," Jace said. Not twins, but similar facial features and body type. The woman handcuffed into her seat in the main cabin *could* be Madeline Cole. Or she could have gone to extraordinary lengths to look like her. It was his experience that people involved in international espionage would do whatever it took. His own parents, for instance.

Him.

"They do. Our facial recognition software says the woman you caught and the woman in the photo is the same person. But it's not perfect, especially when the photos of Calypso aren't as crisp as we'd like them to be. And we didn't know about the existence of Madeline Cole when the comparison was run."

"We know for sure that Madeline Cole isn't also Calypso?"

"The timelines don't match for other jobs. They aren't the same person."

"So you're telling me I might have grabbed an art historian?" *Fuck.* And he'd forcibly handcuffed her to her seat. Not to mention shot at her.

Jesus.

"Maybe. I think it likely Calypso and the Gemini Syndicate orchestrated the whole thing as a way to gain access to Sokolov's compound. We have to consider that she might have killed the historian and assumed her identity."

"We'll need to take DNA."

"Yes."

"And if she's really Madeline Cole? What then? She could be in danger from the real Calypso." They couldn't ignore that fact. If she was really Dr. Cole, then Calypso and her handlers had gone to extraordinary lengths to use her. Because that resemblance wasn't a coincidence.

"We'll cross that bridge when we come to it. In the meantime, Sokolov is safe and I've been in touch with his security. They swept the compound and found 7.62 NATO shell casings in Dr. Cole's room. But the weapon was fired from the room next door—that's where the gunpowder signature was heaviest. The door between the two rooms was open."

Jace frowned. "No rifle?"

"Not there."

That didn't mean much. A sniper rifle would be worth money on the black market. One of Sokolov's employees—or a temporary staff member brought in for the party—could have lifted the thing before security searched for it. It wouldn't be all that unusual. On the other hand, somebody could have been there to sweep up after Calypso. Give her a chance to get away.

"We'll need to check her clothing for powder residue."

"Got everything waiting. Just get her here and we'll find out who she is."

"Who did she kill? I saw two men go down."

"A colonel in the Russian army named Fyodor Isaev, and Muscovite businessman Pavel Popov. Popov was an arms manufacturer. Isaev was an intel officer."

"Fuck."

"Yeah. We're still working on the connections. It's

possible one of those was her target all along. Or both."

"Want me to ask her?" He didn't know why he said that since he was beginning to believe he hadn't captured her after all.

"Let's wait until we get confirmation on her identity."

"You got it, boss."

They ended the communication and Colt met his gaze. "It'd be really good for us if that's Calypso out there. Because the idea she's still at large isn't a pleasant one."

Jace frowned. "Yeah, I know. But if she is, then Dr. Cole is probably dead."

And that wasn't an idea he liked. He didn't know Madeline Cole, but she didn't deserve to be murdered so that Calypso could assume her identity and kill a target. He'd done a lot of dirty shit in his day, but he drew the line at innocent people dying for no reason.

Colt sighed. "There is that. Guess we'll find out when we get her back to HQ."

Jace tapped the edge of the table. He really wanted to have captured the mysterious Calypso. It would be a major coup if he had. Not to mention it could throw the Gemini Syndicate off their game as they worried about whether or not she would talk.

But he wanted Madeline Cole alive even more. Because he knew what it was like to be dragged into something he hadn't chosen and have it affect the course of his life in ways he'd never be able to change.

It wasn't fair and it wasn't right, and he didn't wish it on anyone.

Still, he'd done this job long enough to know that innocent people got killed sometimes. And there was nothing he could do about it once it happened. He fished the handcuff key from his pocket and stood. Time to unleash his prisoner.

Chapter Five

MADDY DOZED. HER SLEEP WAS STILL SCREWED THE hell up and now she had stress to add to the mix. She saw blue eyes in her dreams, a bearded stranger who held her down and called her Calypso. What the hell?

She awoke with a start, blinking into the darkened interior of the cabin. The lights had been turned down and the shades were pulled closed. It took her a moment to realize she wasn't alone. He sat across from her, watching her. The man from her dream. The real-life James Bond who'd kidnapped her and taken her on an adventure she still couldn't wrap her head around. He leaned forward and unlocked the handcuffs, snicking the side open that held her wrist. She tugged it free and rubbed her skin even though he hadn't fastened them too tight. Still, he'd fastened them—and she'd never been trapped like that before.

His gaze dropped to where she rubbed her wrist for the briefest of moments. If he felt guilty, he darn sure didn't show it. "Tell me, Dr. Cole, how did you learn Russian?"

Her heart skipped. Did he believe her? She was hopeful—but then she realized that, no, he probably did not. He was trying to trip her up. Except he couldn't because she wasn't who he thought she was. She was herself. "College. Well, high school and college. My dad was a Russian linguist in the Air Force for a while, then he was a government civilian. S.A.L.T. inspections, that kind of thing. He encouraged it, and I wanted to be like him so I took courses. He'd already taught me a few words and phrases so I had a leg up, I guess. It came naturally to me."

Way to tell him everything, Maddy. Could she have babbled a touch less? Probably. But she was nervous and she had an unfortunate tendency to talk too much in that case.

"You have an American accent."

"Because I *am* American?" There was no small touch of sarcasm in her voice. Maybe she shouldn't antagonize him, but she couldn't help it. She was upset and scared and this whole situation was outrageous.

"It's not bad, just noticeable."

"That's not a crime, Mr. Whoever You Are. Don't you think you could tell me your name now? We're in a plane, thirty-thousand feet in the air, and I don't know who you people are." She glanced at her surroundings. Whoever they were, this wasn't Delta Airlines. This was the kind of private jet that people with money owned. There were two flight attendants, and they kept disappearing into the back of the aircraft where this man and his friend had gone once the plane reached altitude. Presumably, there were more people back there and the flight attendants were busy serving them.

"You can call me Andrei."

"Andrei. You're Russian?"

He shrugged. "Something like that."

"Then why are we going to the States? And who is Calypso?"

"Either you know who she is or you don't. And if you really don't, then you don't need to know."

Maddy threw her hands in the air. "That's the stupidest thing I've ever heard. What is this? A James Bond movie? *Mission Impossible*? I'm an art appraiser. My specialty is Russian art of the thirteenth through seventeenth centuries. Particularly icons, of which Mr. Sokolov has an impressive collection."

"So you only appraise Russian art?"

"No, I'm capable of evaluating other art, though I sometimes need to consult with a specialist. That's why I work for Barrington's. We specialize. I have a whole company of experts to consult if I'm unsure about a piece."

"So you were there to appraise Mr. Sokolov's artwork. How long have you known you were going on this job?"

Maddy frowned. She wasn't sure why he needed to know, but she didn't see any harm in telling him.

The more details she revealed about her life, the more he had to realize she was telling the truth. Who would make this stuff up? Maddy Cole was kind of boring, really. Her job was often interesting to people, but it wasn't as exciting as they thought. And her personal life wasn't exciting at all.

"I got the assignment a few days ago."

He looked thoughtful. "A few days. How many?"

She thought back. Her days were running together. "I think it was six days. Maybe a week."

"You don't know for sure?"

"If I had my purse and my cell phone, I'd know. It's in my calendar. Life is busy, Mr. Bond. Days can rush by in a blur sometimes."

He seemed to accept that. Or at least he didn't ask again. "Did you know Mr. Sokolov was having a birthday party?"

"Not until today, no. Why would I?"

"When did you arrive?" He ignored her question.

She'd expected he would. It made her want to ignore his, but considering he had the upper hand here, she was in no position to do so. "I landed in St. Petersburg on Thursday and stayed the night there. Friday afternoon, a car came for me. When I got to Mr. Sokolov's, I went to work."

"Tell me again how you ended up on the second floor of his house where the shots were fired from."

Maddy blinked. "They were fired from the second floor? I-I thought they were fireworks. It was loud, but..."

"They were fired from the room beside yours. The one with the connecting door that was open."

"It wasn't open," she blurted. "I tried it."

He lifted an eyebrow.

Maddy's gut twisted. "Look, I was in Mr. Sokolov's office when the party started. He has a very large collection of icons, and I stayed there until I went to get batteries. I need to take pictures of every piece, and my batteries were dying. The spares were in my suitcase. So I went up to get them—and that's when I thought I heard fireworks. When people started to scream, I tried that door because the maid had been in there to turn down the room and I thought she might know what was happening. But the door didn't work and I ran into the hall."

"There was a maid?"

"Yes, of course. She was there to turn down the room. I said that already. But she must have finished and left. The door was definitely locked."

"So you say."

"I do say. Why would I make it up?"

"I don't know. Why would you?"

"Stop it," Maddy said. "You're irritating. And no thanks to you, my shoulder aches." She shrugged it as she glared at him. She didn't know why she'd added that bit of information, but he annoyed her so much that she had.

"I did tell you to stop," he murmured.

Heat flared in her belly, spread to her extremities.

"Yes, well, did Jerry stop for Tom? Not if he wanted to live."

He tilted his head, a confused look on his face.

She rolled her eyes. "It's an old cartoon. *Tom and Jerry.* Tom is a cat and Jerry's a mouse—look, never mind. Just, no, I wasn't going to stop because you said so. I don't know you, and you aren't the police. Even if you do have a gun," she finished under her breath.

"I apologize if I hurt you."

She started to tell him it was okay, she was fine. Because that was the polite thing to say and Mimi always told her to be polite—but fuck that. Not this time. She'd been attacked, kidnapped, and now she was on her way somewhere she hadn't agreed to go. She'd also lost her work computer, her camera, her purse and passport—everything that belonged to her—and this man with the glacial eyes sat there and said he was sorry?

No.

"Not accepted, Andrei. If that's really your name. Which I don't believe it is. And believe me, when you verify the truth about who I am, I'm going to sue your ass—and that of your employer—into the next century."

His eyes widened for a moment. And then he laughed. She didn't know whether to scream or slap him. She settled for glaring.

"You'll find that a bit impossible, Dr. Cole. But if you are who you say you are, you'll be compensated for your time."

"Compensated?" Her voice rose at least two octaves. She sounded like she'd inhaled helium.

But, really? He'd upended her life, physically assaulted her, and all he could do was laugh and say she'd be compensated? She unbuckled her seatbelt before she realized she was doing it. And then she was on her feet, standing over him, glaring down at him while he gazed up at her with mild interest. He didn't look intimidated at all. Just… smug.

Maddy snapped. She hauled off and slapped his face. That handsome, irritating, lying face. He didn't move, but his gaze hardened to razor sharpness. A hot feeling flared in her breast, threatened to bubble over and erupt in flame if she didn't find an outlet for it.

So she slapped him again. He still didn't move, but those eyes—God, those eyes. Like twin flames of purest blue. She lifted her hand to slap him again, only this time he shot up from the seat and caught her wrist, holding it firmly in his hand. They were inches apart. The heat of him enveloped her. His scent, like steel and spice, stole over her.

Desire flared in the pit of her belly, sent a throbbing tingle into her pussy. It shocked her.

Arousal? Now? Over *him?* She hadn't gotten any action in so long that she was pretty sure her libido had lost its mind. Because she wasn't the kind of woman who liked autocratic men. *At all.*

And yet her body betrayed her with heat and melting and the desire for more. So much more.

"That's enough," he said. "I think maybe we're

even on the part where we physically assault each other."

She curled her hand into a fist but she didn't try to break free of his grip. "You deserve a lot more than that. But I think I can refrain for now."

His gaze dropped to her mouth. She felt those eyes on her lips as if they were a caress. It melted through her like hot wax. She didn't want to melt. Not for him.

"I like nice men. You're not nice."

His gaze lifted. That was the moment she realized she'd said the words aloud. *Oh hell.*

She didn't expect him to grin. His face was beautiful when he smiled. Breathtaking, really.

"I'm nice," he told her. "You keep looking at me like that, and I'll be happy to show you how nice I can be. It's really, *really* nice, by the way."

"Let me go," she whispered, her heart slamming her ribcage.

His grip eased though his grin didn't. She pulled away, rubbing her wrist even though he hadn't held her tightly at all. She wanted to erase the sizzling on her skin where he'd touched her, but it wasn't subsiding quickly enough.

He turned away. "Do you want something to drink?"

"A very large bourbon on the rocks." He turned back with an arched eyebrow. "But what I'll really have is some sparkling water, thank you," she added.

"You can have bourbon if you want it. It's still night time where we came from."

She shook her head. "I was joking. Besides, it's too close to morning for me. I'm not really much of a drinker."

She liked the occasional bourbon, and red wine, but she didn't keep her head very well after the second glass of anything. She got really happy and super talky. Which was why she was careful about what she drank because who needed the embarrassment?

Andrei snorted as he went over to a cabinet set into the wall and retrieved a small bottle of *Perrier*. Then he poured a healthy amount of vodka into a glass for himself. He came over and handed her the water. "We'll have lunch in about an hour. Unless you need something now?"

"No, I'm fine, thank you." Were they really back to polite inanities? It seemed so. And yet her insides churned with anger, fear, curiosity—and desire. Couldn't forget that one. She was going to have a lot of hours to consider how and why she was attracted to this man. Yes, he was majorly fine-looking in his tux, but looks weren't everything. She knew that from her mother. A beautiful, shallow woman who'd broken her father's heart when she'd left him for a man with money to burn. Dad had his work, but it hadn't been enough. Two years after her mother abandoned them, her dad suffered a massive heart attack and died. He'd been on a work trip to Moscow. The next time she'd seen him, he'd been in a coffin.

Maddy bit back sudden tears. She missed him, and she missed Mimi, who was sinking farther and farther into delusions. She even missed her mother sometimes, but that wasn't a fruitful relationship so she'd given up trying.

"You okay?"

Maddy blinked hard. "I'm fine. Why?"

Andrei had discarded the tux jacket and untied his tie. He'd rolled his shirt sleeves, revealing tattooed forearms that she wanted to see more of. Judging by the way those sleeves bulged at the top, he had some impressive muscles. Not huge, but solid and defined. Sexy.

Stop that.

"You looked upset there for a second."

"Duh. I'm here with you, accused of being someone I'm not, and I'm worried about my job. I need it, by the way."

"Don't worry. Your job is safe… so long as you're really Dr. Cole."

She sat down again, crossed her legs, and glared at him. "I am. What about you?"

"What about me?"

"Is Andrei really your name?"

"It is today."

At least he was honest. "Will I ever know your name?"

"Probably not. When we reach our destination, you're going to be questioned." He sat across from her again. Buckled his seat belt and set the vodka on the small table beside him. "If you aren't who we're looking for, you'll be returned to your life. You won't see me again."

"You make it all sound so easy, and yet you've upended my life in ways I'm not likely to forget."

Andrei picked up the vodka and took a sip, his gaze never leaving hers. "Best if you do, sweetheart. Some things are better left in the dark."

The blood beat hot in her temples. "Yes, well I wish you'd stayed in the dark and not crawled out of it."

He arched an eyebrow, but that was all. "You would rather be back at Sokolov's place with a gunman on the loose and the house in chaos? He's not even there anymore—airlifted out, same as you and me. But maybe when we're done with you, assuming your story checks out, I can drop you back there. Let you find your own way out with the police looking for suspects and your room so conveniently located to the shooter's position."

She felt herself growing pale and she sipped her water to hide it. But she was pretty sure he saw it anyway. "That's okay. I'm good."

His gaze didn't waver. "Be glad I crawled out of the dark, lady. Be *very* glad."

THEY REACHED Black Defense International's Maryland headquarters during the late afternoon.

They hadn't needed to stop for fuel because Ian managed to get a KC-135 to service them mid-air. Jace didn't always know how Ian did what he did, but it certainly made the job better. Safer.

A limo waited at the private airstrip where they'd landed. Jace and Colt hustled their charge into the car and then they were on their way. It took about fifteen minutes to reach the HQ building. The car entered the darkened garage and stopped. Colt got out and Jace followed. Other BDI personnel had been on the plane, but they'd been careful not to let Dr. Cole—or maybe it was Calypso—see them. Either way this went, the fewer people she could ID, the better.

Jace held out a hand for her. She pushed it away and climbed to her feet. Then she swayed in her high heels and Jace caught her before she plopped back down on her cute little ass. Her fingers curled into his arms for a second before she released him and stepped back, holding her hands up to ward him off. He watched her carefully, in case she was acting and this was about to turn into an escape attempt.

"Thank you."

"You bet."

"So where are we?" she asked as Colt led the way toward the freight elevator that would take them up to BDI's offices.

"Maryland."

"I know that. I live in Annapolis. But what is this place? It's not the NSA or the CIA."

"No, it's not."

They got into the elevator and Colt pressed the number four button. Five was the command center and operational heart of the group, but four housed the public offices and boardrooms where Ian Black pretended to be nothing more than a security contractor for hire. Colt peeled off to do something of his own once they entered the offices and Jace walked his charge down the hall toward the examining room where Ian had said he would be waiting with a technician.

"This the room?" Jace asked the man standing outside it.

"Yes, sir." His gaze slipped to Jace's prisoner with interest. Jace started to growl, but the man turned and rapped on the door.

"Enter," Ian said from inside.

The man pulled the door open for them. Jace stood back and motioned for Dr. Cole to precede him. She took a step into the room—and stopped so abruptly that Jace nearly knocked her over. Instead, he gripped her arms and kept them both from stumbling. He could feel the shudder roll through her. She really didn't like him. Probably a good thing because he could like her more than he should. She was sexy and sweetly appealing. Even if she wasn't really sweet, she pulled it off like nobody he'd ever met. He wanted to wrap her in his arms and protect her. Which worried him because if she was Calypso, then his instincts were shot to hell.

"Hello, Dr. Cole," Ian said, standing up and

coming over to offer his hand. "You're safe here. We just need to swab your clothes for powder residue and your cheek for DNA. Nothing painful or invasive, I promise."

Jace let her go, but he could still feel the anger vibrating from her as she faced down the boss man.

"That's not acceptable," she said, sounding as haughty as a princess. "It's an invasion of my privacy."

"I realize that, Dr. Cole. Madeline. May I call you Madeline? I'm Ian."

"Is that really your name?"

"In fact it is." He glanced at Jace. "But there's a reason you shouldn't know everyone's name. It's safer that way."

"Are you asking for my consent for these tests? Or performing them anyway?"

Ian spread his hands. Shrugged. "I'd prefer your consent, but it's not necessary. We need to prove your identity. If you really are Madeline Cole, then you can walk out of here and never see us again."

She folded her arms and glared. Jace had to admire her spirit. The lady was overwhelmed and outnumbered and yet she still stood up for herself. Which he'd expect if she were Calypso, so maybe it wasn't so unusual after all. But that sixth sense of his that always told him when a situation was about to go bad had been throbbing to life in his gut for hours now. Deep down, he suspected this woman wasn't who they wanted her to be. And if she was who she said she was, then the real Calypso was still out there and this entire mission had been for naught. Not a thought he relished.

"I don't need to prove my identity. I know who I am. And I've told *you* who I am. Which you can verify with my employer and my address, driver's license, credit report—hell, so many ways to verify, so why should I submit to tests?"

"There's been an international incident. *You* are on the list of suspects." Ian turned and picked up a photo from the folder lying on a nearby table. Turned it face out so she could see it. "Is this you?"

She looked closer, frowned. "No, it's not. Wow."

Ian turned the photo and looked at it, then back at her. "That's right, she looks like you. A lot like you. So much so that a facial recognition scan says the two of you are the same person. But this woman is a spy. She's wanted for murder in at least ten countries. Now you can insist you aren't her, or you can submit to a cheek swab and powder tests and shut down speculation for good."

"I thought you said my submission wasn't necessary."

"It's not, but I'd like to have it. Makes it easier than holding you down."

She took another step closer, peering at the photo he still held up. "That's not a very good photo. But she looks familiar in a way… So creepy. The shape of her face, her body type—those appear the same. Maybe even her nose. But still, the resemblance between us is physical size and type, not genetics." Her voice was low, almost as if she were talking to herself. "I see where the confusion lies. Fine, I'll take your tests. But when you get the results, I want an apology. And I want compensation for the things I had to leave at Mr. Sokolov's. My equipment, my clothes, my passport."

"You'll get your apology. You will also get your things. I had someone collect them for you." He looked at his watch. "A few more hours, I expect, and they'll arrive."

She seemed surprised. Jace could have told her that Ian Black was thorough and deliberate, but she wouldn't have believed him.

"Now if you'll come sit over here, Madeline, and allow Ms. Barnes to swab your cheek and clothing, we can get this done and get you on your way."

"Dr. Cole," she corrected, and Jace snorted. Girl was a freaking firecracker. He liked that more than he should. Because as soon as her identity was proven, he'd never see her again. He found he didn't care for that idea. If he'd met her in a bar somewhere, he'd romance her, bed her a few times, and then be on his way. Far more enjoyable than what was currently happening.

"Dr. Cole then," Ian said, shooting Jace a look. Jace shrugged.

She walked over to the chair where the technician stood and sank onto it like a queen on a throne.

Within moments, the samples were bagged and the technician was off to the lab.

"Andrei will take you to a place where you can wait," Ian told her.

Madeline Cole stood and brushed off her clothing, tugging on the ends of her jacket to smooth out any wrinkles. "I need to call the office."

"I'm afraid not," Ian said. "No outside communication until we know the truth."

Her eyes could have shot daggers. She lifted her chin and sniffed. "I guess I have no choice. But you're going to regret this when the results come back. I'm suing you for—well, I don't know what for, but I'll find out once I call Barrington's attorneys."

"You can try," Ian told her as he walked to the door. "I predict you won't get very far."

"And I thought *you* were an asshole," she said when Ian was gone.

Jace laughed. "Hazard of the profession."

She tilted her head. "What profession is that, exactly?"

"I could tell you..."

"But then I'd have to kill you," she added with an eye roll. "Fine, take me to this waiting area for now. I still expect an apology when the results come back, by the way."

"And you'll get it," Jace said. He was starting to hope like hell she *was* Madeline Cole. Because he liked her. He might as well admit it to himself, even if he wouldn't admit it to her.

She tossed her hair. It was long and dark gold and glorious. Interest flared in places he'd rather not think about right now. He pushed his reaction down deep and led her to a suite that had a couch, chairs, and a television. There was a connected bathroom, a small fridge with drinks, and snacks in a basket on the counter. One wall was covered by a mirror. She stopped and frowned.

"Seriously, you plan to observe me in here?"

Jace raised an eyebrow.

"The mirror," she said, flinging her hand toward it. "It's two-way, isn't it?"

He didn't see any point in lying. "It is. Standard procedure, I'm afraid."

She rolled her eyes. "God, you people are really too much." She went over and flung herself on the couch, grabbed the remote. "I'll just be sitting here, doing nothing, until you come back and say you're sorry."

Jace had a nearly uncontrollable urge to apologize right then. He didn't though. Somebody was watching. And listening. "If you need anything, just say so. Someone will hear you."

She crossed her legs and arms and huffed. "Of course they will. Bye now, Andrei. It's been fun."

Chapter Six

Maddy was trembling when he left the room. She *was* angry, but she was scared too. Because this was so out of her league. Andrei had grabbed her at Sokolov's house, bundled her onto a helicopter, and brought her back to the States *without* a passport. What kind of organization could do that?

A spy organization, that's what kind.

Maddy flicked the channels angrily, finally landing on a Russian language station. There was footage of Leonid Sokolov's home. A reporter stood outside the gates and talked about a shooting at Sokolov's fiftieth birthday party. She didn't say who'd been shot, which meant they didn't know. Indication that the government was controlling the information. The billionaire was currently in seclusion, and the police were questioning guests. Nobody knew anything, including the identity of the shooter.

Maddy changed the channel to something soothing. HGTV, where Chip and Joanna Gaines were demolishing the interior of an ugly house so they could turn it into something spectacular for the cute couple with the two-hundred thousand dollar budget.

Maddy rubbed her forehead. How nice would it be to move to Waco and buy a fixer upper? Just change her life entirely, cut the travel, and spend her days selling artwork at a little gallery of her own.

Yeah, right.

Not with Mimi needing care. The bills were too much to take such a risk. Not to mention she'd be too far away to visit Mimi anymore.

God, she wished she could call Angie. Angie had been her best friend since high school. Angie was no nonsense, organized, and logical to a fault. She took care of Kitty whenever Maddy was traveling. Fortunately, Kitty loved Angie. Other than having to get into her carrier for the short trip to Angie's house, Kitty was completely content whenever she was with Angie.

Maddy missed her cat. And her friend. She sucked down sudden tears and gritted her teeth. Not crying. No way. Wasn't worth it. She'd be out of here soon and these people would be a memory. Had to be because she wasn't who they wanted her to be.

Maddy watched television for at least two hours before she dozed off. When she woke, it was to the sound of a door opening. She was momentarily disoriented, but she blinked at the man who'd walked into the room and her memory came flooding back.

He was tall, handsome, and had the body of a god. She knew because she'd been pressed to the carpet beneath it.

He looked different. He no longer wore a tuxedo. This time he had on faded jeans and a black polo shirt. The muscles of his forearms were more exposed than before. He had tattoos, though not too many. Tribal designs mostly. And his biceps were definitely drool-worthy as they flexed beneath the short sleeves of his shirt.

"You awake, Maddy?"

She didn't remember him calling her Maddy before. The sound of her name on his lips dripped down her spine like hot wax. She sat up straight and mentally shook herself. My God, what had the assholes behind the mirror seen while she'd slept? Did she snore? Drool? *Lord.*

"I'm awake. What do you want, Andrei?" *Don't ogle.*

He held up a folder. "We have the results."

"Oh really? So who am I? Will I be surprised?"

He snorted. "You really are a firecracker, aren't you? You know damn well what this says. You're Maddy Cole, art historian and appraiser. You're thirty-one, you live in Annapolis in a small house off Back Creek that belonged to your grandmother, and you commute to New York City on a regular basis for your work. Your dad died when you were fifteen, you like Greek food, you have a cat named Kitty—and you broke your arm when you were twelve."

Maddy's jaw dropped by degrees. "You know all that from a cheek swab?"

"No, I know all that from the public information available on the person whose DNA was on that swab. Maybe consider covering the camera on your laptop and removing the remote treat dispenser for your cat. The camera on that thing is ridiculously easy to hack."

"You were spying on me?"

He stood over her, shaking his head. "Not us. But somebody was. The info is readily available if you know where to look."

Anger flooded her. "Where to look?" she parroted. Because what kind of people hacked into a pet camera inside a person's home and spied on her?

Bad people, that's who. She wasn't naïve, but she was also nobody. Why would anyone want to watch her through her cat's treat dispenser? She shivered.

"Yeah, Maddy. Where to look. You think that shit is harmless? Trust me, it's not. Go home and unplug the dispenser. Put a sticky note over the laptop camera. Don't buy anything that connects to the internet by voice, and don't talk about anything you don't want anyone to know, okay? You never know who's listening."

Maddy got to her feet. Fury swirled in her belly. Her cheeks flamed as the blood pulsed beneath her skin. "Do you think this is right? Watching people without their permission? Listening to their conversations, following them around their home?"

His eyes flashed. "It depends on the person, doesn't it? You never know what people are up to."

She shook her head. "I'm sure that's illegal. You can't just listen to people—record people—without their permission."

He took a step closer, his body throbbing with leashed tension. "Yeah, well, when you're concerned about saving the world, you absolutely can do anything the fuck you want to do in pursuit of that goal."

Maddy sucked in a breath. Saving the world? What did she have to do with that? "And maybe you need to be careful that you don't become the thing you despise. We have rights in this country for a reason."

His brows lifted. He hadn't been expecting that answer. "We're the good guys."

"Are you really?" She shook her head. "Never mind, don't answer. Am I free to go now?"

"You are. I need you to tell me everything that happened when you went to your room to get the batteries, and then I'll drive you home."

Her heart leapt at that idea. She swatted it down like a fly at a picnic. "I'll tell you, but I don't need you to take me home. I'll call a taxi. Or an Uber."

" 'Fraid not, Maddy. I plucked you from Sokolov's place. I'll take you home and make sure you're safe."

"Why wouldn't I be safe?" She really needed to tell him not to call her Maddy—but she liked the sound of her name on his lips. He'd spoken such perfect Russian, but his English was perfect too. So perfect she wasn't certain which country he hailed from.

"You will be. I'll make sure of it."

The door opened again and the man called Ian entered. He was handsome too, but he didn't make her heart throb the way Andrei did. She closed her eyes. Neither one of them needed to make her heart throb. Jerks, both of them.

"Well, Dr. Cole, you were right," Ian said.

"Of course I was right."

"I'm sorry for the inconvenience, but we did what we had to do."

She'd wanted an apology but somehow this one didn't quite hit the mark. Truthfully, she was no longer interested. She just wanted to go home and take a hot bath. Then she wanted to sink into bed with take-out from her favorite restaurant and binge on television. Maybe *Covert Affairs*, which was about a CIA agent who went on adventures.

And had an illicit romance with a rogue agent…

"I'd like to go now," she said with as much haughtiness as she could muster. She'd gotten that from her mother so she knew it was pretty good. But inside she was really just a puddle of mush.

"And you may just as soon as you can tell Andrei everything that happened when you went to your room. But Dr. Cole," Ian said, "it'd really be in your best interests not to talk about any of this when you return to your life."

She'd thought she was going to call her employer's attorneys and sue, but she'd realized over the past few hours that it probably wasn't a good idea. What would she tell them? That she'd been kidnapped by a secret agent and spirited back to the US where she'd undergone a DNA test to make sure she wasn't this person named Calypso? She'd bet anything that if the attorney's office called this place, they'd deny everything. And what proof did she have?

"Who is Calypso?"

Ian and Andrei exchanged a look. "The truth?" Ian asked. She nodded. "She's a criminal, Dr. Cole. If you'd been her, you'd be on your way to Guantanamo right now."

Guantanamo? That's where the US sent dangerous terrorists. Not a place she'd want to end up.

"How do I explain to my employer why I'm home again and not in Russia doing my job?"

"We'll take care of it," Ian said. "Barrington's will be happy you escaped the situation. Now if you'll answer Andrei's questions, he can take you home."

"I will do my best. But what about my things? You said you'd have them."

"In the car waiting."

She shot a look at Andrei. He seemed like the safer of the two of them right now. Odd feeling but there it was. "I'd say it's been a pleasure meeting you, but that would be a lie."

Ian didn't laugh. "I know you're angry, Dr. Cole.

But I suggest you guard your tongue once you're home again. Don't speak of this to anyone. Not even Angie."

Daggers of ice pierced her belly. Her heart froze. They knew too much about her. And she knew nothing about them. "I don't intend to. Who would believe me anyway?"

"No one," he said coolly. "No one at all."

"I CAN'T BELIEVE you got my things. It's almost like I was never there."

Jace glanced at Maddy and then turned his eyes back to the road. He didn't know what to tell her. That it was part of the job? That it's what they did? That BDI made things—and people—disappear when necessary?

She turned in her seat to gaze at him. He felt the heat of that gaze like a blowtorch. Was she really safe now that they were letting her go? He'd asked Ian if it was wise. Ian said there was nothing else they could do. They'd watch her place for a few days, tap her phones, see if anything weird happened. Unless Calypso or the Gemini Syndicate came after her, they couldn't justify keeping her from her life.

Jace got it, but he didn't like it. Still, orders were orders. He'd drop her off, meet up with the detail watching her place, and then go home and try to forget everything about her before heading off on the next mission.

He'd questioned her about those moments between when she'd gone to get her batteries and he'd intercepted her in the hallway. She'd spoken to a maid who'd entered the room next to hers, then she'd gone inside to get her batteries. She didn't know how long she'd stayed before she'd heard the shots, though she swore it was only a few minutes.

Jace's dilemma was the maid. Could she have been Calypso? But Maddy didn't recognize her as the woman in the photo she'd been shown. And there could have been enough time for the maid to retreat and Calypso to enter the room and take the shot. A professional like Calypso wouldn't need much time to set up, just like she hadn't needed much time to break down. She could have already been in the room and hidden in the closet when the maid entered. Turning down a bed took no time at all and the maid could have been gone again.

But if the door was locked when Maddy tried it, why was it open when Sokolov's security had found it? These were the things that didn't make sense to Jace, and also the reason he wanted Maddy watched. What if Calypso was waiting for her to be home and unguarded? If she *had* seen the assassin, then she was the only person who could identify Calypso.

He shot a glance at the woman beside him. When had he started to think of her as Maddy anyway? He remembered her saying her name to him, telling him that friends called her Maddy. That wasn't the moment, but somewhere over the Atlantic, that's when it happened. He'd caught himself thinking of her as Maddy from time to time during the flight. He corrected himself, but it felt right to think of her that way. And then they'd gotten the results, and she'd become Maddy in truth.

Maddy.

"So now what?" she asked. "You didn't get her, and she's still out there."

His gut twisted. Yeah, she wasn't Calypso. He was relieved and disappointed at once. Calypso was still out there, still willing to kill for whoever offered her enough money to do so. Not that he cared if she wanted to kill terrorists, illicit arms dealers, drug lords, human traffickers, etc. But some of her targets were innocent of those crimes. Some of them were merely people who'd gotten in the way of those who wanted to commit that sort of crime. That wasn't something he could approve of at all.

"We'll get her."

"Was she using me, or is it all a coincidence?"

Jace glanced at her as he turned down one of the quaint streets in Annapolis. He liked this city. He liked coming down here and eating in the restaurants fronting the bay. Liked seeing the Midshipmen from the US Naval Academy in their uniforms as they hung around the harbor on a weekend and caroused. It felt quaint and profound all at once. The most powerful navy in the world, and their academy was in this cute, historic city on the Chesapeake Bay with the tiniest of town squares that fronted the harbor. He liked it. It was very American.

He *was* American, but he was something else too. It was the American part of him he wanted to nurture, the Russian part of him he wanted to forget. Guilt was his constant companion, even though he'd been a kid and hadn't made the choice to betray his country.

Not your fault, Ian said. *Never your fault.*

"Andrei?"

Jace swung his gaze to her as he came to a stop at a red light. "Sorry. I was thinking. Truthfully, I don't know. But Maddy, you can't talk about this stuff to anyone. You can't mention Calypso or Sokolov or what happened at the party. It's safer for you not to."

"Who would believe me?" she asked with a shrug. "I don't plan on talking about any of it. Ian said my job was safe—are you sure? I need it, Andrei. It's how I make sure my grandmother gets the best care." She dropped her chin. Shook her head. "Before you ask, the house is mortgaged—or maybe you know that. I've already tapped it to pay for her room at the Oaks."

"It was in the report, yes."

There were a lot of things in the report, some of which he was still processing. The part about her father speaking Russian and being involved in more than translating, for instance. He liked how loyal Maddy was to her grandmother though. But it wasn't something he understood. His parents hadn't thought about him or his sister when they'd done what they'd done. How much would they have sacrificed for their kids?

Nothing. They'd sacrificed nothing. No, they'd forced him and Natasha to sacrifice their entire lives for a cause that wasn't theirs.

"Is there anything that wasn't in this report?" She sounded annoyed and tired at the same time. Resigned, maybe.

"First boyfriend. Wasn't there." A lot wasn't there, but he reached for the first thing he could think of. Just to make her laugh. It worked.

"Seriously?"

"Yes, seriously. Wasn't there. Who was he?"

She snorted. "I don't like you—and here you are, making me laugh. I'm not telling you."

"Might be important."

"It's not important. You're trying to distract me."

He shot her a grin. "No, it's not important. And I am trying to make you laugh, Maddy."

She frowned, her fine eyebrows drawing low. Her nose wrinkled. He didn't think she knew it.

"You know my name. But your name isn't Andrei. What is it really?"

His heart thumped. "I can't tell you. I wish I could."

"Are you Russian or American?"

The million dollar question. "Both," he said before he knew he was going to say it.

She turned to him. "Really? That's so cool."

It wasn't cool. She had no idea. "It's no big deal. I was born in the States. I have a Russian parent." Parents, actually. Spies. Not that he intended to tell her that. "We moved to Moscow when I was ten. Then we moved to St. Petersburg a few years later."

What the fuck are you doing, dude?

He didn't tell people these things. Not ever. Yet here he was, spilling his guts to Maddy Cole like she was his therapist or something.

"That must have been fascinating."

"It was certainly interesting." He turned into the driveway of a small Cape Cod-style cottage and put the car in park. "Here we are."

She looked at the house. "I wasn't sure I'd see it again. When you tackled me, well…"

"I'm sorry about that."

She smiled at him, and his heart flipped. *Why?*

"Look, it wasn't pleasant. But I understand. You're CIA—or something like that—and you had to do what you had to do. I'm home now, and it's over."

He hoped for her sake that it was. He took out a card and handed it to her. It was a generic card, but the number was genuine. "If you need us, dial that number. Someone will come."

She took it, turning it over as she read what was on the card stock. It was basic. Just three words—Black Defense International—and a number.

Wide green eyes met his. "Is this real?"

"Yes."

She nodded solemnly. "So I guess this is good bye then."

There was no need to prolong it. Her house had been thoroughly checked by a team from BDI. Just to be sure. There was nothing in there to hurt her. Nobody was waiting.

He opened the car door. "I'll get your suitcase."

She exited the car, shouldered her purse and picked up her computer case. He came around the car with the suitcase. "I can take it from here," she said softly, her gaze dropping from his as he approached.

He let go of the handle, oddly disappointed and frustrated at the same time. "If you're sure."

"I am." She took the handle, rolled the case toward her, and dropped the computer bag on top. It fit perfectly. Then she sucked in a deep breath and met his gaze again. She was smiling, but he wasn't sure how genuine it was or if she was just being polite. Probably the latter. "I travel alone so I make sure I can handle my luggage."

"A good idea."

"Yep." She extended her hand. Took him a moment to realize she was offering it to shake.

He put his palm against hers, clasped her gently. The heat that rolled through him wasn't something he expected. In another world, he'd tug her to him and kiss her right this second. She gazed at him, her mouth dropping open slightly, her eyes blinking more rapidly. She felt it too, whatever this thing was. Pissed him off he couldn't explore it.

"Well, good bye. If I see you around sometime, I'll be sure to pretend I don't know you." She smiled and he knew she was teasing him. He didn't tell her she wouldn't see him unless he wanted her to.

"Bye, Maddy Cole. For what it's worth, I think you handled everything with class and bravery."

"Thanks, Andrei." She let him go and turned to walk up the sidewalk to her door.

"Maddy," he called when she reached the porch.

"Yes?"

He hesitated for a second. And then he did something he knew he shouldn't do. "My name is Jace."

She smiled again. A genuine smile this time. Jace cursed himself six ways to Sunday, but he'd had to do it. It didn't feel right to leave without telling her. Not after everything.

"Jace. I like it."

She put her key in the door and disappeared inside. Jace stood there for a long minute, wondering what the hell was wrong with him. Then he did what he always did.

He walked away.

Chapter Seven

MADDY LEANED HER FOREHEAD AGAINST THE DOOR and sucked in a deep breath. What the heck was wrong with her? Her heart pounded and her blood beat and her skin felt way too sensitive inside her clothes.

Jace.

His name was Jace. She put her palm to the door, curled her fingers. Pretended it was his chest for one split second. Then she straightened and spun away from the door. She didn't even like him, so why the regret? Why did she want to spend more time listening to him talk about his life? He was a total jerk and she never wanted to see him again.

Except she did.

"Stop it, Maddy. You're being an idiot," she grumbled. Mimi's house—her house now—was small, but perfect in its own way. Maddy still had a lot of Mimi's furniture. The antique pieces were her treasures. She would sell them if she had to, but she hoped she never did. They weren't terribly valuable, but they had value to Maddy.

She spied the treat dispenser with its camera sitting on the floor and she marched over to it, unplugged it. Indignation filled her. Somebody had been spying on her through the camera and microphone. She'd asked Jace why on the ride over here. He'd told her that hackers did it for kicks usually. Hoping to glean information like credit card numbers or other personal information. It wasn't that someone had targeted her specifically, but the information was out there for those who knew how to find it.

Poor Kitty. Well, Maddy didn't need to feed Kitty treats from a dispenser when she was home anyway. She could always plug it in when she was out so she could check on her cat and give her a treat. Then unplug it again when she got home. Seemed like a pain in the behind, but she no longer trusted that it was a harmless device.

Maddy took her phone from her purse. She'd checked everything in Jace's car. It was all there. She hadn't looked in her suitcase, but her purse and computer bag were fine. All her work was there. She figured the suitcase was fine too. If somebody wanted to steal something, they'd take the equipment, not her clothing. She dialed Angie's number.

"*Dosvedanya,* Mads," Angie said on the second ring. Her friend was at work, but if she was answering then she was free of clients right now.

Maddy laughed. "That means good bye, Ang. You mean *privyet.* That's hello."

"Whatever. How's it going over there? Meet any handsome Russians?"

Maddy thought of Jace and her skin heated. He wasn't exactly Russian, but he fit the handsome part. Not that she was telling Angie anything about it. "Actually, I'm home. The job was cut prematurely short when the collector got sick, so I came back."

That's the story Jace had told her to use, so she assumed it was the official story. It grated to lie, but on the other hand he and Ian had done a good job of impressing upon her how important it was she stick to the script and not mention them or this Calypso woman who bore such a strong resemblance to her.

"Oh, sorry. I knew you were looking forward to spending some time in St. Petersburg for the White Nights."

"I was, but I've been before. I'm sure I'll get to do it again."

"Okay, so what about handsome Russians?"

"Sorry, not this time. The most excitement I had was leaving almost as soon as I arrived."

"That sucks, huh? I can't imagine all the flying was pleasant."

It would have been worse on a commercial plane. At least there'd been a lay-flat seat on the private jet. Barrington's didn't spring for those on regular flights. "It wasn't the best, but it wasn't too bad. I didn't really have time to get on their schedule, so I guess I'll get back to my own pretty quickly."

"Did you want to get Kitty? Or I can bring her by later."

Maddy wanted to see her cat pretty badly. But until she knew what Barrington's was going to do, it was best if she left Kitty where she was. They might send her back out again. She prayed they didn't fire her over this, though Ian had promised they wouldn't. She wasn't sure she trusted him. She thought of the card Jace had given her. She'd tucked it into her pocket before she'd unlocked the door. She took it out now.

Black Defense International

Would they really come if she needed them? "I'll get her tomorrow. I might have to head out again since this job didn't pan out as expected. I should know in the morning. I'd hate to bring her home and then have to take her back tomorrow."

"Totally understand. She's perfectly fine, by the way. I left her sleeping in a sunbeam this morning. I expect she'll be waiting for me in the kitchen when I get home."

"You know she will. She wants her evening meal."

"Like she doesn't have dry food all day long. You spoil that animal."

"You love her and you know it."

"I do. Silly beast. Think you might want to get some dinner with me later?"

Maddy gazed out the window at her neighborhood. It was still light and she wasn't scared, but the thought of being out after dark and then coming home alone unnerved her. And that made her mad because she'd been living alone in this house for the past three years now. "I can't tonight. I feel like I'm going to crash hard. I'll just order something and stay in."

Angie sighed. "I get it. If you find you can't sleep and you want to get out, let me know. A group of us were thinking about going to Dock Street later."

"I'll text you if I change my mind. Kiss Kitty for me. Hopefully I'll see her tomorrow."

"Oh hell, here comes the boss. Gotta run!"

"Bye, Ang."

Angie had already ended the call. Maddy sighed and put the phone down. She really needed a shower, and then she was going to binge some TV. She knew just the show too. *Covert Affairs.*

But first she checked all the doors and windows, closing the blinds as she went.

It didn't help. She still felt vulnerable.

"Get over it, Maddy," she muttered. "If it was dangerous, he wouldn't have left you here alone."

IAN READ a report about human trafficking in the southern states. Anger simmered hot just below the veneer of his cool whenever he had to think about the kind of scumbags who would drag innocent girls into such terrible situations. He felt like his skin was going to split open from all the chaotic feelings rolling beneath it.

He looked up and met Jace's gaze as the man strode toward him across the command center. The expression on his face made Ian sit up and pay attention. Jace walked into his office after a cursory knock. When he closed the door, Ian knew it was serious.

"I told her my first name. I shouldn't have done it."

Ian arched an eyebrow. "Is that all? I thought you'd come to resign or something."

"Isn't that enough?"

Ian sat back and flipped the folder closed so he didn't have to feel the oiliness of the report anymore. "I knew you were going to do it. It's fine." There was a common thread between Jace's life and Maddy Cole's, and he knew Jace was thinking about it.

Jace frowned. Hard. "You knew?"

Ian shrugged. He'd gotten good at reading people after all these years in covert ops. He'd been so deep beneath the surface of the muck himself that he sometimes wondered if he had any humanity left. But then he read about innocent girls being trafficked to disgusting old men and his humanity surged to the surface again. Still, one of the benefits of this life he'd led was that he knew people's emotions almost before they did. He got it, and he could predict people's breaking points with a certainty that bordered on psychic. It wasn't psychic, but he didn't mind letting them think so. Made him into one scary motherfucker when he needed to be.

"You kept looking at her, but it wasn't disgust. You knew she wasn't Calypso." He held up his hand when Jace started to protest. "You thought she was at first, but your instincts told you fairly quickly you'd gotten the wrong woman. Still, we had to bring her in and test her. So you doubted yourself. But you knew. And then there's the intel on her father. He was an agent and she never knew it."

Jace was frowning. "Not uncommon for spies, is it?"

"No, it's not. You would have never known either if your parents hadn't gotten caught."

"But they did."

"They did." There was nothing else he could say. Even if he wanted to.

Jace blew out a breath. "So what's any of that have to do with telling her my name?"

"Guilt. And attraction, I expect. She's pretty. And feisty as hell. Told me to piss up a rope, right? Not in so many words, but her dismissal was pretty obvious. I like her. You like her more."

Jace shoved a hand through his hair and shook his head as if to deny it. But he didn't. "Yeah, I like her. She's interesting. But I meet a lot of interesting women and walk away. And I don't tell them my name."

"You've got good instincts, Jace. Even if she talks about you, it's not enough to jeopardize the mission.

She may talk, but she won't talk about what happened."

"You sure of that?"

Ian thought of the fire in those pretty eyes of Maddy Cole's. The dislike of him, but the curiosity toward Jace. Her eyes had dilated, her skin flushed, and her breathing quickened when she looked at Jace. Hell, if he were gay, he'd look at Jace that way too. The dude was walking, talking sex-on-a-stick. And since Maddy Cole was attracted to Jace, Ian figured she wasn't going to do anything she feared would endanger him. "I'm sure."

"Are you sure Calypso won't come after her?"

"Nope. That's why I put the detail on her."

The corners of Jace's mouth tightened. "Maybe we shouldn't have let her go so soon."

"If someone comes after her, we'll get more information than we would if we kept her here against her will."

Jace straightened, his nostrils flaring. "Are you seriously telling me that you let her go so you could use her as bait?"

Ian felt the pinch of guilt in his soul. But he did what he had to do. "Tell me what choice I had. We couldn't keep her. The next best thing we can do is watch her closely. I've got assets I could be using elsewhere watching her carefully. You talked to them. You know."

"Put me there too."

Ian studied Jace carefully. Interesting twist. "You

sure about that? It's a typical stake out. Watch her every move. Could be boring as hell."

"I'm sure."

"It's not your fault she's a part of this, you know. You grabbed the wrong woman because you were meant to grab the wrong woman."

He'd been thinking about it for a while now. Why hadn't Calypso eliminated Maddy Cole and taken her place? BDI hadn't known about Maddy, so they wouldn't have been able to stop the assassin. Either something had gone wrong on Calypso's end or Maddy had always been meant to be a smokescreen. Ian's instincts told him it was the second one, which caused him no small amount of worry.

Why? Why her?

Her father had been a low level operative, no one important. There was nothing in the files to indicate he'd ever been involved with the Syndicate. Still, Ian had assigned Brett Wheeler to dig into Maddy Cole's background. Not that he expected Brett would find anything significant, but they couldn't be too careful.

He was also trying to get the camera feed from Sokolov's compound. The grounds were surveilled, as were some of the hallways and public rooms of the house. Which meant they might just have footage of Calypso entering the room beside Maddy's. He'd been interested in the maid, but Maddy hadn't recognized her in the photo of Calypso, so that was out.

"I know I grabbed the wrong woman," Jace said.

"But now she's in it. And I feel like I owe it to her to make sure she's safe."

Ian made a split decision. "All right. If you want to stake out Maddy Cole's place, then I guess I can't stop you."

One of Jace's eyebrows went up. "Really? You're giving in that easily?"

"Easily? No. But giving in to the inevitable? No sense fighting it. You're not going to be worth a shit if you can't stop thinking about that girl."

Chapter Eight

STAKEOUTS WERE BORING AS HELL. IAN WAS RIGHT about that. He was also right that Jace couldn't stop thinking about Maddy. He could still see her standing on her porch, her face lighting with pleasure when he told her his name. He shouldn't have done it, but he couldn't take her calling him Andrei for one more second. It grated on his nerves.

The bitch of it was that it shouldn't have mattered at all. But it did. He still wasn't sure why.

So now he was here, in a rented house across the street from Maddy's place, watching her come and go. It had been five days since he'd tackled her in Sokolov's house. Five days in which he'd replayed that moment again and again. She'd been soft in all the right places, and she'd smelled good. His brain had been focused on the work because it'd had to be, but the rest of him had noticed. Now that it was in the past, his body was treating his brain to the memory on repeat.

Good times.

"She's walking out her door," Tyler Scott said. "Who's following her this time?"

"I've got it," Jace replied before Brett Wheeler could, standing and grabbing the car keys. He wasn't worried about losing her. They'd tagged her car with a GPS device so they always knew where she was. He wasn't following her to see where she was going. He followed to make sure nobody attacked her while she was out.

He got into the nondescript navy sedan and started it up, being careful to wait until Maddy was already at the end of the street before he pulled out. He had the GPS tracker on his phone and he glanced at it from time to time. Maddy was heading across town. She could be going any number of places, but her trajectory told him she was headed for the Oaks, the memory care facility where her grandmother was staying.

He'd followed her there once before, waited an hour for her to reemerge. She'd gone to lunch with her friend Angie afterward and he'd watched the two of them sitting at a restaurant by the harbor, eating crab cakes and fries and laughing. Maddy lived a quiet life when she was home. She hadn't gone out on a job again and Jace was glad. Ian had arranged that. She'd been working for Barrington's for six years, and while she traveled a lot for work, she also did a lot of work from home. There were reports to go over, research to be done.

Eventually, she'd have to travel again. They'd figure it out when she did.

Jace pulled into the parking lot of the memory care facility as Maddy strolled toward the entrance. She was wearing a yellow top with a cream blazer, distressed jeans, and some kind of high heel today. Not a stiletto, but he didn't know a whole lot about shoes so he had no clue. Her hair was loose, hanging down her back in thick dark gold curls that bounced when she walked. When he saw her like that, he had a hard time believing he could have ever thought she was a cold-blooded killer.

Admittedly, it would be the perfect cover if she was. She was so sweet and wholesome, and she traveled a lot. She *could* be Calypso if she'd ever been in the same places where the assassinations took place. Hiding in plain sight would be something he'd do if he were an assassin.

But he wasn't and they still had no reports on her whereabouts. Or even if she'd really been the trigger person during the shooting at Sokolov's.

Today, however, he was concerned with Maddy, not Calypso. He waited for an hour and then she emerged again. Her expression was a little sad, a little bewildered. His protective instincts went into overdrive. He had to stop himself from opening the car door and going to her, asking her what was wrong.

She stopped beside her car and folded her arms

over her chest. Turned to stare at the building for a long moment. He got the impression she was preparing herself for something. Then she unlocked the door of her Honda Accord and climbed inside. She started the engine. He waited for her to move, but she didn't.

And then his heart twisted as he realized what was happening. She sat there with her forehead on the steering wheel, her shoulders shaking. Maddy was losing it. He put his hand on the door handle, determined to go to her and ask what was wrong.

He tugged and the door came free. Maddy sat up again. Her brake lights went on and then the reverse lights. Jace swore and shut his door again. Maddy pulled out and drove past him. If she'd turned her head she would have seen him, but she didn't so much as glance in his direction.

He followed her toward the city center. He figured she was meeting Angie again, but when she parked and got out of her car, she didn't head for one of the restaurants that fronted the harbor. Instead, she seemed to walk aimlessly, wandering into shops and coming out again with no bags. She did that for almost forty minutes before she reached Ego Alley and kept going toward Susan Campbell Park. When she got to the end of the park, she stood and stared out at the waters of Spa Creek where it met the Severn River.

His phone rang. It was Ty. Jace wasn't miked up

because this wasn't an active mission and phone communications were fine. "Yeah?"

"You've been wandering around for an hour. Just checking."

"It's Maddy. She's the one wandering. Think she had a hard time at the nursing home."

"Shit."

"Yeah."

Ty hadn't met Maddy personally yet, but he knew her file as well as Jace did. It was part of the job. The fact Ty understood and cared said a lot. Some of BDI's operatives were questionable but that was because Ian had a cover to maintain. Those guys didn't get anywhere close to the truly important stuff. They were off in remote locales, doing whatever minor tasks Ian needed done and feeling like Rambo whenever they did it. They were all former military of some description, but former military didn't always mean they were worth a damn.

"I'll let you know if anything changes. She might be meeting her friend. Maybe she's early."

"Copy that."

Jace ended the call and stood near the park entrance, watching as Maddy continued to gaze at the water. A few people wandered by, but no one who looked suspicious. One woman jogged by him and into the park, made a loop, and then sat on a bench not too far from Maddy. She took out a phone and started to scroll.

Maddy still hadn't moved. Jace wondered what

she was thinking. Wondered what had happened at the nursing home to make her feel this way. His heart throbbed, urging him to go to her.

He shouldn't. Of course he shouldn't. But he wanted to.

"Shit," he muttered. Where the hell was this tenderness toward her coming from? He didn't get attached to anyone or anything. He knew how precarious it was. How quickly it could be ripped away.

But he wanted to.

He took out his phone. Dialed Ian.

"What's up, precious?"

Jace snorted. Ian was simultaneously the most irreverent guy he'd ever known and the most serious. "Think it fair that you know I'm considering talking to her."

There was silence on the other end of the line for a long second. Then a sigh. "Can I ask why?"

A light wind ruffled Maddy's hair, playing with the strands the way he'd like to if they were in bed together. "You can ask. I don't have an answer."

"That's an answer. Whether you realize it or not. So why are you telling me this if you plan to do it anyway?"

"I thought you might talk me out of it."

"Okay, let's give it a whirl. Talking to her might compromise you. If they're watching her, and you get involved, they'll know who you are. Where to find you. You've been hidden a long time now—do you really want to risk exposure?"

Jace clenched his jaw tight. Did he? "I'm not worried. I can take care of myself."

"All right."

Jace blinked at the sudden capitulation. "That's it? Just *all right*?"

"Can I stop you?"

Jace watched the lonely girl staring at the water. He had no softer emotions left. They'd burned out of him a long time ago. Yet here he was, feeling soft. Needing to know why. "You can order me not to."

"I've been in this business a long time. When something pegs your instincts, it's best to listen to it. Besides, you're an experienced operative. You know what's right."

"You're helpful, boss."

Ian laughed. "It's part of my charm. Now get the fuck off the phone and either follow the girl or talk to her. Your choice."

IT WAS a cloudy day with the threat of rain. Maddy stood and watched the sailboats plying the Severn River that connected to Spa Creek. Some people would sail no matter what. Didn't have to be a sunny day, or even a warm one.

She could see the Chesapeake Bay Bridge in the distance, tall spans seeming to rise into the clouds. She had such good memories of living with Mimi. Mimi had been a sailor, and she'd taken Maddy out and taught her how to sail. They'd had a sailboat, *The Miss Madeline*, that Mimi had bought when Maddy was still a baby living with her parents. Maddy had to sell it a few years ago now.

She missed that boat. Missed Mimi. Today was the first day Mimi hadn't known her at all. There were times when Mimi didn't know her at first but remembered, or a memory would come out that involved her and suddenly Mimi would look lucid again and peer at her, "Maddy girl, where have you been?"

The answer was always the same. "I've been working, Mimi. But I'm here now."

Today, Mimi never remembered her. Hadn't even talked about her. She'd talked about her son, Christopher, and told Maddy all about his big important job in the Air Force and how he was coming by to see her later today.

He wasn't coming, of course. He'd been dead for sixteen years. Maddy missed her dad and today had made it even worse. It was like the family that she loved so much existed somewhere else without her entirely. Like she'd never been born. Of course she knew it wasn't true, but it hurt.

Days like this, she almost wanted to call her mother just for some connection. Except her mother wasn't the connecting type, plus she was too caught up in her life with her husband Richard and their two kids to even care about Maddy.

Maddy dashed her fingers beneath her eyes as the

tears pooled and spilled over. "Stop it," she hissed. "Just stop."

But it wasn't that easy. It never was.

And standing here wasn't helping. Maddy whirled. Best to just get her car, pick up take-out somewhere, and go home and binge some more *Covert Affairs.* It got her mind off Mimi, but it made her think of Jace and Russia. And dwelling on what happened there brought its own kind of angst.

What she really needed was a work assignment where she could lose herself in someone's art collection. Lately, all she'd been getting were things she could do from home, and that didn't occupy her mind nearly enough.

She rubbed the tears from her cheeks and kept on walking until she was amongst the shops and restaurants of the quaint City Dock again. Her car was in the parking garage over on Gorman Street and she was making her way toward it when someone bumped into her in front of one of the restaurants on Main Street.

She stumbled backward. Strong hands gripped her shoulders and steadied her. Maddy looked up to apologize for bumping into him. Her breath stopped as blue eyes in a handsome face stared back at her.

"Jace?" *Oh, idiot.* Of course it was him, and she had to ask a question like she couldn't put two and two together. Like maybe his identity had changed? Though knowing him, maybe it had.

"Hi, Maddy." He smiled down at her and his grip eased. "How are you?"

Her heart decided to take about a hundred leaps forward, pounding so hard she felt a wave of heat wash over her. Any second and she'd be sweating under her light blazer.

"I-I'm fine."

He reached up with a finger and skimmed the back of it over her cheek. It was shockingly intimate—and also shockingly sexy. Her body responded with more heat.

"Looks like you've been crying."

"Oh, does it? Must have been the wind. I was standing by the water for a while."

He frowned, and for some idiotic reason all her defenses crumpled. She was feeling too raw, too alone, and here he was. Someone she'd been thinking about. Someone she'd been attracted to, but had resigned herself to never seeing again. Someone who confused the hell out of her and somehow—paradoxically considering their first meeting—made her feel safe.

Maddy burst into tears. "Oh God, I'm so sorry," she choked out, waving at him as if sending him away from the crazy.

She didn't know what to expect, but strong arms going around her and tugging her gently into the circle of his embrace wasn't it. He pressed her cheek to his chest and murmured something soothing. It took her a moment to realize it was in Russian. She clutched his shirt, curling her fingers into the soft cotton of the polo he wore. He stroked her hair and she struggled between embarrassment and relief that he was holding her and comforting her.

"I'm so sorry," she repeated, pushing away from him when she felt as if she could finally get herself under control. He let her go and stood tall, shielding her from prying eyes like her own private wall of muscle.

"What happened, Maddy?"

There were two damp spots on his dark shirt. Embarrassment swirled. She forced herself to meet his gaze. Her heart flipped. Why was he so attractive? Why was she so damn needy right now?

"It's my grandmother." His expression changed and she realized how that had sounded. She rushed on. "She's fine… but she didn't know me today. Not at all. Not even a glimmer."

It sounded kind of lame now that she said it. Because dementia was a thing and it wasn't about her, it was about Mimi. Wasn't it selfish to be upset because Mimi was lost in happy thoughts of the son she thought was still alive and couldn't remember her granddaughter at all? Maddy should be happy that Mimi wasn't in pain right now.

"I'm sorry, Maddy. That had to be hard."

She sniffled. "It was. And now I feel guilty about it because she's fine, you know? She thinks my dad is still alive and well, so why should I feel sorry for myself because today she didn't know me?"

"I think you're entitled to be upset. She's your

family. You have a wealth of memories about her, and she had none of you today."

"I didn't expect it. It hit me hard. She usually recognizes me at some point." Maddy dragged in a breath. "They told me it would get worse. That one day she wouldn't know me at all. But she *could* remember me again. Just in the tiniest of slices though. She'll never be who she used to be."

"I'm sorry."

"So am I." She shook her head. "You don't want to hear about this. How are you? What are you doing in town? Am I interrupting something super important?"

Oh jeez, what a way to ask if he was on a mission.

"Nothing important. I'm on my way to lunch. You want to join me?"

Maddy blinked. "I—yes, thank you." No way in hell was she saying no. Maybe she should—she knew what he did, after all, and it wasn't safe—but she really didn't want to. She'd called Angie to go to lunch earlier, but her friend had a new client today and couldn't get away.

"Good. I know a place you'll like."

He offered his arm. She looped hers inside it, shivering just a little at the thrill it gave her to do so.

Oh Maddy, this is a very bad idea….

Chapter Nine

THEY HAD TO WALK A LITTLE DISTANCE, BUT JACE took her to a small restaurant on a side street where the tourists didn't tend to go. The proprietor seated them at a table in the back and Jace pulled out her chair before taking the one opposite. The one that faced the entrance. He was armed, of course. He didn't expect trouble, but he was always prepared for it. He didn't walk into a restaurant or a store—or anywhere really—without scoping out the entrances and exits. He always knew where he was and how he was going to defend himself. Occupational hazard.

Maddy fiddled with her menu. She seemed nervous, nibbling the inside of her cheek and studying the menu like she was going to be tested on it and the results meant the difference between life and death.

Jace watched her, which probably didn't help her nervousness. He knew she could feel it. Just like he could feel it when anyone stared at him. Between the two of them, however, there was something more.

A wicked attraction. The desire to get naked and sweaty. He knew she felt it too. He could tell by the way her voice hitched in when she'd accepted his invitation to lunch. The way she'd clung to him as she'd cried.

He wanted to strip her and see everything. Then he wanted to run his fingers and tongue over her body, exploring all her soft sweetness. He wouldn't do any of it without an express invitation though. She might be attracted to him, but until she said the actual word *yes* he wasn't acting on the hot, dirty thoughts swirling in his brain. He wasn't the kind of guy who forced a situation at all.

He shouldn't be here. He shouldn't have approached her at all, but he'd known he was going to do it. Ian had known too. Jace had tried to walk away. When she'd turned in the park and started walking back, he'd slipped away to follow her. Watching her hunched shoulders and downcast head, he'd made his decision. He'd needed to know what was wrong. What was making her so sad. If he knew, maybe he could help.

So here they were in a restaurant, facing each other across a table, and the sexual heat was flowing fast and strong. And he couldn't fix a damn thing for her. Her grandmother was losing her grip on reality, and nothing could bring that back. He didn't know from personal experience, but he knew. Dementia claimed its victims, dragging them beneath the surface of memory and reality until they drowned in their own confusion. Nothing fixed that.

The server arrived, interrupting Jace's study of her.

"Hi, I'm Bobby and I'll be your server today. What can I get the lady to drink?" he asked.

"Uh, water."

"And the gentleman?"

Gentleman? Jace didn't know who the dude was kidding, but whatever. "I'll have a water too. But bring a bottle of your best Cab and two glasses, please."

He already knew that Maddy drank red wine or bourbon when she drank. It was in her file. It was also in her file that she didn't drink often, but he thought she might need it today.

Bobby lifted one eyebrow. "I can bring sir a wine menu. The best is subjective. And some are pricey."

Jace appreciated his honesty, though he also found himself wondering if the guy was thinking he couldn't afford it. In truth, Jace could afford a lot. Covert work paid *very* well. It should considering what he risked to get it done. He saved it because he never wanted to be in a position where he couldn't buy himself privacy or a new identity if he had to. You never knew in this business…

"You like wine, Bobby?"

"Yes, sir."

"Red wine?"

"Yes."

"Then you choose for me. Just make sure it's good."

"Very well, sir. Did you know what you want to order for lunch or should I come back?"

"Maddy?"

"I know what I want," she said, her voice soft.

"We'll order now."

Maddy ordered the grilled fish and Jace did the same. Hard to be in Annapolis and not eat fresh-caught fish. Bobby took their menus and disappeared. Jace told himself to act like a normal guy on a date, not a covert operative seeking an angle. "How have you been, Maddy?"

Green eyes the color of sea glass stared back at him. "I've been okay. You?"

"Fine."

"I thought you'd be on a trip somewhere."

"Busy here. What about you?"

She shrugged. "I've got a few things to do, but nothing exciting. No trips to Russia."

"What about Sokolov's collection?" He knew she wasn't being sent back yet, but he asked anyway.

"I expect to return in a week or two. The job isn't done."

"How much did you finish?"

"Considering the size of his house, not a lot. But I catalogued about half the icons. Most of the artwork has already been appraised, but my job was to verify. And authenticate his new acquisitions. There were a few."

"Anybody else in your organization who can do it?"

She bristled. "I'm the best. Why would they send anyone else?"

"You aren't worried about going back?"

Bobby returned with their drinks then. Two waters and a bottle of Napa Valley Cabernet Sauvignon that he opened with a flourish before pouring a taste into a crystal stem for Jace to sample. Jace sniffed, swirled, and sipped. "Excellent."

Bobby smiled. "Very good, sir." Then he poured two glasses and disappeared.

Maddy picked up her glass and took a taste. Her eyes closed for the briefest of moments. He thought she might have moaned. "This is really good. But I shouldn't be drinking at lunch."

Jace lifted his glass. Swirled it to release the scent. "Life's short, Maddy. Drink up."

Her sea-glass gaze was troubled. He wanted to wrap her in his arms and tell her it would be all right. Even if it wouldn't. She tipped the glass up and took another big sip. "You've got that right."

"You didn't answer my question."

"Which question?"

"Are you worried about going back to Sokolov's?"

She twisted the stem of the wineglass on the table, swirling the wine gently. "Are you planning to be there too?"

Was he? If she went back, then Ian would probably send someone. Just in case. He didn't know if it would be him. Though he could always insist. Still, he wasn't telling her that. "I don't know. Probably not."

"Then I think I'll be safe, don't you?"

Her eyes twinkled and it took him a second to realize she was ribbing him. "Cute. You're safer when I'm there. Don't you know that by now?"

She sipped the wine again. "I don't think you're safe at all. Jace," she added softly, as if testing his name. He loved the way it sounded on her lips. Soft, sweet, welcoming. Like coming home.

No. He shook his head. There was no home for him. No coming home. He didn't know what that was like. At *all.* And he didn't need to grasp at straws now, to wish for it in the arms of a woman he hardly knew.

"I'm not safe," he told her. Growled at her, really. He set the wine glass down, leaned toward her. "Don't you know what this is, Maddy?"

She licked her lips. Shook her pretty head. Her eyes were wide. Not scared, but slightly shocked. She didn't speak.

"It's a seduction," he told her. "I want you beneath me. On top of me. Surrounding me. I've never even kissed you, and I want you so badly my knees are weak with it."

Her mouth was a soft, round O. Delicate pink heat flared over her cheeks. She lifted her wine glass. Sampled. He could see the pulse beating in her throat. She was a hunted animal, and he was the hunter. He wanted to dominate her. Fuck her into oblivion. Make her feel good and forget her pain.

She didn't say anything for a long moment. Then her eyes lifted, and he felt as if she'd speared him. "My heart tells me I want the same thing you do." She sucked in a breath. "My head tells me you're bad news and to run. My heart refuses to even stand up."

"Here we are," Bobby said, arriving in a sing-song of server-speak with their meals, which he sat down in front of them with a flourish. "Fish for the lady. Fish for the gentleman. Can I get you anything else?"

A cold shower? A reality check?

"Nothing," Jace said. "Nothing at all."

HER HEART BEAT SO FAST she was dizzy with it. The food was fragrant and appealing, and yet she worried she couldn't eat a bite because her stomach was twisted with heat and need. He'd told her when he'd dropped her off a week ago she wouldn't see him again unless he wanted her to.

Yet here he was. It wasn't an accident, was it?

Her brain could hardly wrap itself around the fact. Her body was already pressing the accelerator. *Let's get naked. Now. It's been too long…*

Yes, it had been too long. But getting naked with Jace—oh my God, she didn't even know his last name—wasn't the answer.

Is too!

Her body was insistent. Get naked, spread her legs, feel his hard cock inside her. But what if he didn't know how to use what God gave him? What if he was a lousy lay?

He must have read the confusion on her face. He took her hand, twisted his finger in hers. "Maddy, I'm not trying to push you into anything. I'm happy to have lunch with you. Talk to you. Get to know you. You don't have to make a decision right now. I just thought it fair to tell you where I'm headed."

Was he for real? Men like this one didn't tell her they wanted her—but only whenever she was ready. Did they? *He just did.*

She didn't remove her hand from his, but she picked up her fork in the other and gently poked at the grilled fish. Her nerves were a tangled mass of quivering jelly. He squeezed her fingers softly and then let go and picked up his own fork. Doubt pricked her. Should she have bent her attention to the fish? Or should she have kept staring into his eyes and let him know she wasn't uninterested even if she didn't know how to tell him she definitely wanted more?

"Eat, Maddy," he said gently. "We've got time to figure this out."

She ate fish and grilled zucchini and fragrant rice and contemplated her life. She'd been devastated over Mimi, but then Jace arrived and threw her a curve ball. And now she couldn't stop thinking about what he'd said. She watched him furtively. He ate his fish, drank his wine, and every movement made her want him more. How was that possible?

"Why don't you live in Russia now?" she asked.

His head snapped up. She hurried to explain. "You said you moved there as a kid. When did you leave?"

The lines on his forehead seemed to relax. "About seven years ago."

"Is your family still there?" He'd said he had an American parent and a Russian parent. But where did they live now?

His expression changed. Hardened. He didn't look up from his food. "No. They are gone now."

She picked up on his tone. "Gone? You've lost them?"

His gaze crackled with emotion. He nodded. She reached for his hand impulsively. Squeezed his fingers in hers. She thought he might pull away but instead he squeezed back. "*Da*," he said, acknowledging her in Russian. "They are dead."

"I'm very sorry for your loss."

"I know you are," he said. "You're a sweet girl, Maddy Cole."

She didn't want to be sweet. She wanted to be sophisticated. Interesting. Sexy as sin. *He said he wanted you, idiot.*

He had said that. Didn't mean she was sexy as sin though. She stabbed at the fish. It was delicious but it was also hard to taste because she was nervous.

They finished the meal with small talk she wouldn't remember an hour from now, then Bobby arrived again and sold them on a chocolate cake that he swore was *to die for*. Maddy asked Jace if he wanted to share and he said he did. So the cake arrived with two forks, some whipped cream, and two cups of coffee. She'd drank half a bottle of wine and her head was swimming so she reached for the coffee like a lifeline. It was rich and fragrant and she just knew it would fix the swimmy-ness of her head.

She downed two cups, ate half the cake, and then Jace was asking for the check. "I'll pay for mine," she said, rummaging in her purse for her credit card.

Jace frowned. "I've got it."

"I can't let you do that—"

"You can. I asked you to lunch. I'm paying."

Mimi always said never to argue with someone who insisted on paying. You could offer, even offer insistently, but if someone wouldn't accept your offer you graciously thanked them and let them pay. Which is what Maddy did now.

Jace dropped several twenties onto the tray and stood, holding out his hand for her. Maddy put her fingers in his, thrilling at the sizzle of heat that passed through her as he helped her to her feet. She was a little unsteady, though not terribly so. It wasn't the wine anymore because they'd lingered over the cake and coffee for quite some time. It was him. Heat slid through her veins at his touch. Sadness pressed at the back of her mind, but right now she was happy and she didn't let it bust through her barriers.

Jace kept holding her hand as he led her from the restaurant. She didn't question him, just walked along with him until he asked her, "Where did you park?"

"The garage on Gorman."

"Me too," he told her. "I'll take you to your car."

They walked together, looking in shop windows and laughing at things she would later have trouble recalling. Her heart beat high and hard and Jace was like a sun in her orbit. Intense, hot, full of life. He led her to her car, then backed her against it and caged her between his arms. He was close. So close, his blue eyes hot as they skimmed over her face. He lingered on her lips, which tingled at the touch that wasn't a touch.

"I want to kiss you," he said, his voice deep and throaty and masculine.

Maddy tried to tell herself why it was a bad idea. Why she was still pissed at him and always would be. He'd shot at her and hand-cuffed her to an airplane seat, for pity's sake! But it was futile. She wasn't pissed and she could think of nothing better than a kiss. Nothing she wanted more.

"Yes," she said almost helplessly. "Yes."

His mouth captured hers hotly, and her body melted like wax beneath a blow torch.

Chapter Ten

HE'D KISSED A LOT OF WOMEN IN HIS THIRTY-TWO years of life. None had ever bowled him over with the first touch of her tongue the way this one did. Maddy tasted like coffee and chocolate and wine, and he couldn't get enough. He'd backed her against her car door, trapped her there, and when she'd said yes to a kiss, well, he hadn't given her time to change her mind.

Her fingers curled into his shirt, her head tipped back. She'd opened to him with all the trust in the world. And he took advantage, sliding his tongue into her mouth to tangle with hers.

The drumbeat of desire pounded in his veins, throbbed to life in his cock. Any second and she'd know it too. He could back away, make sure she didn't. But he wanted her to know. Wanted her to say yes.

But then he thought of her standing in the park,

her back to him as she stood with hunched shoulders and thought about her grandmother, and he knew that now wasn't the time. She was sad and lonely and maybe she'd say yes out of a desire to forget her sadness. He didn't want that. He wanted to be with her because she wanted it, chose it, not because it was an alternative to her melancholy.

The hardest thing he ever did was gentle his kiss and put space between them. So she wouldn't feel the insistent press of his hard-on against her belly. Her fingers still curled in his shirt and her mouth still welcomed him, but now he wasn't pushing for more.

The kiss went on for long minutes while he explored her mouth, nipped her lips, sucked the lower one softly between his while she moaned. And then he released her. Her eyes drifted open and she stared up at him, the green depths vulnerable and raw and filled with swirling emotions that told him he was right not to push her into more at this time.

"You okay?" he asked her.

She nodded. "You?" Her sudden grin was cheeky.

His laugh was rustier than he expected. "I will be. Give me your keys, Maddy."

She fished them out of her purse and handed them to him. He unlocked her door and shifted them sideways so he could open it. "So this is good bye?" she asked.

He gave her the keys and stepped away. "For now."

She seemed disappointed. He appreciated that. He was disappointed too.

"Will I see you again, Jace? Or was this an exception?"

It should be an exception. It needed to be. One afternoon, one kiss, the end. "Give me your phone."

She took it out and unlocked it. Handed it to him. "Do you always give orders instead of requests?"

"Sorry," he said as he called his number so they would each have the other's. "It's a habit. In my business, I don't make requests when orders are what keeps me and my guys alive."

"That makes sense. But try asking me sometime, okay?" The cheeky grin was back.

He laughed. "I will."

"So when will I see you again? I assume giving me your number means I will."

"Soon, Maddy. Very soon." He looped an arm around her, tugged her back in for a kiss. Need sizzled through him, scorched his soul. *So sweet.* Yeah, this girl was sweet and he wanted so much more.

But patience had seen him through a lot of tricky situations in his life. It would get him where he wanted to go now.

"Wow," she breathed as he ended the kiss. "That's some secret weapon you've got there. Is your mouth licensed to kill?"

He liked her corny James Bond jokes. He liked her. "No—but it is licensed to give you one of the best orgasms of your life."

Her breath hitched. "Only one of the best?"

"Yeah. Got another weapon licensed for best orgasms too." Corny, but he was a go with the flow kind of guy. And she made him feel playful. Something he didn't recall feeling in a very long time.

"I'm going to withhold judgement for now. You'll have to prove it to me."

His heart flipped. His belly clenched. And his balls squeezed tight at the idea. "I'm planning on it, *zvyozdochka*."

He held the car door for her as she got inside. She twisted the key and looked up at him. "Thank you for lunch, Jace."

"You're welcome, Maddy. I hope it helped."

"It did. I needed a friend, and you were there. Who would have thought it a week ago? Life is crazy sometimes."

"It can be." He knew it better than most.

She hesitated. Then she smiled. "Okay, bye."

"Bye."

He closed the door and watched her back out of her spot. Then he went over to his car and followed her home.

KITTY LOOPED around her ankles as Maddy emptied a tin of moist food onto a plate. "Hang on, baby, Mama's getting it ready."

She set the plate down and Kitty dove in like she

was starved. She wasn't because she had dry food in her bowl. Still, she was a cat—and cats wanted what they wanted when they wanted it.

Maddy gave her a stroke down her back, then straightened and returned to fixing her own meal. It was after seven, later than she normally ate, but the lunch with Jace had been big and she hadn't been hungry again until now.

She couldn't stop thinking about him. About that kiss. Her knees had nearly buckled when his mouth touched hers. Everything about Jace was intense and that kiss had been no exception. It had consumed her. She'd have done anything he wanted right then. But he hadn't asked. She'd thought for certain he was going to take it as far as she let him. He hadn't though. He'd stopped.

At the time, she'd been confused and a little nervous. The more she thought about it the more she wondered if maybe he wasn't as attracted to her as he pretended to be. Maybe he was back because they needed something from her. She didn't know what, but she'd watched enough *Covert Affairs* to know she might still be useful to them.

"That's just a silly television show," she mumbled as she stirred the pasta in her Lean Cuisine before putting it back in the microwave.

It was a fun show, but she was certain it bore little resemblance to reality in many cases. She couldn't divine Jace's intentions based on television.

Her phone pinged. She picked it up, hoping it was Jace. But it was Angie.

Can you talk?

Sure.

A second later the phone rang. "Hey, babe, what's up?" she asked.

"So," Angie began. "Liam said he saw you today."

Maddy's heart thumped. "And?"

Angie blew out a breath. "He said you were with a guy. A very sexy guy, I might add. I can't believe you met a guy and you didn't tell me about it!"

Maddy frowned. Oh, boy. "He's just someone I know. It's nothing, which is why I didn't mention him. I ran into him after I went to see Mimi. I was upset and he asked me to lunch. No biggie."

"No biggie? Babe, Liam said the guy was big and pretty and sexy as hell. I'd expect, even if it's nothing, that you might at least introduce *me* to him if you aren't interested."

"I don't know him all that well, Ang. He's a work acquaintance." Well that was certainly true. Sort of. "Honestly, I didn't expect to see him today—or ever, really—which is why I didn't say anything. I met him on a job and never thought to cross paths again."

She could practically hear Angie's wheels turning. "So does he live around here or what? And what's his name? Do you think you'll see him again?"

"He lives in the metro area, but I don't know where. His name is Jace and I don't know."

Angie sighed. "Okay. Do you want to see him again?"

Maddy's belly twisted. Did she? Oh hell yes, she did.

Insanity, that's what it was. She'd lost her damned mind. From him capturing her and forcing her onto a plane to lunch today where he'd kissed the daylights out of her, she'd certainly come full circle.

"I wouldn't say no if he asked," she replied.

"Do you think he will?"

"I think it's possible. We exchanged numbers." Her heart raced and her skin prickled with heat. Maybe she didn't need to be talking about this, but she suddenly had to tell someone or she'd burst. She and Angie typically talked about everything, but she hadn't intended to mention Jace unless things got a bit more certain. Since Angie's coworker saw them at lunch, though, all bets were off.

"Oooh, sounds like a distinct possibility then. What kind of guy gives you his phone number if he doesn't want to see you again?"

"I don't know. I'm rusty on the whole dating thing, remember?"

"I know, hon. That's not your fault though."

No, it wasn't. She'd been taking care of Mimi and building her reputation at Barrington's. She'd had the occasional drink with a guy, but she wasn't typically the sort of woman who hopped into bed with a man on the first date. She didn't think there was anything wrong with it, but it wasn't the way she was wired.

She needed to know somebody first. Not everything about them, but enough to make her comfortable with the sort of person they were.

Did she know what sort of person Jace was? She thought so but she couldn't be certain. Which made her reaction to his kiss earlier a little bit frightening. Like jumping off a mountain without being certain the hang glider was attached.

"Well, he may not call. Maybe he was just being nice. He could tell I was upset when he ran into me and he was nice enough to ask me to lunch. That might be the end of it."

"Except for the part where you exchanged numbers. What else happened?"

Did she dare tell Angie about the kiss? If she did, her friend would analyze it for an hour at least. Maddy loved Angie but she wasn't sure she could handle that right now. On the other hand, if she didn't spill, she'd feel guilty for days. Angie was her bestie and besties were there for each other through thick and thin.

"He kissed me—but I don't want to analyze it to death, okay? It was a hot kiss with tongues—and if he'd kept going, I'd have let him screw me right there against the car in public. But he didn't. He backed away and said good bye."

"Honey, a hot kiss with tongues and numbers being exchanged sounds *very* promising."

"I thought so too."

"And you said it was nothing."

Maddy laughed. "I did, didn't I? I think I'm trying to set myself up so I'm not disappointed when it doesn't work out."

"Don't doom the whole thing before it begins. Think positive."

"You're right. I'll try. So how did your new client meeting go today?"

"It went well. I think they'll switch their accounts to our firm." Angie was a junior accountant with a big firm that had branches all over the country. She'd been a math teacher for a while, until she'd realized that teaching wasn't her calling. Then she'd gone back to school and got the accounting degree. Maddy wasn't certain that Angie was happy yet, but she hoped her friend would find the thing that made her excited to get up in the morning. It was disheartening to see Angie push off plans and dreams while she worked hard to make her bosses value her.

But then wasn't that what Maddy did too? She worked a lot, took every job they threw her way, and didn't have much of a social life. She told herself it was about Mimi—and it was—but the truth was more complicated than that. She worked out of fear—for Mimi, for herself, for what life could bring when you weren't vigilant.

She talked to Angie a bit longer and then they ended with a promise to get together for lunch this week. Maddy went into her bedroom and changed into her pajamas in the bathroom. When she went to close the blinds, there was a woman pushing a stroller along the sidewalk. Maddy didn't recognize her, but the neighborhood was getting gentrified and new people were moving in all the time. Paying a premium for the land, too. One day, Maddy would have to give in and sell even though the idea saddened her too much. This house was the last link she had to her childhood and her family. If she sold it, what then?

Maddy returned to the living room and flipped on the TV. Out of habit, she turned to the Russian language news station to see if there was anything new on Leonid Sokolov or the shooting at his home. The media had been utterly silent on it after the first night, and tonight was no exception. Whatever had happened, they were done with it.

She considered more *Covert Affairs*, but decided that what she really needed was a dose of HGTV. Watching people flip houses was entertaining and exciting all at once. There was a marathon of *Fixer Upper*, her favorite remodeling and decorating show, so she pulled up a blanket and settled in for the night.

She was just starting to doze off to the sound of Chip Gaines's voice when her phone dinged with a message. She pulled it up—and her heart rocketed into outer space at the number on her screen: *Jace.*

JACE FELT LIKE A VOYEUR. Here he was across the street, watching Maddy's house, peering at her through the blinds—wanting to shout at her to close them until she finally did—and listening to her phone conversations with her friend. BDI hadn't tapped her phone, but a special listening device aimed in the right direction caught everything she said—and everything Angie had said to her.

His gut had clenched at the part where she'd said she would have let him screw her against her car. He'd been both thrilled and disgusted at the same time. Disgusted with himself for spying on her, not at her for saying it. If anything, he'd wanted to rewind the day and make it happen just like that.

Colt was with him tonight while Ty had the evening off. Brett had left earlier to do something for Ian. Colt was watching *John Wick* on Netflix and cheering Keanu Reeves as he battled his enemies. Jace had been listening to Maddy's call and trying not to hang on her every word.

But fuck that shit because she was off the phone now and he wanted contact. So he'd picked up his phone and texted her. In Russian, just to test her. She spoke it well. Did she read it equally as well?

Her reply was swift. *Who is this?*

Jace frowned. *Seriously? I gave you my number today.*

She sent back a laughing emoji. *I'm kidding. I know it's you. How's it going? Kidnap any innocent women tonight?*

Damn, she was hardcore. *Not tonight. Yet….*

Night's early. You've got time.

He wished he could see her. Wished he could see the expression on her face and divine her mood. If she hadn't just been telling her friend she hoped he'd call, he might think she was pushing him away.

Not tonight. Too much trouble.

I had fun today, Jace. Thanks.

You feeling any better tonight?

I think so. I know it's part of the journey. One day she won't know me at all.

I'm sorry.

Not your fault. Why are we texting? Can't you talk?

He glanced at Colt. Then he stood and headed for the back door. "I gotta make a call," he said.

Colt grunted. "Yeah, fine."

Jace went out the back door and stood in the growing darkness, listening to people in a yard nearby argue about something he couldn't quite hear. He dialed Maddy's number. She answered on the second ring.

"This good enough for you?" he asked.

"Hello to you too." There was silence for a moment. "We could keep texting, but I have to backspace and retype half the words. Talking seems easier. Unless you're on a mission or something."

"I wouldn't be calling you if I were."

She sighed. "I'm sorry. I shouldn't have said anything. If you'd rather text, it's fine."

"I wouldn't rather text. I just didn't want to call you without texting first." He frowned. God he was so out of his element here. He usually seduced a woman into bed, gave her a good time, and walked away without a second thought. "I've been thinking about how we said good bye."

"Have you? I haven't given it another thought."

He snorted. How could she be so cute and interesting—and why was he intrigued this much? Ian said it was because her dad had been a spy and she didn't know it, which paralleled his life until age ten. It was more than that, though. "Liar."

"Fine, you caught me. I've thought about it a lot. I even thought maybe the whole thing was a set up, and you and Ian still need something from me."

"It wasn't a set up," he swore—though guilt pricked him anyway because he still wasn't telling her the full truth. *We're spying on you, Maddy. Hoping you aren't in danger but also hoping Calypso shows up.* "I broke the rules to be with you this afternoon."

He could hear the hitch in her breathing. "You did? Why?"

"Didn't I already tell you? I want you."

"But why? I'm nobody special. You meet far more interesting people in your line of work, I'm sure."

He walked over to the side of the house. Around to the front. Stared across the road at her cute little house with gray siding and blue shutters. The front door was a bright, happy green. Light glowed softly behind the closed blinds. He could only imagine where she was in there. What she was doing.

"You *are* special, Maddy. And you're beautiful. I like you."

"I like you too. I shouldn't. I really shouldn't after Russia. But I do."

"I'm one of the good guys, swear to God."

"A good guy who tackled me, shot at me, and cuffed me to a plane seat."

Jesus. It was a wonder she was even speaking to him. "For which I am profoundly sorry. But I thought you were someone else. Do *not* repeat that name over this line," he added.

"Is someone listening?"

He loved how she leaped to the logical conclusion. It wasn't that he thought she wasn't smart enough to do so. It was simply that most people didn't consider all the ways in which they could be spied upon.

"Probably not. But some names are volatile and bring attention."

"Kind of like *Beetlejuice*, huh? Say his name three times and he'll appear."

Jace was confused. "Wait—isn't that a star in Orion?"

"Oh my God, you've never seen the movie?"

"I don't even know what you're talking about." American pop culture escaped him sometimes.

"It's a movie about ghosts and demons and the afterlife—but it's a comedy. You should watch it sometime."

"Maybe we can watch it together."

"Maybe. Mimi loved it. We watched it every Halloween. It was just scary enough without being terrifying when I was a kid." She paused. "So you still haven't found her, huh?"

She meant Calypso. "Not yet. We will."

"I hope so. She sounds like a terrible person."

"I don't know if she is or not." Ian probably wanted to hire Calypso if he could find her. Jace didn't think it would happen that way, but Ian never wrote off anybody until he had to. Jace was a prime example of that. If not for Ian, who knows where he'd be right now. Dead, probably. "But it's best if we don't discuss her anymore."

"Trust me, she's a bad person if how you treated me when you thought I was her is any indication. But fine, I'm done talking about her."

"Good." He didn't think her curiosity was at an end, but he was relieved she didn't want to talk about Calypso anymore. He could hear the back door open and he knew Colt was looking for him. If Colt had checked the listening device at all, he knew Maddy was on the phone. But did he know who she was talking to? "Something's come up, Maddy. I have to go."

"Okay."

He heard the doubt in her voice. She still didn't trust him. Not that he blamed her. "Meet me for lunch again tomorrow."

"When?"

"One o'clock. Same place."

She didn't say anything for a long moment. "I'll be there."

Chapter Eleven

Patience was a virtue, or so they said. Calypso wasn't sure she believed it was a virtue so much as it was absolutely vital to her profession. It wasn't satisfying to pull the trigger too soon—metaphorically speaking since she didn't only use guns to eliminate her targets. No, it took time to do the job properly. Time and planning.

And sometimes there were rewards for patience. Huge rewards. This time was going to be one of them.

She ditched the stroller she'd stolen off someone's porch in a yard the next street over and kept on walking. If she'd popped Madeline Cole too soon, she wouldn't know about the men who watched over the art historian from the house across the street. She also wouldn't know that one of those men was someone she'd been searching for for years.

He was there now. In that house, unsuspecting. She could kill him before he even knew he was in danger. She'd have to kill the others as well, but she didn't mind. Still, where was the fun in doing it now? The reward?

No, it would take patience to do it right.

To make him pay for what he'd done.

But she would. She always did.

MADDY DIDN'T KNOW why she was doing this. She parked her car in the garage, then got out and made her way toward the restaurant where she'd lunched with Jace yesterday. She hadn't heard from him again other than a text that said, *See you at one.*

So here she was, striding into the restaurant—which was more crowded today—and waiting for her eyes to adjust to the darkness. The hostess looked her up and down. "Are you Maddy?"

"Yes," she said, closing her umbrella since it was drizzling outside and dropping it into the designated spot at the restaurant entrance.

"Your lunch companion is already seated. Please follow me."

Maddy tried not to be nervous as she smoothed the fabric of her dress and followed the hostess. Oh God, why had she worn a dress anyway? She was trying too hard. It was lunch, not the symphony. If she could have turned and left without Jace seeing her, she would have. But he was right there, waiting. He stood as they approached. He was wearing jeans and a button down shirt today, and he looked utterly delicious. Her heart throbbed as he smiled. He took her hand and the world melted away. The hostess disappeared—or at least Maddy didn't see her anymore—and Jace leaned in for a kiss. Her brain tried to process everything that was happening but all it did was short circuit. Their lips met and she sighed.

The kiss didn't last long, plus it was chaste. Jace pulled away first, then helped her into her seat. She plunked into it because her knees were weak. Then she pasted on a smile even though she felt like an idiot. "Hi," she said.

"Hi," he replied, sinking down opposite her. "You look gorgeous today."

"So do you." Maddy stared at his handsome face for long moments. Then she shook herself. "What on earth are you doing to me? I shouldn't even be talking to you, yet here I am."

His expression didn't change, but she thought his eyes looked bleak for a second. "If you're uncomfortable with me, you don't have to stay. I'll understand."

Maddy bit the inside of her lip as she picked up her menu. She could feel him watching her. Waiting. "I shouldn't have said that. The truth is I couldn't stop myself from talking to you if I tried. And I don't want to try."

He reached across the table and threaded his fingers through hers. She looked up into glittering eyes that made her heart skip. "You need to know that it'd probably be safer for you to walk away."

Her heart kept on skipping. "Oh, you mean safe like I was before I met you? Because apparently I wasn't, was I? That shooting at Sokolov's the night I was there was no accident." She shook her head. She'd had time to think about everything and she knew that whoever was out there, whoever this Calypso person was, Maddy had been chosen specifically because of her job and her resemblance to the assassin. So she could get into Sokolov's party and eliminate her targets. "Why didn't she kill me so she could use my credentials to get into the party? That's what I don't understand."

"She had a way in already. Had to, right?"

"Yes. But why involve me at all if so?"

"Maybe you were her back up plan."

Maddy blinked. "Wow. I hadn't thought of that. I guess it's a good thing she didn't need me then."

"You might have also been her way out. If we had you, we wouldn't keep looking for her. And we didn't."

"But how could she have known I'd be in the right place at the right time?"

"I doubt she did. But she probably had a plan to make sure you were where she needed you to be."

Maddy thought back to the moments leading up

to the shots. "I keep thinking about the maid. But she didn't look anything like the photos you showed me—or anything like me. She had short black hair, for one thing. She was white, pretty, but I think it would be kinda hard to mistake me for her. She was shorter than I am, heavier. And her chest was, uh, larger."

Bobby from yesterday arrived and Jace let her go. "Well, hello again, you two lovebirds. What can I get you to drink? Another bottle? Same as yesterday or something different?"

Maddy held up her hand. "Oh, no wine for me today. Just water." She wanted to keep a clear head. She was already out of her depth with Jace, and she wasn't adding wine to the mix.

"Very well, madam. Sparkling or still?"

"Sparkling, please."

"And what will sir have?"

"Sparkling water sounds great," Jace replied.

"Fabulous! Now let me tell you the specials, and I'll be right back in two shakes to take your order."

After Bobby named all the specials and disappeared, it seemed suddenly quiet and awkward. Maddy pulled in a breath and tried to focus on the menu.

"You seem nervous," Jace said with a frown. "Is it what we were just talking about?"

Maddy thought about telling him yes, that was exactly it. But she didn't. She opened her mouth and the truth came out. "I am nervous. I haven't, uh, been involved with anyone in years now. Not that we're involved, of course. But I don't know what I'm doing or if I should even be doing it. I also know more about you than I would if we'd met at a party or in a bar. And what I know is kind of frightening, I guess—which does relate to what we were talking about in a way. What happened at Mr. Sokolov's was terrifying."

Jace nodded. "I get that, Maddy. I appreciate the honesty, but I am who I am. That's not going to change. I have a job to do—an important job—and I'm going to keep doing it. You need to know that."

"I know."

"The way I see it, you have two choices. Keep going or walk away. I won't stop you if you walk away."

She really should get up and leave right now. It would be so much easier. Just walk away and not get involved. But she also knew she wasn't going to do it. Yet. "I don't think I want to."

"I'm glad to hear it. But if at any point you change your mind, all you have to do is tell me."

Bobby returned with their drinks and took their order. The restaurant was hopping today, but they were in a secluded corner. Jace sat with his back to the wall and Maddy got the impression, even when he was looking directly at her, that he was also scanning the restaurant for threats. If someone came inside with mayhem on their mind, Jace would take care of business and put a stop to it.

"How's your grandmother today?"

Maddy swallowed the lump in her throat. "She's okay."

"Did you go see her again?"

"No." She swirled her finger along the edge of the glass. "I don't want to confuse her too much, so I don't go every day. But I called to check on her. The nurse said she was fine. Playing cards in the common room and hoarding chocolate kisses. She was talking about her granddaughter today and how proud she was of her. Of me."

God, it hurt to talk about this stuff, but she felt like he really wanted to know. And she was just emotionally raw enough to take advantage of that.

"That's good, right?"

"It is. She'll probably always remember she has a granddaughter—but she won't remember me. She'll think of me as a shy fifteen year-old who came to live with her when my dad died." She shrugged, even though it hurt. "I'm trying to learn to deal with it. Mimi won't forget *me*. But she won't know who I am when I visit her. And as painful as that is, I still have to go see her."

He seemed troubled. "I'm sorry it's difficult for you."

"Thank you." She sipped her water and smiled as brightly as she could. "So tell me something about you." She knew his parents were dead because he'd told her so, but she didn't know much else about him.

"There's nothing to tell."

"I don't know… it seems as if you live a very

interesting life. You said you'd lived in St. Petersburg. How long were you there?"

"Until I was conscripted into the Russian army at eighteen."

"Oh my goodness. I didn't realize."

He shrugged. "How could you?"

"No, I guess I couldn't. But how did that happen? I thought you were American…"

His expression seemed troubled. "I am. I am also Russian. Or was."

"No longer?"

He set his fork down and studied her intently. "It's best if we don't talk about this."

Maddy twisted her fingers into her skirt. She was out of her depth here. "Oh, of course. I'm sorry for prying."

He reached for her hand like he had earlier. Held her fingers lightly in his. "You're refreshing, Madeline Cole. You say what you think, you wear your heart on your sleeve, and you're tougher than you look. And you're here with me again, even though I've told you it'd be best if you walked away and left me sitting by myself."

Her skin warmed at his words. Her nerve endings tingled at his touch. Her breath grew short in her lungs. "Well, I've never been good at hiding what I feel. Or in doing what I should do when my heart wants something different."

WHAT THE FUCK was he doing here? Maddy was too sweet, too good—*too innocent*—for him. She had problems of her own to deal with. Her grandmother's care was huge in her life. He'd checked into it, because that's what he did, and he knew that she'd sold everything of value over the past few years. Except the house. She held onto that, wisely in his opinion, and worked hard to pay the fees that the Oaks charged. They were a top notch facility, and Medicare didn't cover everything.

Her grandmother was a woman of modest means. Maddy's father's life insurance had gone to her grandmother so she could use it to raise Maddy. By all accounts, her grandmother had been a good steward of the money and used it as intended. Maddy had attended good schools, graduated in the top of her class, and went to William & Mary on a partial scholarship.

She'd apprenticed at the National Museum of Art, then gone on to work in museums with Russian art collections. She'd ended up at Barrington's six years ago. She earned a good salary, plus commissions on the art she procured for clients when they were looking for specific pieces that she managed to track down. It was a good living, but not good enough when you had a beloved grandmother to care for and expenses of your own.

He was in danger of losing his perspective where it involved Maddy Cole. Just because her father had been a spy didn't mean they had anything in common. She didn't even know the truth about her father. She thought he'd been in the military. He had, but he'd also been assigned to special duties that took him into danger. Was that why Jace was drawn to her? Because her life had been normal with a spy dad while his had been fucked up beyond belief?

Last night, when he'd gone back inside after Colt opened the door looking for him, he'd found his teammate sitting on the couch, frowning. "What the fuck are you doing, Jace?"

He hadn't pretended he didn't know what Colt was talking about. "Checking on her."

"Checking on her," Colt repeated as if he couldn't quite believe his ears. "Direct contact with the subject. Making dates with the subject. Seems a lot more involved than just checking in."

So he'd heard. Figured. "I told Ian when I made contact earlier today. If you want to report this one, go right ahead."

Colt shook his head. "Nope, not interested. Just be careful, okay? We don't know if Calypso is done with her yet."

"Calypso better be careful," Jace growled. "Because if she comes for Maddy, she's going to have to get through me first."

That had been the end of the discussion, but Jace was still thinking about it. About Calypso not being done with Maddy yet. He laid awake at night thinking of the angles, but he couldn't see the big picture. Her father's past shouldn't affect her sixteen years later, so what was it?

He dragged himself back to the present. Back to what she'd said about her heart wanting something different from her head. "What does your heart want, Maddy?"

Her pretty eyes were the color of sunlight streaming through a green bottle. Bright, achingly lovely. She had thick lashes that swept down to cover those eyes while she thought about her answer. Then they swept up again and her gaze pierced him to the depths of his black soul. "I think it wants more of you, Jace." She shook her head. "I don't even know your last name. It's like that country song by Carrie Underwood."

A shard of desire stabbed into him. Tightened his balls. There was guilt too. Guilt because he knew something about her dad that she didn't. "It's Kaiser. And you can have as much of me as you want. Just say the word."

A soft smile wreathed her face. "I think I just did."

God help him.

The food came and they dug into it, the conversation moving to lighter topics for a while. Eventually, however, it was time to finish and pay—he insisted on paying again, even though she fought him over it—and then he helped her up and guided her toward the exit, his gaze firmly on her ass in the short dress she'd worn. Her legs were long and slim and pale, and he found himself wondering what they might look like hooked over his forearms as he spread her wide and drove deeply into her.

"Are you in the parking garage?" he asked.

"Yes."

"Do you need to get back right away, or do you want to walk to the waterfront?"

"The waterfront sounds good."

He took her hand and led her down the slight incline toward Spa Creek and the City Dock. Once they reached it, he continued toward the park where he'd watched her yesterday. They walked in silence, holding hands, and he found it comforting somehow. Reassuring. When they entered the park, her footsteps slowed. He cursed himself for bringing her here after the way she'd stood by the water yesterday and cried.

"Do you want to leave?" he asked.

"No."

"You seem hesitant." He couldn't tell her he knew what had happened when she'd stood in the park alone only twenty-four hours ago.

"Mimi and I sailed past here many times on our way to the bay and a day of fun together. It makes me miss her, that's all."

He spun her toward him, caught her in his arms. "Lean on me, Maddy. Let me help."

She curled her fingers into the fabric of his sleeves. He could feel her touch like a brand on his skin. "You already help me just by being here. Thank you."

He couldn't stop himself from tipping her chin

back with two fingers and pressing his mouth to hers. Lightly, in case she wasn't interested in more. But her mouth, when it met his, was like flame. She opened to him, hot and wet, and he speared his tongue between her lips with a groan.

She clung to him, kissing him back just as hotly as he kissed her. His dick grew solid as stone. If he wasn't careful, he'd be running his hands up the smooth skin of her thighs, beneath her skirt, cupping her sweet ass in his palms as he dragged her against his erection.

"Maddy," he said on a groan, breaking the kiss and pushing her back just enough to give himself some breathing room. "I can't."

She frowned. "Can't? What do you mean, can't?"

He sucked in a lungful of briny air. "I can't keep kissing you like this. I want more." But he didn't deserve it.

She studied an imaginary spot on his sleeve, picking at it softly. "What kind of more?"

"You have to ask?"

Her long dark gold hair rippled in the breeze as the wind caught it and ruffled it against her cheek. "Maybe I do."

He dropped his nose to her hair, sucked in her sweetness. He shouldn't say it, but he couldn't help himself. "Okay," he said in her ear, stiffening with need at the soft shudder that vibrated through her at their closeness. "Tell me if you want this kind of more. You, me. Naked, Maddy. Hot and sweaty and lost in each other. I want to slide that sweet skirt up your hips, drag your panties off, and fuck you on the nearest surface. Then I want to strip you and do it all again. I want my name on your lips, your fingers digging into my shoulders, and my cock buried in your pussy. Is that the kind of more you're ready for?"

Chapter Twelve

Oh hell. Maddy's thighs clenched tight as a ribbon of desire uncoiled inside her. Her brain told her this was probably a bad idea since she barely knew him, but her heart urged her to go for it. To take the leap and see where it led. Her life had been very dull until Jace careened into it little more than a week ago. Since then, her thoughts had been filled with him. With the spark of his blue eyes, the handsome cut of his jaw, the mysterious and dangerous air that surrounded him. He was the embodiment of that boy from high school. The one that mothers—and grand-mothers—told their girls to avoid. The bad boy who smoked cigarettes and thumbed his nose at authority—and academics—while being so appealing and tempting that teenage girls often lost whatever good sense they possessed just for a few exciting weeks as his girlfriend.

There was nothing so tempting as a bad boy. And

Maddy wasn't an innocent schoolgirl anymore. She was a woman who could make decisions for herself. Though this decision was probably going to come with a lot of regret at some point, the ride was too wild and too promising to refuse.

Maddy ran her fingers up his biceps, hooked them around his neck, and stood on tiptoe to deliver a sweet kiss to the corner of his sensual mouth. "I'm ready," she whispered, her heart pounding recklessly, dizziness swirling in her brain.

His hands on her waist tightened for the briefest of moments. And then he stepped back and took her hand, retreating toward the City Dock and the parking garage. When they finally reached her car, he turned her and backed her against it like he had yesterday. His gaze swept over her face, studying her. Probably for signs of second thoughts. Maddy leaned up and kissed him again.

"It was a long walk, but I haven't changed my mind. In case you're wondering."

"Good." He kissed her again and her stomach flipped. *So good.*

When he stopped kissing her, she was dizzy, and she clung to him so she didn't slide down the side of her car and collapse in a puddle on the pavement.

"I still want you to think about it," he told her, his voice rough and soft and warm all at once. Like smooth bourbon whiskey on the rocks. She loved bourbon.

"I don't need to think about it."

"Go home, Maddy. I'll talk to you later."

Disappointment swirled inside her like smoke. "You're a very confusing man, Jace Kaiser. Is that really your name?"

"It's my name now." She must have frowned because he continued. "I wasn't born with it, but it's the name I chose for myself. So yes, it's mine."

"I don't understand anything about you."

"Which is why you're going to go home and think about this."

She sighed. "Fine. You're far more noble than I would have believed possible when I met you. Infuriatingly so at the moment, I might add."

He grinned. "I can be." Then he opened her car door and helped her inside. Bent to kiss her before straightening, his eyes still on hers. "See you later, beautiful."

He shut her door and walked away. Maddy turned her key while she watched his ass. Faded jeans never looked so good as they did on that man. Once he was gone, Maddy backed out of her spot. Frustration tapped a steady beat inside her brain. Her body was all *hey, what the heck happened? Thought we were getting laid…*

"Not yet," she muttered. "Maybe not ever." Because she wasn't sure about him. Still. Except why would he meet her for lunch, kiss her so hotly, and then back off when she said yes? Why kiss her at all if he wasn't interested?

Maddy hit the button for the hands free and

instructed the computer voice to dial Angie. Ang answered on the second ring. "Hey, babes! What's up?"

"Sexual frustration," she grumbled.

"Whoa, whoa, whoa! Hold the phone, Mads, and tell me *everything.*"

Heat seared Maddy's face. She cranked the air conditioner up to max, even though it was damp today and not as hot as it could be. "It's Jace. I saw him again."

"Saw him as in bumped into him, or saw him as in spent time with him?"

"Lunch. He texted last night after I talked to you."

Angie snorted. "I'm really going to have to school you on what it means to keep your bestie informed."

Maddy laughed. "I'm sorry. I guess I don't know what to make of this whole thing yet, so I don't know what there is to tell you. Except now. Now, I'm confused as hell."

"Go on," Angie said as if she was a queen granting an audience.

"He kissed me again, Ang. And then he told me what he wants to do to me—the words hot and sweaty and fuck were used."

"And the problem is? You don't want him? What?"

Maddy pulled into traffic. "Oh no, I want him. I even told him so. I thought we were going to do something about it—but then he walked me back to my car and told me I needed to think about it."

"Seriously? Is he gay?"

Maddy rolled her eyes. "No, he's not gay. At least I don't think so. I guess a gay guy could fake-kiss a woman. Or maybe he's bi—oh hell, I have no clue about him. I really don't."

"Which is why you've called me."

"Pretty much."

"So tell me what kind of kisser he is."

Maddy thought back to the moment Jace's lips had touched hers. To his silky tongue gliding into her mouth. Her body clenched with hot need. She was so wet she'd need to change panties when she got home. "He's pretty amazing. Not the kind of guy who rams his tongue down your throat, or gropes you while he does. Somehow, he gives you just enough to want more."

"Okay, so he's a decent guy who kisses like a dream and wants you to be very certain about having sex with him. Why is this a problem?"

Maddy would have gaped at Angie if they were face to face. "You don't think it's weird that he put me off?"

"No. I think it's sweet. Old-fashioned even."

"The things he said he planned to do to me are *not* old-fashioned."

"It's still decent of him not to push you. You've been out with him twice, right? Or are you hiding something from me?"

"I'm not hiding anything," Maddy lied. "When I

first met him, it was work related—and not under the best circumstances. We didn't get along at all."

"So what changed?"

Maddy was glad that Angie didn't push her for details on the first meeting. She didn't know what she'd say if Angie had. As much as she wanted to share with her best friend, there were things she couldn't. "I'm not quite sure. But when I saw him again yesterday and he asked me to lunch, we got along just fine. I think there were sparks. There must have been, right? Because he asked me out again today."

"Maybe he wants to do the romantic gesture. You know, book a hotel, flowers, champagne—really make it special."

Maddy pulled into her drive and hit the button for the single car garage. The old door ratcheted up slowly and then she drove inside and cut the engine. "Maybe."

"Or maybe he doesn't want you to make a decision in the heat of the moment and regret it."

That sounded more realistic to her. Not that she knew how Jace thought, but he didn't strike her as a romantic. Could be wrong, but the second option seemed most likely.

"I thought of that too."

"Then wait and see if he calls you. Or call him later and tell him you're ready right damn now. You don't have to wait for the man to make the move, you know."

"I know. Thanks, Ang. I just got home, so I'm going to go in and feed Kitty and get some work done."

"Glad I could help. Now if he calls you and wants to come do the nasty, you let me know. At least I can get some vicarious excitement from your love life."

Maddy laughed. "I don't have a love life."

"Honey, neither do I these days. Love you. Talk later!"

"Yep, later."

They ended the call and Maddy got out of the vehicle. A woman in a car pulled up and stopped in front of the house across the street. Somebody had rented the place recently, but she hadn't met them yet. The woman didn't get out. A moment later she pulled away, the car rolling down the street and turning at the end. The rain picked up, splattering the sidewalk and driveway, making everything dreary and gray. Maddy powered the garage door closed and went inside. Kitty let out a yowl as she entered.

"Hello, precious girl," she said with a pat. She set her purse on the counter and went about freshening Kitty's food. When she finished, she headed for the bedroom to change. Her door was closed and she frowned. She never closed the bedroom door because Kitty liked to sleep on the bed sometimes. Still, the cat could have knocked it closed somehow.

But how had she gotten out if so?

Maddy's heart hammered as she leaned her ear against the door and listened. She didn't hear anything. In fact, she was being paranoid. A few hours in a spy's company and she was imagining things. Slowly, she twisted the knob. Then she pushed the door back.

Her bedroom was as she'd left it. The curtains fluttered in the breeze of the open window and the suction pulled at the knob in her hand. All very normal.

Except Maddy froze as realization hit her—she hadn't opened the window today.

JACE WAS JUST PULLING up behind the house across the street from Maddy's when his cell phone rang. He glanced at it, saw that it was her number, and snatched it up, some sixth sense telling him that she wouldn't be calling if it wasn't important.

"Hey, beautiful."

"Jace," she wheezed, and the hair on the back of his neck stood up.

"Maddy, what is it?" He shoved the car in park and jumped out, ready to run across the street and do battle for her.

"I think someone is—or w-was—in my house."

His blood ran cold. "I'll be right there." He didn't know for sure she was there, but he figured that Colt or Ty would have warned him if she'd left again so soon after arriving. They'd parted twenty minutes ago, and he'd stopped by the store to pick up the snacks those two had asked him to bring.

"Hurry. I'm in my car in the garage, but I don't know if I should go. What if it's a trap?"

He heard a cat meow loudly. "Stay there and keep the doors locked. Open the garage and start the car. If anyone comes at you, go. I don't care if you have to fucking run them over. But don't run me over because I'm coming on foot and I'll be there in three seconds."

He was already on his way through the yard. He could see her garage door sitting open, see the exhaust coming from the pipe. He had his hand on the pistol grip beneath his shirt, ready to pull it if necessary.

"I see you," she said. "How did you—?"

"We'll talk about that later." He reached the garage and darted in to the driver's side of her car. Her eyes were wide and frightened as she rolled down the window. "I'm going in. Stay here. I need to put you on hold and call somebody, but don't hang up, okay?"

"Okay."

"Put the window up." He didn't tell her that if he wasn't back in three minutes she needed to book it out of there. He'd make sure Colt and Ty took care of her.

She did as he told her and he drew the gun from the hidden holster at his waist. Then he put her on hold and dialed Colt.

"Yo," his teammate said.

"Did you motherfuckers see anyone go into Maddy's house?"

"What? No. Why?"

"Because she just called me. I'm here now."

"Shit."

"Yeah, shit."

"I'll be right there."

"Stay and watch for trouble. I'll clear the place. If there's nobody here, we need to discuss this."

"Copy."

Jace ended the call, tucked the phone into his shirt, and breached the door. It took him only a few minutes to clear the house. There was nobody inside, but the open window in her bedroom gave him pause. He checked the sill for scrapes, then shoved the pane closed and locked it. He took out his phone and unmuted Maddy as he stalked back through the house.

"It's safe," he told her. "Turn off the car. I'm coming." When he got there, she was still inside, her forehead on the steering wheel. Her cat had two paws on the passenger door windowsill. Jace could hear the meowing even with the windows up. He pulled open the driver side door and Maddy looked up at him, took a deep breath.

"I'm sorry," she said. "I overreacted. I must have." The cat darted for the open door but Maddy caught her. "No, Kitty-girl. Not happening."

"You didn't overreact. Never think that. It's always better safe than sorry." He called Colt, who answered on the first ring. "Nothing here. But a window was open. Back bedroom. Need to check the surveillance."

"We should have gotten a motion alert. Hang on." Jace waited while Colt checked the video feed of the camera they'd installed on a tree nearby. He could hear his teammate swearing in the background. "No feed. The damn thing is dead."

Jace felt a chill sweep down his spine. "That's not typical."

"No, definitely not. The battery should have been good for a few more days at least."

"We need to sweep her house for devices."

"On it. Be there in a few."

Jace ended the call, his insides boiling with anger and even a little bit of fear. For Maddy. Her window was open and they had a dead camera? She'd gone inside her house like everything was normal, but somebody could have been waiting for her. If they had been, she could have been killed and he wouldn't have known it for hours. The thought chilled him to the bone.

He held the car door while Maddy emerged with her little black and white cat. She took the animal inside and set her down on the kitchen floor while Jace closed the garage and then closed the kitchen door behind him. When she rose, she faced him with an apologetic smile. "I should have called the police. I don't know why I called you."

"If you'd called the police, you'd still be waiting. Not because they don't do a good job, but because they're stretched thin and responding takes time. Better that you called me."

She tilted her head. He knew what was coming next. "How did you get here so fast? And where's your car?"

This wasn't a conversation he'd wanted to have just yet. Still, there was no way around it. "You feel okay to leave your cat for a few minutes?"

"I think so. Why?"

"Lock the door and come with me."

She grabbed her keys and they went outside. He took them from her and slid the key into the lock, making a mental note that she needed an alarm system. And cameras of her own.

He threaded his fingers in hers and led her across the street. "Where are we going?" she asked as they hit the sidewalk.

"Not far."

He took her up the walkway to the front door. Then he pulled the screen door and knocked. Colt swung it open a moment later, his gaze landing on Maddy with a frown. "Dude," he said. "Seriously?"

"Seriously. Maddy?"

She stood on the stoop with eyes that darted between them. Her jaw hung slightly open as she recognized Colt. Color stained her cheeks. "I don't… I can't… You're *spying* on me?"

"Yes. I'm sorry, but it's necessary. You could be in danger."

Her skin mottled with anger. Jace began to think

this wasn't going well at all. When she smacked her hand against his chest, shoving him back, he knew it wasn't.

"Fuck you, Jace Kaiser! Fuck all of you! How dare you do this to me?" She flung her arms wide. "Was it all a set up? Lunch? Kissing me? The things you said?"

Colt's eyebrows climbed his forehead. Ty wasn't visible but he also wasn't far enough away not to hear. Jace knew he was appalled as well. Jace turned his back on his teammates and grabbed her wrists, forcing her arms to her sides before she could do damage. He didn't doubt that she would if left to her own devices.

"It wasn't a set up," he growled, bending his face close to hers. "None of it. I've risked a hell of a lot for you—and I'm still fucking doing it. Do you think these guys are happy to know I just compromised them? Compromised the mission? We're here for *your* safety, Maddy. Because you could be in danger and I'll be goddamned if I'll let anyone hurt you. I'd fucking kill anyone who tried."

Her gaze fixed on his for a long moment. Her jaw went slack. She was still red, and she still trembled. But maybe he'd gotten through to her. Somewhat.

"You could have told me," she whispered.

"No, I couldn't. And I shouldn't be telling you now, but I can't keep lying to you, Maddy. If I have the ghost of a chance with you, I have to tell you the truth. I know that, and I'm doing it. So give me some credit for that at least."

"It's not a set up? You weren't romancing me for the mission?"

"No. I like you. I've told you that more than once."

"I know you have. But I don't know if I believe you."

Chapter Thirteen

MADDY WANTED TO BELIEVE HIM. SO MUCH THAT IT physically hurt. But how could she? Nothing about Jace Kaiser was simple. He'd even admitted to her that his name wasn't real, though he'd sworn it was the one he used now. But was it all a game? An elaborate set up? Why?

Her gaze darted behind him to the man she recognized from their trip out of Russia. Another man came into view then. He smiled at her, but she didn't smile back.

"Better bring her inside," the man from the plane said. "We have to call Ian."

Jace's nostrils flared but he stepped to the side and motioned for her to go up the steps. "Maddy."

She threw a glance over her shoulder. Kitty was alone in the house. Not that it was a problem, but someone had broken in. Or she thought they had. What if they came back?

"Your cat is fine," Jace said. "Whoever was there is long gone. But we can go get her if you like."

"No. She was traumatized enough when I flung her in the car. But I don't want to be gone long."

"You won't be." He reached for her arm and she shrugged out of his grasp.

"I don't need your help."

His hand dropped to his side. "Okay."

She stomped up the steps and into the tiny living room of the mid-century ranch house. The walls were paneled but someone had painted them white at some point. She'd never actually been inside the house before, even though she'd lived across the street from it for many years. It had been empty for so long that she'd been surprised to see activity recently. Now she knew.

She folded her arms over her chest and glared at the three occupants of the house. They had a lot of computer equipment set up in the room.

"All this to spy on me. Wow."

"After what happened in Russia, did you just think we'd let you go back to your life like nothing happened?" Jace asked.

Ugh, why did he have to be so handsome? So commanding and forceful? And why the hell was she attracted to commanding and forceful? She never had been before. All the guys she'd ever gone out with were nice guys. The one she'd had a relationship with, until Mimi got sick and Maddy broke it off with him, was a literature professor whose most bad boy trait was that he smoked French cigarettes whenever he drank Scotch and expounded at length on the manly virtues of Hemingway.

Maddy drew herself up and glared harder at him than the other two. "Well, yes. After all, that's what you told me. Why ever would you lie?" She said that last with such mockery in her tone that one of the other guys coughed and turned away.

"For your safety, Maddy. If we'd told you that we were planning to watch your house for a couple of weeks, shadow you whenever you went out just in case one of the bad guys showed up to hurt you, would you have slept at night or would you have sat up shivering with terror and wondering when someone was going to break in?"

Heat stabbed behind her eyes. *Anger*. "Don't even try to tell me you didn't inform me for *my* safety. It was for you—" She swung a hand to encompass the room. "—For this. For *you*, not for me. You're so afraid that somebody will know your names, or your faces, so you hide behind aliases and smokescreens. Well, I'm done with that. With this."

She turned to make her escape, but a firm hand landed on her shoulder, stopped her. She shuddered at his touch. Even without seeing him, she knew it was Jace who'd touched her. She would always know when it was Jace.

That thought sent hot, angry tears springing to life in her eyes. *Why him? Why not some normal guy?*

"This isn't over, Maddy. The danger isn't over. We

have to sweep your house for recording devices. It might be best if you don't stay there for a few days."

She spun back to him, uncaring of the tears that spilled over. "And just where in the hell am I supposed to go? I have responsibilities—my cat, my grandmother. I can't rack up hotel charges just because you think I need to go somewhere else. And I can't impose on my friends either, not if I'm really in danger like you seem to think."

He gripped her shoulders gently. "We'll figure it out. I promised you that anybody who wanted to hurt you would have to go through me. That hasn't changed. Whatever else you might think about me, I keep my promises."

She searched his gaze, the hardness there. The tenderness that surprised her but seemed to be there just for her. She thought about the past two days, about how he'd held her while she'd cried helplessly into his shirt. He hadn't needed to do that. If all he'd been doing was spying, he could have done it without showing her that bit of humanity.

"Were you following me yesterday?"

"Yes."

"So bumping into me wasn't an accident."

"No. But it was against the rules. I broke protocol to do it."

"Why did you do that?"

"Because you seemed to need someone. I couldn't let you suffer."

Maddy pulled in a trembling breath. Either he

was the best liar God ever created or he meant it. Judging by the looks on the other two guys faces, she decided he meant it. They weren't happy with him for making contact with her. That much was clear.

"Okay, fine. So what happens now?" Because they weren't letting her walk out of here like nothing had happened. And, to be honest, she didn't want to go home alone anyway. Not when she didn't know who had opened her window.

"We're going to check the police reports for any burglaries in the area—could be that someone opening your window had nothing to do with Russia or us—and I'm taking you back home and sweeping for bugs. Once we get the results of that, we'll have a better idea about what to do next."

Maddy shot a look at the other two men. They were both tall and handsome, one dark-haired and one a dusty blond, and they watched her and Jace with grim expressions.

"I'm on the reports," the dark-haired one said.

"I'm calling Ian," the blond added.

Jace went over and rummaged around on one of the desks they'd set up. He pocketed a small device and came back to her. "You ready?"

"Yes."

He led the way out the door and across the street. It had stopped drizzling, but the sky was gray and misty and the clouds felt as if they were perching heavily on the city today. It was the kind of day that Mimi always said was a good reading day. She'd fix tea and they'd sit in the big bay window seat at the rear of the house, feet up on the cushions, and read books. Sometimes they took turns reading aloud, and sometimes they curled up with their own book, only stopping for meals and restroom breaks.

On other misty gray days, they'd rent movies and have a marathon. God, Maddy missed her Mimi. She swiped her fingers beneath her eyes, angry with herself for being so emotional. Life moved on, and she had to move with it. Mimi was safe and warm and she seemed happy most of the time. If she was ever scared or upset, Maddy didn't know about it. The doctor had told her that it was different for people. Some were terrified. Others weren't. She hoped Mimi was one of the ones who was not. So far, she seemed content though she sometimes wanted to go home.

They reached her front door and Maddy unlocked it. She started to go inside, but Jace stopped her. "Let me go first."

She followed him inside and waited while he took the device from his pocket and flicked a switch. Kitty came sauntering over, meowing, and Maddy picked her up and buried her face in the soft black and white fur. "Baby girl," she murmured. Kitty purred and turned her head to blink at Jace.

He moved through the house, sweeping the device into corners and up to the ceiling. He also swept it over the whole ceiling. He was very thorough and by the time he was done, fifteen minutes had passed. He took out his phone and called the guys across the street. "Nothing here. You got anything? ... Yeah?" He blew out a breath, raked a hand over his head. "Maybe that's all it was, but I don't like it. Too convenient. ... Yeah, okay."

He pocketed the phone again and turned to her. Kitty struggled to be let down and Maddy set her on the floor. Her cat promptly went over to Jace and started sniffing his leg.

"Hey, sweet girl," he crooned, dropping to his haunches and holding out his hand for her to sniff. A second later she rubbed against his fingers and arched her back. He stroked her soft fur as she flopped onto her side. He looked up at Maddy and grinned. "I think she likes me."

Maddy frowned. "No accounting for taste, I guess."

He cocked his head. "Either you're really pissed at me or you're teasing me. Can't decide which."

"I am pissed at you. Don't think I'm not."

"But you still like me."

She did, dammit. Though she wasn't going to admit it. "You wish."

He kept stroking Kitty. And she kept right on letting him. *Traitor.* "Yes, I do."

"Do you plan to tell me the results of your scan and their research? And do I at least get some fake names so I don't have to call them *they* and *them* and *those guys* all the time?"

"I'll let them tell you their names. But there are no listening or recording devices in your house. And there've been reports of burglaries in the neighborhood this week. One last night just after ten, and it was one street over."

She hadn't realized that. "I don't think anything's missing."

"It doesn't appear they even got inside. Probably startled by a car or person walking by. The people burgled last night reported prescription drugs missing. Somebody looking for opioids probably."

While she wasn't happy someone had tried to break into her home, she was happy it wasn't anything sinister. "I might have left the window unlocked by accident."

"These are old windows," he said, looking around. "It's not hard to slip them open if you know what you're doing."

"Well gee, thanks. That's reassuring."

He straightened. "Don't get upset, Maddy. We're installing an alarm system ASAP. And cameras. Nobody's getting in here without you knowing about it."

She rubbed her arms absently. "I was planning to install a system. I just haven't had the time. And monitoring costs money," she added, dropping her gaze to the floor.

"Yeah, well it's a good thing you met me. I know people."

She looked up to find him grinning. And suddenly she was feeling warm all over. Just from that megawatt grin he had. Too attractive. Too damned smooth. "I'm still mad at you."

"I know, babe. I'd be mad at me too if I were you. But I'll make it up to you."

"It's not going to be easy," she said coolly.

"Nothing worth having ever is."

SHE LOOKED AWAY SHYLY and the need to take her in his arms flared hot. Jace didn't know what the hell this was anymore, but the idea of her being in danger made him crazy. He wanted to protect her, and he wanted to possess her. He'd been so close to getting her naked today, but he'd had to be all noble and give her time to be sure. Then this happened, and now she was mad at him.

He *would* make it up to her. He wasn't sure how yet, but he would.

"I need to go back over there and talk to the guys for a few minutes."

She looked at him again, arms folded loosely around her middle, long hair curly and wild. She bit her bottom lip and desire lanced through him.

"I'm not stopping you. You can stay there for all I care."

"I'm not staying. I'm coming back here until we get your alarm set up."

She shrugged. "Whatever."

He wanted to shake her. Or kiss her. He did

neither. "Lock up behind me and don't open the door for anyone but me."

"It's broad daylight, Jace. And you're going across the street. I think I'll be fine by myself for a few minutes."

He gave in to the urge to touch her. Ran his fingers down her cheek while she trembled. But at least she didn't pull away. "Lock the door, Maddy. Stop arguing with me."

"Fine," she whispered.

He stepped outside and listened for the locks turning. Then he walked across the street. He should be relieved there was apparently nothing sinister to the attempted break in, but the whole thing left him vaguely uneasy. He'd feel a lot better once they got her set up with an alarm system and placed more cameras on the back of the house. Some lowlife casing the neighborhood, jiggling locks and trying windows in an attempt to get prescription drugs made sense.

But he didn't like it. And he didn't trust that's all it was. The camera dying was too a strange coincidence for him to accept. But if the break-in was tied to Russia and Calypso, why wasn't there more to it? Calypso was a professional. If she'd killed a camera and opened a window, why didn't she wait to eliminate the target before disappearing again?

It didn't make sense. Nothing did. But sometimes the simplest explanation was the correct one. So a drug addict—or someone who wanted to sell to drug addicts—was stealing prescription drugs from easy targets. If Maddy *had* left the window unlocked, then the thief could have been surprised by something and left before going inside.

Colt and Ty were waiting for him when he walked in, both looking a little surprised and a lot concerned.

"What did Ian say?" he asked.

"You mean after he stopped swearing? Or did you want all the swear words too?"

Jace sucked in a breath. Yeah, well, he hadn't expected Ian to be happy, had he? He'd call Ian himself just as soon as he got a minute. "I can imagine those for myself."

Colt rubbed the back of his neck. "He said you'd better fucking hope you know what you're doing. There's a lot at stake if this goes wrong. If she talks to the wrong people about any of this."

Did he know what he was doing? He wasn't so sure anymore. He knew how to kill people. How to hide in plain sight. How to get the goods and protect the innocent. But did he know how to handle Maddy Cole?

"She won't talk to the wrong people. I'll make sure she doesn't. Besides, she's smart—and she already knows about Calypso and the fact they resemble each other. How much worse could it be?"

"It can always be worse, brother. You know that." Colt looked grim and Jace knew he was thinking of other missions, other civilians. Things went wrong sometimes. Terribly wrong. They'd seen it. Been involved in it. Would always be scarred by it.

"Yeah, but I'm not letting it happen to her."

"Careful, Jace. You're letting your emotions get the best of you."

Jace clenched a fist. He was. First rule of covert ops was not to get involved. He'd left that one behind miles ago. "Maybe so, but you ever think that sometimes you can't stay uninvolved? That some people get to you in ways you don't expect and you can't ignore the feeling?"

"We both know that happens. We also know that we're supposed to squash it out of existence. She's not an operative. You can't drag her into this world and expect everything to come out fine. She'll get burned if she stays. And you'll blame yourself for it."

Jace glanced at Ty. He was new to BDI, but he wasn't stupid. He didn't say anything. So Jace tipped his chin at him. "What do you think?"

Ty shoved his hands in his pockets. Shrugged. "Man, I think if you care about this girl, you have to do what's best for her. Right now that's protecting her. But later? You'll have to ask yourself what that is."

Yeah, he would. But for now he was jumping in all the way. He already felt responsible, for fuck's sake. If he hadn't tackled her and dragged her onto that plane, maybe she'd still be living her life untouched by any of this.

Except she wouldn't. Calypso and the Syndicate knew she'd be there. They knew who she was.

And that was why he couldn't stay uninvolved. There was more to come. He knew it. Felt it.

Colt shook his head and rolled his neck to pop out the kinks. "Look, she's in now and we're going to do everything we can to keep her safe. You know that."

"I do."

"Ian's sending over a team with the equipment. They'll be in a security company van so it looks legit. Better go tell her they're coming."

"I'm staying with her until we're sure she's not in danger."

Ty snorted. Colt did too. "Man, you tell her that yet? Because she didn't seem too pleased with your ass when you left outta here."

Jace grinned. "Nope, didn't tell her. Feel free to listen in while I do. But then I expect you mofos to give us some privacy, you copy?"

"Whatever you say, dude. Better not get your hopes up though. That was an angry woman."

He'd dealt with angry women before. But he'd never really cared if they stayed angry. This time he did. "I can handle her."

He hoped.

Colt shook his head. "Dunno, man. Better watch your balls."

IAN BLACK STARED at the report that had just come across his desk. He didn't like what it contained, but that didn't change the facts. He kicked back in his seat, put his hands behind his head, and stared at the television above. It was muted, but he could read the news crawl. Always some shit going on in the world. Always people who didn't have a problem with rape or murder or mass destruction. Sometimes he wondered why he didn't just get a bunker of his own, fortify it against disaster, and sit it out for a while.

Except he wasn't wired that way. Goddamn hero complex always had him riding out to save the day—or die trying.

There was a knock at the door and he looked over. Brett Wheeler leaned sideways to peer through the glass. Ian motioned. The door swung open and Brett strode in.

"You sent for me, boss?"

Ian sat up straight and turned his chair around to the desk. He hated desk work. What he really needed was to get back in the field for a few weeks. "Yeah." He picked up the folder and handed it to Brett. "Better sit down."

Brett sat and opened it up. It only took a few seconds. "Shit."

"Yep."

"You planning to tell Jace?"

"Nah, not yet. He's got enough going on right now."

"What do you need me to do?"

"Watch him. He's not thinking clearly at the

moment. I don't want him getting into trouble because his dick's leading the charge."

"You don't have any doubts about him—?"

"No," Ian cut in. "None at all."

Brett nodded. "Neither do I. But I had to ask."

"Yeah, I know." Ian jerked his head toward the door. "Get over to Maddy Cole's place and help them secure it. Let me know what Jace is up to."

Brett stood and dropped the folder on the desk. "I'm on it."

Brett walked out and Ian turned his attention back to other things. A few minutes later, his phone rang. It was one of the techies in the IT department. "We finally got the recordings from Sokolov's house, boss," he said. "You're going to want to see this."

Ian was already in motion. "Be right there."

Chapter Fourteen

Maddy was watching out the window when Jace emerged from the house across the street. She thought about not unlocking the door, but that would be a childish thing to do. And idiotic, considering that he and Ian had thought it dangerous enough to spy on her in the first place. But if her attempted break-in was only someone looking for drugs, why was Jace still here? Why the cameras and security?

She didn't know, but she wasn't stupid and she wasn't demanding he go away just yet. As if she could ever demand such a thing of a man like that. He'd do what he wanted to do, regardless of what she thought about it. It made her mad, but it was also a little bit thrilling. God, she hated admitting that to herself.

No bossy men.

It was bad enough being a professional woman in a world where her male colleagues got more credibility than she did, even though her skills were equal or better in some cases, yet here she was thrilling to the alpha male take-charge attitude Jace Kaiser wore like a second skin.

Maddy unlocked the door and opened it before he got up the sidewalk. His gaze met hers, looking all growly and sexy, and her belly twisted into a knot as she remembered kissing him not that long ago. Telling him she wanted him.

Before she knew he'd been spying on her. A pang of sadness pierced her. It had been easier when she'd thought he'd been interested in her just because he liked her. Now she knew differently, and it hurt more than it should. She gritted her teeth and prepared to be as cool to him as she could.

He came up the steps and through the storm door and she stepped back. He closed both doors behind him and locked them. Then he turned to face her.

"Now what?" she asked.

"Now we wait for the security system to be installed."

"And then what? You and Ian and your friends disappear in a few days and call it a parting gift? Or will you be taking it all back when this is over?"

"We're not taking it back. And I'm not disappearing."

"But that's what you do, isn't it? Swoop in, do the job, and disappear again? Why should I believe you'll still be around in a month? You said this was a seduction—well, once you've got what you want, you'll be gone again, right?"

Oh God, could she sound any bitchier?

He was frowning. Hard. "I have a job to do, Maddy. But I also have a life. And right now, I want you in my life."

Her throat grew tight. "You'd say anything to get me to believe you."

"Are you fucking kidding me right now? I told you my name, Maddy. *My name.* Do you have any idea how dangerous that could be for me—for both of us?"

She sniffed. "You said it wasn't your real name either."

"I said it wasn't the name I was born with."

"Is there a difference?"

"Yes, there's a difference. For me, it's a huge difference. And don't ask me what my birth name is. I can't tell you."

She swallowed. "Okay. But why not?"

He shook his head. "It's dangerous. For you. For me. That person is dead, and he needs to stay that way."

She didn't understand. But she also knew he wasn't going to tell her any more than he already had. He looked troubled and she suddenly felt bad for pushing him. What right did she have to demand more than he'd already given her? They weren't a couple, even if she felt drawn to him in ways she hadn't with anyone else. They were two strangers who'd almost gone to bed together. That was it, really.

"I'm sorry. I shouldn't have asked."

"I don't blame you for wanting to know more. I

get why you don't want to trust me. I'd be stupid if I didn't understand that. But what you need to know is this—I'm committed to protecting you. To making sure none of the ugly stuff that's out there—the ugly people—touch you. I won't let them hurt you. I gave you my word on that, and I meant it."

Her heart throbbed. "I believe you, Jace. I really do. I know you aren't here to hurt me, no matter what the bigger picture might be. And though I'm really bothered that you were across the street the whole time, spying on me, I also know you wouldn't be there without a reason. So thank you—thank you all—for not just dumping me the second you knew I wasn't who you wanted me to be." A little shiver slid over her. Maybe it was the damp weather, but more likely it was the idea that the danger wasn't over. That a shadowy person was waiting to strike her dead for reasons she didn't know. "Do you have any idea where she is?"

"At this moment, no."

"So your plan is to stay across the street until she's found?"

"I don't intend to stay across the street, Maddy."

Disappointment pricked her but she lifted her chin and pretended not to be bothered by it. It was impractical to expect him to stay over there indefinitely. "When are you leaving?"

He arched an eyebrow. "I'm not leaving. I'm staying here. With you."

HE WAITED for the inevitable explosion. Maddy's eyebrows climbed her forehead. Then she thrust out her jaw and folded her arms over her chest. "No way are you staying here when you have the house across the street."

He advanced on her. She didn't back down, though he thought she might want to. He stopped a foot away. Definitely in her space. Close enough to smell her sweet vanilla and peaches scent. Close enough to kiss her if he just leaned down and did it.

Not that she'd take that very well. But God how he wanted it. Then he wanted to slide that sweet dress up her thighs and bury his face in the warm paradise between her legs. If this shit hadn't happened, he'd be well on his way to doing it.

"Sorry, babe, but a line's been crossed. Someone tried to break into your house."

"And you're putting in an alarm and cameras. You'll be across the street. There's no reason for you to stay."

There were plenty of reasons, but he wasn't telling her that. Most of them were personal. Like he wanted to be with her. Needed to be with her. Needed to make sure nothing happened to her. What if Calypso came for her and he didn't get there in time?

"Think of me like a very mean guard dog. I'll be by your side, ready to bite someone's head off. Can't do that from across the street."

Her eyes glistened. It threw him for a moment. But he wasn't backing down.

"Jace, I don't—. I can't—." She sucked in a breath and he knew she was trying not to get emotional. "Look, this might just be a job to you, but this is my home. And having you in it when you've been spying on me and not just asking me on dates because you're attracted to me—well, I just don't know if it's something I want to do."

He put his hands on her shoulders. Gently. "Honey, I'm sorry, but I need to be here. And I *am* attracted to you. I want to be deep inside you right this minute, and if you give me half a reason to do it, I'm going to strip you naked and make you come."

Her gaze dropped. Her chin quivered. "I want that, Jace. I really do. But I can't. Not after—" She waved her hand in the vague direction of the street. "I need time."

He gave in to the desire to press a chaste kiss to her forehead. "Yeah, I get that. But honey, I still have to be here with you. If not me—if you're too pissed off at me—then Colt or Ty. Your choice."

She looked up at him. Sniffed. "Were you supposed to do that?"

"Supposed to do what?"

"Their names. If those really are their names."

"They are. And yeah, you're part of this now so you can know their names. It's your life we're protecting first and foremost. But of course we want to capture Calypso. And while it's probably not likely she's coming here, we're prepared for it anyway."

His phone buzzed and he dropped his hands from her shoulders to slide it from his pocket.

Ian. Great. "I have to get this. Are you okay?"

"I'll be fine," she said.

He tapped the answer icon. "Hey, boss, what's up?"

Ian snorted. "Man, you're killing me with all this protectiveness toward Dr. Cole. You know that?"

Jace watched her turn and walk away. He didn't know if she was giving him privacy for the call or if she just wanted to get away from him. That thought banged up against old hurts he'd thought he'd buried. He didn't like needing people. He'd learned long ago not to let it happen. Yet here he was, getting twisted up because Maddy was upset with him.

"You said to listen to my instincts. I'm doing that."

"You sure it's your instincts and not your dick?"

A tiny blue flame flared inside him. Much more of that and it would turn into an inferno. Not because he was insulted by the idea of his dick making decisions—dicks did that for most men at one time or another—but because of what it suggested about his intentions toward Maddy. That she was somehow only a potential lay and he'd be done with her as soon as he'd fucked her.

"I'm sure."

"Yeah, well if it's any help, I think you might be right."

Jace blinked as he processed that bit of information. "I'm listening."

"Need you to bring her in. I've got something for her to look at."

"When?"

"Immediately."

Shit. He knew better than to ask for more on the phone. "I'll tell her."

"Tell her it's important, Jace. No time to waste."

"Yeah, got it, boss."

Maddy came sauntering out of her bedroom as he ended the call. She'd changed into jeans and a baggy rose-colored top that made her so achingly pretty it hurt. She stooped to pick up her cat. And then she took one look at him and groaned. Was he getting that bad at maintaining a poker face?

"What now?"

"Need to go to HQ."

"So go. I won't open any doors for anyone. Except Angie. And take-out."

"Need you to come with me."

"What? Why?" She hugged the cat, whose tail flicked at the sudden squeeze. "I can't leave Kitty here alone after today."

"I'll get one of the guys to come over."

"Jace, seriously? I still have a job, you know. And I have files to go over this afternoon. Barrington's is going to fire me if you people keep interfering in my life."

"I'm sorry, babe, but it's important. It shouldn't

take too long. Colt can stay with Kitty. I've watched him feed stray cats in Rome and Greece, and on the kind of shit details in remote villages that you wouldn't believe. He likes cats and they like him."

"Oh for fuck's sake," she muttered, and his balls tightened at the word *fuck* coming from her mouth.

She didn't curse much so it was sort of shocking when she did. Like hearing a Sunday school teacher say filthy things. It was kind of a turn on, to be honest.

Not now.

"Great," she said, oblivious to his train of thought. "Call Colt—but if Kitty doesn't like him, I'm not leaving her with him."

"Fair enough."

THEY RETURNED to the building he'd taken her to the first time. Maddy sat quietly in Jace's car as they drove through the wet streets. Kitty had of course loved Colt. And he'd loved her. Jace hadn't been lying about the guy liking cats. He'd come in, promptly laid on the floor, and let Kitty sniff him from head to toe.

Dammit, she didn't want to like these guys. But she did.

Their first meeting in Russia not withstanding.

Jace drove into the garage and found a slot. They went to a different elevator than before, and they didn't go to the fourth floor. He pressed the button for the fifth and then turned to her.

"Where we're going this time is very secure. You're cleared to enter—or should be—but don't be surprised if it takes a little time to get in, okay?"

"Okay." She was still thinking about what he'd said to her earlier. About wanting to be deep inside her. She was mad at him, but she wanted it too. Badly. Her body was twitchy when he was near, her skin burned, and her senses were achingly heightened. One kiss and she'd go off like a Roman candle.

She'd protested about him staying in her house, but it wasn't because she didn't want him there. She wanted him there too much, which scared her. Jace Kaiser was hotter than an inferno, and she didn't know if she was going to get burned. The longer he stayed, the more likely she thought it was.

The freight elevator chugged upward and rocked to a stop. The doors opened into a plain hallway.

Jace led the way to another door, stopping to look up at a monitor perched over the entry. A moment later, a disembodied voice broke the silence. Maddy nearly jumped out of her skin.

"You're cleared to enter, Mr. Kaiser."

"And Dr. Cole?"

"Yes. Scan her palm, please."

Maddy took a step back as Jace turned to her. "Standard procedure, Maddy. Just need you to come over here and put your hand where I tell you."

She went to his side and waited. He didn't tell her

where to put her hand though. Instead, he took her hand in his, big palm covering the back, and gently lifted her arm to place her palm and fingers on the wall beside the door. Her breath shortened as he pressed her hand beneath his.

"Did anything happen?" she asked as they waited.

"They're checking your prints. Just another second."

"Why didn't they check yours?"

He glanced up at the monitor. "Retinal scan."

The door clicked open. Jace let her go and stepped through, turning to motion her inside. She halted as she entered the room. It was—wow, it was like a movie set or something. Banks of computers, giant screens ringing the walls, people sitting at the computers or standing and conferring with each other.

It was like the scenes at the CIA in *Covert Affairs,* with people going about top secret business while the world outside had no idea. It felt like she'd stepped through the wardrobe to Narnia, if Narnia was filled with spies and covert ops centers.

"Welcome to Black Defense International, Dr. Cole."

Maddy jerked her gaze to where the voice emanated. It was Ian, standing with legs spread and arms crossed, observing her. He was wearing gray trousers and a button-down Oxford with the sleeves rolled partway up. Not for the first time, she thought that he was a striking man—and a scary one.

"Thank you. I think."

"If you'd like to follow me, I want to show you something."

Maddy didn't think she had much choice as he turned and walked away. She glanced at Jace. He nodded. "I'm going too."

She didn't know why, but she felt better hearing that. She followed Ian, trying not to stare at the people who barely spared her a glance. The giant screens were interesting, but she realized they didn't actually show anything other than a world map that circled the room. There were no dots, no words, nothing. What was the point if there was nothing on them?

Ian opened the door to a conference room and held it while she walked inside. When she turned, Jace was there. He went over to the table and held out a chair for her, then took a seat beside her. Ian closed the door and walked over to join them.

"Thank you for coming on such short notice," he said as he powered up a computer on the table in front of him.

"I didn't think I had a choice."

He chuckled. "You always have a choice, Dr. Cole. Some choices are wrong, but we attempt to persuade you of the error."

"But then you do what you want anyway, right?"

He speared her with a piercing gaze. "Sometimes." He tapped at the computer and a video flared to life on the television at one end of the room.

"That's me."

"Yes," he said. In it, she was walking down the hallway toward her room at Mr. Sokolov's. It had to have been when she was going for the batteries, because she didn't have anything with her and Sergey wasn't leading the way.

"Please don't tell me he was recording in my room too."

"No. Sokolov has cameras in the common areas and the hallways. He's not a man who trusts people."

"And why would he? With that kind of money, somebody probably always wants a piece of you." She'd met a lot of rich people and that was always the way of it. Some of them were jerks and she didn't feel sorry for them. Some, however, were not. She suspected Sokolov was probably one of the jerks though.

"Ah, here we go," Ian said.

Maddy had just reached her room when the maid appeared. But the maid's back was to the camera while Maddy was head on.

Ian zoomed in as much as possible, but the maid's face never made it into the frame. Just the back of her head and then a partial profile when she turned toward Maddy at the door. "The maid goes inside the room after you enter yours. But she emerges from your room after the shooting, and she never turns toward the camera. She disappears into one of the other rooms, and that's the last we see of her. She doesn't appear on any other cameras, either in the house or on the grounds."

"I don't understand what you want from me then. I told you she didn't look like me at all. If the picture you showed me was correct, this woman didn't look like that. She was shorter than me. Heavier-set, and she had short hair and brown eyes. I remember because she was wearing dark eyeshadow, very elaborately done, and I was jealous of the smokey eye she pulled off. I'd look like a raccoon if I tried it."

"Tell me what else you remember about her."

Maddy frowned. "She was friendly enough, but it wasn't genuine. Just a job thing, I figured. Be nice to the guests. She said she was turning down the rooms. That was it."

"She wasn't carrying anything?"

"No, nothing."

"Any distinguishing features?"

"No… but she had a tattoo." Maddy swept her fingers from her elbow to her wrist. "Here. I didn't get a good look at it, but it looked like a mermaid, though there could have been more to it than that."

"A mermaid," Ian said.

"Describe the mermaid, Maddy." It was Jace this time.

Her gaze darted between them for a second. "I… I mean it was ornate, but done in black and gray. The mermaid had a trident in her hands, I think, and, um, hair that might have been tentacles. I only saw a flash of it, but it was striking."

Jace took her hand in his. She didn't realize how cold she was until the heat of his fingers sizzled into her. When had she gotten cold?

"Maddy. Jesus, honey. Why didn't you mention that before?"

"I… You didn't ask. With everything else that day, it didn't seem important. Not after you showed me the picture and the maid didn't look anything like that. You didn't ask for anything distinguishing, and quite frankly I was overwhelmed by the two of you."

Jace turned to Ian. "Do you think it's her?"

Ian was frowning hard, his fingers steepled beneath his chin. "I think it's possible. She's an operative, Jace. She knows how to run a con."

"Wait," Maddy said even as her temples began to throb. "What do you mean you *think* it's her? The maid is supposed to be the woman who looks like me? I'm confused."

Jace hadn't let her go. His touch warmed her. Made glowy lights flicker inside. "Yes, we think it could be. She looked like you because she intended to look like you. Or she really does look like you but she donned a disguise for the maid."

"Did she have an accent? Anything else you remember?" Ian fired the questions at her and she thought hard about that day.

"Her Russian sounded like a native speaker. Not that I'm an expert, but I'd say Central Russian. She wasn't from the north or the south. Her voice was distinctive though."

"How do you mean?"

"She was a woman, but if you spoke to her on a phone you might think she was an adolescent. Her voice was… girlish."

Ian leaned forward. "Interesting. Now tell me what you hear when I speak Russian."

Maddy frowned as she processed the words. "You sound native to me too. I don't hear an American accent. Central Russian, I'd say."

"What about Jace?"

She turned to look at him. He didn't speak to her, but he didn't need to. They'd conversed quite a bit in Russian. "He has the barest of accents every once in a while. Traces of American, as if he didn't learn to speak the language until he was a little older. Like me."

Jace lifted an eyebrow and one corner of his mouth quirked in the ghost of a grin. "It's true. I didn't learn a word of Russian until I was ten." He jerked his head at Ian. "I don't think he learned a word of it until he was seventeen. Bastard."

"Sorry, kid. I'm talented at languages. Anyway, you hear that Jace has a slight accent but didn't hear one from Calypso. Which means she's either Russian or she's exceptionally good at language." He turned and tapped the computer. A photo appeared. The one he'd shown her before. The one they'd thought was her.

There were a couple of other photos too, but they seemed different to Maddy. Different women.

"Study them, Dr. Cole. Tell me if you see any commonalities."

She stood and went over to be closer to the screen. There were four photos. A fifth appeared and she gasped. It was her. She whirled. "Not funny."

"Necessary."

She turned back, darting between her photo and the one they'd shown her the first time she'd come to this place. "The hair is very similar. You can't really tell how tall she is, but the build is similar too. Not heavy like the maid. I wish you had the maid. I'd love to compare her with this one."

"We do too. What about the others?"

"They're blurrier, aren't they?"

"Yes."

She studied them. They were different than the one that looked like her. But the more she studied them, the more familiar the faces seemed. Which probably just meant she was staring at them too much.

Familiar. Creepy.

She remembered thinking those words when she'd first seen the photo of the woman who was supposed to be her a few days ago. She peered at that one again. At the expression on the woman's face. Cool, haughty. Superior.

The maid had looked at her with that same superior gleam, but was that enough to say they were the same person?

She turned away from the screen. "I don't know. I

think there's a similarity of expression. But that's not enough to damn anyone, is it?"

"Nope, but it was worth a try." The screen blacked out. "Do you think you could describe the maid to a sketch artist?"

She glanced at Jace for support. It hit her how much she trusted him in that moment. He gave her a nod, a firm look, and she turned to Ian again. "I can do that."

He came over to where she stood. "Thank you, Dr. Cole. I know this is rough for you. I know it doesn't make sense. But it's important. If that maid is who we think she is—well, you're the only person we've found who can identify her."

Chapter Fifteen

Jace stayed with Maddy while she described the maid to the sketch artist. The portrait that emerged prickled a memory, but Calypso was nobody he could pinpoint. It was more that she had an everywoman look. A valuable skill for an assassin.

The tattoo was the interesting part. Maddy hadn't seen enough detail to really create a portrait of the ink work, but knowing they were looking for a woman with that particular art in that particular place was more helpful than all the grainy photos and potential sightings in the world.

Add in the girlish voice—though Calypso could have been putting the voice on as well—and they had enough information to search for her. It was a huge coup—and they had Maddy to thank for it.

Except that information also put her in danger, which he didn't like at all. While Maddy continued to refine the portrait with the artist, Jace stepped out of the room and went to find Ian.

Ian was in the ops center, viewing a heat map for Southeast Asia. They had a small cell there, operating in the murky world of human trafficking and arms deals. Trying to dismantle the local organizations and sow discord whenever possible.

The map had been carefully blank when Maddy walked through earlier, but now it was alive with activity. It would go dark again when she emerged from the conference room.

Ian looked up as he approached. It was hard to tell what Ian was thinking most of the time, but this time he jerked a nod, as if pleased with something. Then he stood and motioned for Jace to follow him to his office. Once inside the glass walls, they could observe the ops center but talk in private.

Ian went over to his desk and shuffled some things around, studying whatever intelligence had been dropped off recently. "You've handled her well," he said. "Good work."

Annoyance pricked him. "I wasn't handling her, boss."

Ian's gaze lifted. "No, maybe not. But your instincts were good and it amounts to the same thing."

"Her information is game-changing."

"It is. Going to suggest something to you, Jace. You aren't going to like it."

"What's that?"

"Walk away. Let Colt and Ty handle her security. If Calypso is Russian, and from central Russia at that, you're the best equipped to hunt her down."

He considered it. He really did. Because he was a warrior and had been his whole life. From the moment his parents turned his world upside down to right this minute, he'd been immersed in the world of secrets and spies. He didn't know how to exist any other way. "What makes you think staying by Maddy's side isn't the best way to hunt Calypso?"

"Oh, it probably is. But you're too involved. Pull back, let them guard her, and you stay on the perimeter, observing. Leaves you free to hunt. If you're concentrating all your brain power on this, you might even find Calypso before she makes a move."

Now that was a seductive idea. Find the assassin before she made a move. Protect Maddy from afar. It wasn't what he'd promised her though. And something about the idea of leaving her made his gut churn.

"Maddy trusts me. And I promised I'd be there for her."

"Your life is dangerous. You're pulling her into your orbit. Is that what you really want?"

Anger flooded him. And doubt. "Are you telling me nobody else around here leads a dangerous life? That having Colt and Ty there with her is somehow safer than having me there? What the fuck, Ian?"

Ian's jaw hardened. His voice came out in a low

growl. "You know your life is more dangerous than most—*Nikolai.*"

Pain gripped his heart in a tight fist. "That's not my name. Not anymore."

"Maybe not, but there are those who haven't forgotten that man. Those who would love nothing better than to find him and make an example of him. And if they do find him? They won't spare an innocent art historian just because she's sweet and thinks the man she's with is somebody else entirely."

Jace wanted to break something. Always, *always*, the life he hadn't chosen intruded on the life he wanted. It was why he never got involved. Why he stayed aloof and disconnected. That had worked for years. Until Maddy Cole. Never before had he wanted to be a normal man as much as he did now.

But he never would be. That was the problem. His life was too unpredictable for a woman like Maddy. If he told her the truth about himself, what then? His parents' crimes were an easy Google search away. They'd been infamous spies, and they'd been deported in exchange for several American spies that the Russians were holding. He and Natasha had been stripped of their citizenship and sent packing too. At the ages of ten and four.

Goddamn. He didn't like it, but it was the right thing to do. For Maddy. He needed to rip off the bandage and move on. "I'll go, but only if you move her to a safe house."

"You know our best hope of finding Calypso is to let her come after Dr. Cole."

"Yes, but you don't need Maddy for it to happen. Send an asset to impersonate her. I'll stay and watch for signs of Calypso."

Ian huffed a breath. "Fine. I've already put a lot of resources on her when we aren't even sure Calpyso is out there, but I'll add another. It'll take me a day or so to get someone here who can do it though."

Relief rolled through him like a shot of alcohol—warm and soothing, with a painful bite on the finish. "That's fine. It'll give me time to sell the idea to Maddy. She'll trust Colt."

Ian nodded. "I know you like her. But she'll be safer with you actively hunting for Calypso. You know it as well as I do."

"Yeah, I know."

"And after?"

"I won't make contact." Bitterness tasted like acid on his tongue. "She's better off if I don't."

Ian looked fierce and sad at the same time. Almost as if he knew the struggle Jace was having with himself. He put a hand on Jace's shoulder and squeezed. "I'm sorry, man. You'll get over it in time."

Jace stepped back, breaking the contact. "I'm sure I will."

He left Ian's office and headed back to the conference room. If his time with Maddy was drawing to a close, he wasn't wasting a moment of it.

JACE WAS silent on the trip back to her house. Maddy shot him glances, but he didn't look at her. Didn't speak. She finally rolled her eyes and took the leap.

"Cat got your tongue?"

He glanced over at her. Did his jaw harden? His fingers tighten on the wheel? "Just thinking. You did good, Maddy. Gave us something we can really use. You have no idea how important it is."

Maddy glowed. "Oh, I don't know. Considering all the trouble you went to when you tackled me and dragged me back to the States, I'd say it's pretty important. You had a private plane reserved for her, and a way to get her into the country without a passport. Impressive."

"You need to be careful how much of that you talk about."

She felt chastened. But she knew he was only looking out for her. "I know. I won't tell anyone. Who would believe me anyway?"

"That's a good way to think about it."

The silence descended again. Maddy frowned, wondering what was wrong with him. He'd been her ally back there. Always at her side, encouraging her. She'd thought hard about the maid, and between her and the sketch artist, she thought they'd come up with something that looked like the woman she'd seen. The tattoo wasn't right, but it was close enough considering she hadn't seen much.

Jace had asked her, since she'd only glimpsed the tattoo, how she knew it was close. She'd had to think about that. But the answer was that she knew. She just knew. There were elements about it that reminded her of artwork she'd seen, but she couldn't remember where she'd seen it.

He'd accepted that. And now here they were, returning to her house, the silence between them stretching into discomfort. She'd felt at ease with him since their first lunch together. And now she didn't. It was odd.

They reached her house and went inside. Colt was sitting on the couch watching television with Kitty curled up beside him. He looked up as they walked into the living room. Maddy's heart squeezed. She was happy her cat was safe and well, and confused about what came next now that they were here. Would Jace really be staying? Or would he go back to the house across the street and leave her here alone? That's the conversation they'd been having before he'd taken her to the building with the secret ops center, but had anything changed between then and now?

Colt and Jace disappeared into the dining room to confer. A few moments later, Colt headed for the front door. "Bye, Maddy. Kitty was a good girl, in case you were wondering."

"She usually is."

He grinned. "She's a purr machine."

"Do you have a cat?"

His smile faltered for a second. "Naw, no time. Travel too much."

"I understand." But her heart ached at the emptiness of traveling so much you couldn't have a pet. She traveled, but at least she had Angie to take care of Kitty when she was gone.

As soon as he left, Jace locked the door behind him and tapped something into the new keypad beside the door. A sharp beep sounded, and another one emanated from his phone. "Need your phone, Maddy. Have to put the security apps on and show you how to use them."

She handed her phone to him after unlocking it. He downloaded an app and logged into it. A few minutes later, he handed it back. "You'll need to choose a code."

She tapped in the last four of her dad's social security number. Jace took the phone again and did a few more things. By the time he showed her how to activate the alarm, shut it off, view the cameras, and look at neighborhood reports of suspicious people, an hour had gone by and her stomach growled.

He met her gaze. "Hungry?"

"What gave that away, Einstein?"

His grin made her want to kiss him. So sexy. It was the first time he'd seemed at ease since they'd climbed into the car and returned to her house. She'd started to think something was wrong, but maybe he was just focused on the task at hand.

"Oh, I don't know. The monster in your belly maybe?"

"This monster needs feeding. It's been a long time since lunch," she said.

"Got anything in the fridge?"

"Do I look like a chef?"

"How would I know?" He arched an eyebrow. "You seriously don't have anything?"

"Sandwich meat. Cheese. I'm not a cook, Jace. Not even a little bit. Mimi tried, but my aptitude is zero."

He shook his head. "So how about pizza? I'll order one."

"Sure. Sounds good." She loved pizza.

"What do you want?"

"Cheese is my favorite. Though if you require meat, I like ham."

"Nope, cheese is excellent." He dialed a number. "Hey, Ty. Need a large cheese pizza over here. And a bottle of cabernet. The good stuff, not that cheap shit they sell as house wine. … Yeah, thanks, appreciate it."

Maddy gaped at him when he pocketed the phone. "You seriously called your friends across the street and asked them to get pizza?"

He shrugged. "Of course. Much faster than ordering from a restaurant."

"What do you mean, faster?"

"I mean that restaurants prioritize orders based on their own criteria. A man standing there waiting for his pizza is going to get it faster—especially a man as intimidating at Ty."

Maddy shook her head, laughing. "That's not even logical. Pizza delivery places have metrics to meet."

He looked horrified. "Baby, delivery pizza isn't what we're getting. Ty will head for Gino's and get the best pizza in town. You'll see."

She hadn't heard of this Gino's. Didn't mean it wasn't great though. The metro area was getting bigger all the time, and she didn't spend a lot of time exploring. Between work and Mimi, she didn't have much time.

Forty-five minutes later, they were watching *House Hunters International* when her phone dinged at the same time Jace's did. She picked it up to a notification that someone was approaching the front door. She could even see who it was. Her eyes met Jace's. He grinned as he disabled the alarm system.

"How much better is that?"

"It's better," she said.

He got up to unlock the door and open it. Ty came in with a pizza, a bottle of wine, and a grocery bag. "Had to stop for snacks anyway, so here's some other crap I know you like."

Jace peered in the bag. "Mm, potato chips and Tim Tams."

Maddy watched the two of them standing

together and a pang of envy filled her. They might be coworkers, but there was something about the ops center where she'd been earlier—and the people who worked there—that said they were a family. Not a nuclear family, but a family forged through bonds of work and duty. She liked some of her coworkers, loved her job, but that sense of family was missing. Looking at these two men, she felt there was a bond between them that she didn't understand.

A few minutes later, Ty was gone and Jace flipped open the pizza box. "Mm, damn that smells good. You want to eat from the box while finishing that episode about Spain or do you prefer to get fancier with plates and shit?"

She thought about it. She was usually a plate kind of girl but something about the way he assumed she'd be fussy made her say, "Box."

He took out the wine. "Need an opener and glasses, baby."

Maddy went to the cabinet to retrieve glasses, taking Mimi's corkscrew from the drawer, and setting them on the counter where Jace had set the wine.

He opened the bottle, poured two glasses, and carried them back to the living room. "Can you get the pizza?"

"Sure." She picked up the box, grabbed a couple of paper plates—that was her compromise, apparently—and napkins, and returned to the living room to join him. Kitty was on the couch, sniffing the air like she was about to get the best treat of her life.

"Get down, fluffy butt," Maddy said, pushing the cat gently to the floor.

Jace made room on the coffee table and took the box from her. Then he sat on the couch and looked up at her expectantly. Maddy swallowed. She could like this life. Eating pizza with Jace in front of the television. Drinking wine.

Making love.

Stop.

"What?" he asked. "Did you forget something?"

"No. It's just… About the only person who ever comes over to eat pizza and drink wine with me is Angie. And I can't remember the last time we did that because she's busy and I'm busy, and, well… I guess I don't really know why I haven't made it a priority."

"Life is pretty chaotic as it is. It's a good idea to spend time with friends whenever you can. You never know when things will change."

Her heart hitched. "Speaking from experience?"

"Yes." He motioned at the seat beside him. "You sitting down or what?"

She plopped down—but not too close—and he flipped open the box. She handed him a paper plate and he took a gooey slice of pizza and handed it back. It was intimate and she found herself blushing as she turned away and took a bite. "Mm, delicious."

"Yep." Jace took a bite of his own slice. Her heart tripped as he managed to brush his leg against hers. He seemed not to notice as he turned and shot her a look. "You want to watch something else while we eat or stick with the house hunting?"

"I'd like to see what they pick. After that, I'm open."

He hit the button to unpause the show and kicked back with his pizza. Maddy couldn't help but be aware of him beside her. Everything about being this close to Jace was intense and her heart was hammering a quick beat that made her dizzy.

After the second slice, she set her plate down. "Jace, what is this?"

He shot her a look. "What do you mean?"

"Eating pizza. Drinking wine. Watching television together. What's it about?"

He set his plate down too. "What do you want it to be about?"

That hadn't been the answer she'd expected. "I want it to be about you and me and getting to know each other. But it's not. It's about you and those guys across the street, about Ian, about Calypso. About so many things that have nothing to do with dating a person. I want it to be real, but it's not real. And I can't quite forget that."

He reached for her hand, squeezed it gently. His gaze held hers. "It's real for me. Every moment I spend with you is real. Yes, I'm a mean-ass junkyard dog who'll tear someone's throat out if they come for you, but I *want* to be here. Ian has a hundred guys who could do this job. I'm the one who wanted it." His gaze dropped to their hands as her heart throbbed at his words. "I'm no good for you, Maddy. So I'm not pushing for anything more than this. But right now, right here, I want to eat pizza with you and watch people with micro-budgets ask for sea views and palatial entertaining spaces."

She laughed at his characterization of the show, but her heart kind of broke at hearing him say he was no good for her. "I make up my own mind about what I want. Nobody gets to decide for me."

He nodded. "I suspected as much."

A motion alert blared from their phones in unison. "That thing's going to be the death of me," Maddy grumbled as she reached for her phone. But Jace was faster, peering at the screen to see what the commotion was about.

He started to rise, his hand sliding along his waistband in a maneuver she recognized as reaching for his weapon. "There's a woman coming toward the house."

Chapter Sixteen

THE WOMAN WAS WEARING HEELS WITH BLACK trousers and a jacket. She didn't appear to be trying to hide as she approached the door. Jace gripped his gun in one hand while he turned the phone to Maddy with the other.

"Recognize this woman?"

Maddy shot past him toward the entry. "Oh my God, yes! That's Angie—don't you dare shoot her."

The doorbell rang. Jace disarmed the alarm because he could tell Maddy wasn't even thinking about it as she barreled over and yanked the door open. Angie stood on the porch, staring at the doorbell with the camera attached.

"Whoa, Mads, you've gone high-tech."

"Angie, what are you doing here? Is something wrong?"

He heard Maddy suck in a breath but he couldn't tell why. "A grabby client. I just wanted to talk."

"Of course, honey. Come in, let me get you something to drink." She stepped back to let Angie in and Angie crashed to a halt in mid-step as her gaze landed on him.

"Oh."

"Ang, this is Jace."

Jace held out his hand to the woman. She was pretty, with red hair and creamy skin, but her eyes were bloodshot. As if she'd been crying. Still, she floated into the room with a smile on her face and put her hand in his. "Hey. Wow."

She turned to Maddy, still holding his hand. He didn't know what she did but Maddy bit her lip and tried not to laugh. "Sorry," Angie said, turning back to him. "It's just that I'm not used to gentlemen callers over here."

"Gentleman callers, Ang? Really?" Maddy laughed this time.

"Nice to meet you, Angie."

"It's Angelica really. Angelica Turner. But my friends call me Angie. Pleased to meet you." She let go of his hand and turned to Maddy again. "I should go. You're busy."

Maddy put a hand on Angie's elbow and stopped her from escaping. "No way, girlie. Sit down. Have some pizza and I'll pour you some wine. Tell me what happened."

Jace hooked a thumb toward the kitchen. "You know what, I'll just head in there and give you two some privacy."

"Oh, no, please," Angie said, holding out her hand to stop him. "I'm interrupting and I don't want to do that."

"You aren't interrupting," Maddy insisted. "Don't make me have Jace bar the door. He can, you know. Just look at the size of him."

Maddy lifted her brows, clearly hoping he'd play along. He kind of liked this unspoken conversation between them. She was asking him if he had her back. He did. Her back, her front—whatever she'd give him.

"I could rustle up some handcuffs if they'd help," he drawled out. Maddy's eyes widened. Then she coughed and he wanted to laugh.

Angie's gaze darted between them, clearly trying to understand what was going on here. Funny that Maddy had just been asking him that very question. What was going on was that he was having fun with her. He'd been trying not to think about how he was going to have to tell her he was leaving her in Colt's hands tomorrow, and trying to convince himself that it was a good thing he'd decided to pull back.

"No," Maddy blurted. "I think that's unnecessary."

"I'll just go get a glass for her."

Maddy smiled her thanks and Jace went into the kitchen. When he returned to pour a drink for Angie, Maddy had her sitting in a chair, a slice of pizza on a plate in her hands. Angie's fingers trembled as she picked it up and took a bite, and Jace's gut clenched.

Somebody had scared her. He'd like to find out who, then go have a talk with them.

"When you're ready, honey, tell me what happened," Maddy said.

"I'm sorry to barge in. I should have called first," she said in a rush after she'd swallowed the bite of pizza.

"It's okay. I'm your bestie, remember?"

Angie looked like she might cry. "Yeah," she said softly, her smile wavering at the corners.

Jace seriously felt like he was intruding. But there was nowhere to go. His phone buzzed then, saving him. He took the call in the kitchen. "Yo."

"Who's the redhead?" Colt asked.

He would have seen her on the camera feed. "Maddy's best friend. Angelica Turner."

The sounds of Colt typing reached his ears. "Running it now."

Jace sighed. Of course they'd run a background check on anyone who showed up at Maddy's house, but he didn't think they were going to find anything sinister.

"Whoa," Colt said.

"What?" He was suddenly on alert, ready to charge back in there and throw himself in front of Maddy if need be.

"She's fucking *hot*. Smart too. Junior accountant at Barton, Barnes, and Blake. She's only been there a year. Gets the shit hours right now. And the shit clients, it looks like."

An idea started to take hold. "Any idea who she met with tonight?"

"No, but I can find out. Why?"

"She came to talk to Maddy because she said a client was grabby with her. She's been crying, too."

Colt literally growled. "Motherfucker."

Jace didn't have any use for men who used their superior strength against women. Neither did Colt, it seemed. "Yeah, figure it out for me. Maybe we need to pay him a call."

"On it. I'll let you know."

"I'll see what I can get out of Maddy. Angie will probably tell her a name. Then you can run a background on the client."

MADDY WAS FURIOUS, but she was trying hard not to let it show. Angie ate a slice of pizza and drank an entire glass of wine. She'd stopped trembling and started talking. Angie was trying so hard to succeed at this new career, and she was doing a good job. But as a junior accountant, she sometimes got the people who weren't as successful or, heck, as decent as other clients.

Tom Walls was that kind of guy. A blowhard with a car repair chain who used Angie's firm for his accounting. He was about forty, full of bluster, and a real bastard with people he perceived weren't his equals. Or people he thought he deserved a piece of, like Angie.

Tonight, he'd wanted her to come to his main store to pick up some paperwork. Angie hadn't wanted to do it, but he was a client and she didn't want to assume there was anything wrong with the request. So she went.

"He pushed me against his desk and kissed me," Angie said with a shudder. "Then he grabbed my breast and squeezed. I could feel his erection." She shivered again and Maddy patted her leg.

"I'm so sorry, Ang. I'll send Jace to beat him up if you like." She wouldn't do any such thing, didn't think she could do any such thing, but she said it to get a laugh.

Jace had disappeared into the kitchen about fifteen minutes ago now. She was certain his phone call was over, but he was giving them privacy. She was overwhelmed with feelings she didn't have time to examine right now.

"He's lovely, Maddy," Angie said, her cheeks glowing with the effects of the alcohol. As a redhead, her skin showed everything.

Maddy felt a blush creep into her own cheeks. "He's a nice guy."

"Shit, girl, he's a *sexy* guy. You need to jump on that. Immediately." Angie tried to rise but Maddy pushed her firmly down again. "I need to go so you can do that, Mads. Don't argue with me."

"You drank a glass of wine. You aren't driving

home."

"I'll get an Uber."

"No, you won't. Stay and visit with me. You can go when you sober up."

Angie flopped against the chair. "Fine."

Maddy stood as Angie lay her head back and closed her eyes. "I need to check on something. Be right back."

"Go. I won't move."

"Better not." Maddy went into the kitchen, keeping an eye on Angie as she did so. Jace was leaning against the counter by the sink, legs crossed at the ankles, scrolling through his phone. He looked up as she peeked in. "Hey."

"Hey," he said. "She okay?"

"She will be. A client tried to force himself on her."

Jace's expression was stormy. "Got a name?"

"Why?"

"Because I'm in the kind of business where I can send someone to pay him a visit."

Her heart skipped. "This isn't the mafia, Jace."

"No, it's better. Name?"

Maddy considered it for two seconds. Then she said, "Tom Walls. He owns Walls Auto Repair. Don't do anything drastic."

"Not going to. But he won't touch her again, promise you that."

Maddy could only stare. The thought she could love him flashed into her head.

"She can't stay here, Maddy," he said, and the warm fuzzy feelings she'd been having evaporated.

"She's my best friend. I'm not sending her home to deal with this alone. Besides, she's had wine. She can't drive."

"You forget I have people. I'll ask Colt or Ty to take her home."

"She doesn't know them. And she just got attacked by a guy—do you really think she'll want to leave with a stranger?"

"You really think she's safer here?"

"Maybe. You don't know that Calypso is after me. You really don't. You just think she *might* be because I may have seen her. You don't even know if the maid was really her."

"No, we don't. But you're my responsibility. And your friend not only doesn't know what's going on, we aren't telling her."

Maddy frowned. "If she wants to leave, I won't stop her. But you get Colt or Ty over here right now to meet her. So if she does want to go, she'll at least know the guy she's going with is your friend. But if she doesn't want to go with him, I'm not making her. You hear me?"

Fierceness flowed through her like a river. She thought he might blow a gasket but instead he laughed. "Yeah, I hear you, honey badger."

Colt was there ten minutes later, waltzing in like he'd been invited the entire time. Angie had woken from her catnap, declined another glass of wine, and sat sipping water instead. When Maddy let Colt in, Jace did the introductions. He left out the last name, but he called Colt by his name so at least Angie wasn't getting a fake name. Maddy thought Angie might be interested in Colt—he was totally her type—but she didn't flirt with him the way she normally would.

And that worried Maddy more than she liked.

They sat and talked for a while. Maddy asked Colt questions while Angie sat quietly. An hour later, Angie stood up. "I need to get home now. Thanks for the wine, Maddy. It was great meeting you, Jace. Colt."

Colt shot to his feet. "Need a ride home?"

Angie aimed a look at Maddy. Then smiled politely at Colt. "Thank you, no. I'm fine."

"But you had wine," Maddy said.

Angie didn't even pretend not to glare. "More than an hour ago, Mads. I can drive myself home."

Chastened, Maddy walked her to the door. "You sure you're fine?" she asked quietly. "You can stay here if you don't want to be alone."

Angie squeezed her hand. "I think alone is where I'd most like to be right now. But I'm good, babes. Thank you for being here for me when I needed it."

"I'm always here for you."

"I know. That's why I love you."

"I'm worried about you, Angie. What that asshole did was wrong."

"I know. But he didn't rape me. He forcibly groped me, kissed me, and ground his erection against me."

"That's assault."

"I know, but I just want to forget it, okay? It won't do me any good to pursue it. I'll lose my job."

It angered Maddy to think that could happen, but she didn't know that it wouldn't. And it wasn't her place to force Angie to report the incident, even if it hurt Maddy's heart to see her vibrant friend so wrecked. "Of course. Be careful going home. Text me when you get there."

"I will."

Maddy watched Angie go down the sidewalk and get into her car. She felt Jace's solid presence as he came up behind her. He put a hand on her shoulder. "Colt's going to follow her home. He'll make sure she gets inside."

Maddy hadn't even heard Colt leave, but he'd apparently gone out the back door while she'd been talking to Angie. "If she sees him, she'll kill me."

"She won't see him." Jace put his other hand on her, drew her back against his solid chest. She shivered at his warmth, his strength. One thing she knew for sure—he would never force himself on her the way Tom Walls had done to Angie.

She turned into him, wrapped her arms around him, and held on tight. He didn't hesitate to hold her close. He maneuvered them so he could shut the door, lock it, and tap commands on the keypad. Then he just held her, his hand rubbing up and down her back. Never touching her inappropriately. Never copping a feel or grinding against her. Just comforting.

Maddy tipped her head back and studied him. He didn't say a word as he looked down at her. His gaze was hooded, careful.

Just like in the parking garage earlier today, Maddy stood on her tiptoes and pressed a kiss to his mouth. He groaned softly, his tongue dipping between her lips briefly before he pulled back again.

"I don't understand you, Jace Kaiser. I don't understand why you make me feel the way you do, but I think more than anything I want you to hold me tonight. Please."

SHE WAS KILLING HIM. Flat out killing him. Jace held Maddy close, his cock swelling, desire a hard drumbeat in his veins. But going there meant crossing a line he'd decided he shouldn't cross. As much as he wanted sweet Maddy Cole, he'd promised Ian he was walking away. Leaving her to the care of Colt and Ty and whoever else Ian sent, and going on the hunt for Calypso.

He was doing it—planning to do it—for Maddy. To protect her. Keep her safe. Give her a life where she could meet a guy, get married, have a couple of kids, and stop being lonely. Have a normal fucking life, unlike anything he could give her.

He was a man without a country, a man on the run, a man who could *never* be close to anyone. Because he was nowhere near normal.

Yet she touched her lips to his and all his willpower—all his formidable self-discipline—was in the toilet. He wanted her. Just one night. One night of aching sweetness before he walked away forever.

He kissed her, letting himself taste her thoroughly while she clung to him. He didn't grind his hips against hers, not after hearing her friend's story—but he didn't have to. She made the move. She arched into him, pushing her hips into the burgeoning hard-on currently pressing itself against his belly.

Goddamn she was sweet.

"Maddy," he groaned, breaking the kiss, pushing her back just enough so he could see her face. Tangling his fingers in her hair and wanting to fan it out over the pillows before he fucked her into blissful rapture. He lifted it to his nose. Buried his face in the strands while she quivered. "So fucking sweet."

"I don't want to be sweet, Jace. I want to be dirty. With you. Please."

"Honey. Baby. God, you're killing me." He kissed her again, told himself it was the last damn time. Just to feel her tongue against his. "Baby," he said, pushing her away again. "Listen to me."

Her arms snaked around his neck. Her body arched into his. She blinked up at him, green eyes wide and trusting. He didn't deserve her trust.

"I'm listening, Jace."

"I want this. I want you. Badly. But I have to ask you something."

She looked so trusting. "Yes?"

Fuck. "If tonight was all we'd ever have, would you still do it?"

She scrunched her forehead adorably. "Why are you asking me that?"

"Because I don't know what tomorrow brings." *Liar.*

Maddy sighed, but her grip on him didn't loosen. "I think, if tonight was all we'd ever have, that I'd be even more determined to do this. To be with you, Jace Kaiser. Because you make me feel things I've never felt before—and even if my heart breaks tomorrow, I want this. I want *you.* You're exciting and interesting, and as much as I don't want tomorrow to be the end, I'd regret if it was and I'd never been any closer to you than this."

Jesus, he didn't deserve her. He shouldn't kiss her, shouldn't undress her and taste her, but the urge was strong. Because tomorrow *was* the end, and he'd never see her again. He'd promised Ian, the only person to whom he owed any loyalty whatsoever. The man who'd saved him.

Yet he owed Maddy too. Because she trusted him. And he cared about her.

"If tomorrow is the end, I need you to know it's not because I didn't want to stay—"

She put her hand on his mouth, silencing him. "I don't want to hear it, Jace. I don't want to know, because I know anything is possible with you. I know you're probably trying to set me up for disappointment, or maybe trying to talk me out of being with you because you know damn well you're leaving tomorrow, but tonight is not tomorrow. Tonight is now." She sucked in a breath. "I've lost my grandmother, my father. My mother, God bless her narcissistic soul, doesn't speak to me more than once a year. You leaving won't surprise me. Believe me. I'm used to it."

Damn if her words didn't threaten to break his empty heart. He thought of her yesterday, standing by the water, looking so lost. Sobbing in her car. He didn't want to do those things to her. Didn't want to be the cause of more heartbreak.

She took her hand off his mouth.

"Maybe we need to go slow—"

"No, Jace. *No.* I'm tired of doing things slowly. Tired of holding back. I want what you promised me earlier. And if you don't want to do that, it's fine—but you need to go back across the street and stop pretending like you want more from me."

"I'm not pretending."

She stepped back and took his hand, threaded her fingers in his. "Then do something about it," she said before leading him over to the couch they'd been sitting on only a few minutes before.

He fought with himself. He really did. But in the end, he swept his arm beneath her knees and swooped her up. Then he lowered her on the couch and came down on top of her.

Game on.

Chapter Seventeen

MADDY'S HEART THREATENED TO BEAT RIGHT OUT OF her chest. Jace tipped her back to the couch and dropped down on top of her. She opened her legs, cradling his hips between them. The ridge of his cock pressed against her in all the right places. She was wet, ready, but she also wanted the excruciating build up. Because once he was inside her, once they came, she knew it was over.

Jace Kaiser wasn't here to stay. She could feel it as surely as she felt the impressive length and width of him. He dropped his mouth to hers, kissed her sweetly and then hotly, his tongue thrusting into her mouth and stroking against her own. His big hands went to her waist, tugged her shirt up until he could put his fingers on her skin. She thought he might strip her quickly, thrust into her, and take them both to heaven.

But he went slower than that. Slower than she expected. His fingers stroked up, glided along the lower edge of her bra, and then up to caress the mounds of flesh above the cups. He dragged one cup down and slid his tongue around her nipple. Maddy gasped at the flood of sensation where there'd so long been drought and deprivation.

Jace drew her nipple into his mouth, tugged gently and then harder, and Maddy thought she might come from the pressure of his mouth alone. Her fingers curled into his shoulders, her legs wrapped around his waist, and she arched her body up to that glorious mouth, urging him to take all she had to give.

He dragged the other cup down and repeated what he'd done while he softly pinched the nipple he'd been sucking previously. Maddy was on fire. Her body was strung so tight it hurt. She put her hands in his hair, cupped his head to her. He stopped and went to her mouth, kissing her deeply. Maddy moaned into his kiss, sucked his tongue, ground herself against him, seeking an orgasm that wasn't self-inflicted for the first time in more than three years.

"Patience," he told her as he lifted himself up and tugged at her shirt.

She sat up enough for him to whip it over her head, then she pulled at the hem of his. He obliged her by tugging it up and off with one hand. Maddy's breath froze. Dear God that was a sexy maneuver, especially watching the way his muscles rippled and popped. He grinned at the look on her face, and Maddy felt herself blushing. Or maybe that was just the heat of her desire.

Jace had muscles that went on for days. He also had tattoos, though not an excessive number. Tribal tattoos on his arms. A clock with a broken face on his ribs, stylized writing in both Russian and English, a bird with colorful feathers that perched on his shoulder and pectoral, the long tail wrapping down and around his ribs. Sexy. So sexy.

She reached up to trace the bird, but then he slid a hand behind her to unsnap her bra and all her contemplation of his ink evaporated. His piercing blue eyes were hot and fierce as he freed her, and she melted in a warm puddle beneath that gaze.

"You're so fucking beautiful, Maddy," he said reverently, cupping her breasts in his big hands and pushing them together.

"So are you," she replied, her blushes heating her skin. He had to know she was blushing, but he didn't mention it. She was grateful.

He bent to suck her nipples, one after the other, nibbling and tugging, until she thought she would come unglued at any second. Then he nibbled his way down her belly, his fingers finding the zipper for her jeans. He opened them up, ran his tongue along the top of her panties, and then dragged the fabric off her hips and down her legs, tossing them to the floor along with her underwear.

She was completely naked—and suddenly very self-conscious. Maddy wrapped her arms over herself, but Jace quietly pulled them open again as he hovered above her.

"Don't hide from me, Maddy. I want to see all of you. Taste all of you. Do you have any idea how fucking crazy you've been making me?"

She shook her head because the power of speech had deserted her.

"Almost from the moment I tackled you in Sokolov's house, I've wanted to uncover your secrets and taste your kiss on my lips."

She bit her lower lip, her heart pounding hard enough that he surely had to see it. "You don't mean that."

"I do, Maddy. I honestly do. I'm drawn to you. I don't know why. It'd be better for us both if I wasn't, but I can't seem to help myself."

"I'm scared," she blurted.

He rocked back to stare down at her. Searched her gaze. She saw the moment he reached a conclusion. "Baby—are you a virgin?"

Maddy spread her palms over his warm skin, stroked his muscles because she could. Because she couldn't help herself. "No, sorry, that's not what I meant." She drew in a breath. "I'm scared of how I feel with you. I feel reckless. High. And happy. I want to say to hell with everything and stay right here with you, just us, but I also feel like there's not enough time. Like tonight is all there's going to be, and I can't stop it or control it. I just have to let it happen."

He dropped between her legs, pushed them open and cupped her ass in his hands. Then he gazed at her over the delta of her body. "A lot is going to happen tonight, Maddy. You're mine for the next few hours, and I'm going to make you feel so good you won't regret a single moment."

He touched his tongue to the wet seam of her body and she gasped with pleasure. She was so ready for him that her juices dripped down her thighs. She was embarrassed, but she quickly forgot her discomfort as he licked his way around her clit before sucking it between his lips and flicking his tongue over her sensitive flesh again and again.

She tried to hold out—really tried—because it'd been so long and felt so damn good, but she couldn't. Everything inside her tightened into a hard spiral before exploding in a shower of sparks that stole her breath and vision for long moments.

"Damn," he breathed. "You're so pretty when you come."

"It's been too long," she offered. "I'm sorry."

He grinned. "You think I mind that you came so fast? Hell no." He slid his thumbs along her pussy lips, opening her up. "Let's see if you can do it again."

This time he teased her first, sliding his tongue inside her, around her, licking his way to her clit with sure strokes that came closer and closer. Until he was there again, taking her in his mouth, slipping a finger inside to fuck her that way too.

Maddy arched her back, her eyes closing tight, as she tried to catch the wave of pleasure sitting just out of reach.

And then she did catch it, and the sensation built

to excruciating levels before exploding in that same hot shower of sparks as before.

Maddy was delirious with joy, but she knew it wasn't yet enough. There was more to experience with Jace, and she wanted it all. When he dipped his head to lick her again, she pushed his shoulders. "No more, please."

His hot eyes met hers. "You don't want more pleasure? "

"I do, Jace. But I want it with you inside me."

He sighed. "Babe, I want that too. More than you know. But what I don't have with me, because I didn't show up for this, is condoms."

"I have some."

An eyebrow arched. "Seriously?"

"Yes. And the box is full—I only opened it so I'd have one in my purse just in case, but they've never been used."

He grinned. "Then let's go use them."

JACE FOLLOWED Maddy to the bedroom, his eyes firmly fixed on her pretty little ass, her taste on his tongue, his body hard as stone. Her long hair brushed the dip in her back just above her ass, and it turned him on for some crazy reason.

Hell, everything about Maddy turned him on. She bent over to get the condoms from a drawer and he groaned. Then he dropped to his knees and licked her pussy from behind while she gripped the dresser and cried his name. When she shuddered hard, creaming his tongue with her release, he stood and turned her in his arms, lifting her against him as he kissed her.

She wrapped her arms around his neck and kissed him back with all the passion he wanted. He walked her over to the bed and set her down, breaking the kiss. She dropped to her knees, her pretty green eyes staring up at him as she tackled the button on his jeans. When she freed him, she gripped him with both hands before pressing a kiss to the tip.

Jace sucked in a groan and fisted his hands at his sides. "Baby, how about we skip you doing that this time?"

She tugged his jeans down his hips. "We didn't skip it for me, so no."

"Yeah, but you make me come this way, it'll be a few minutes before I'm ready again."

She grinned up at him. "I'll keep it in mind."

She took him in her mouth, sucking him as deep as she could—which wasn't deep but he didn't care—before running her tongue along his length and tickling his balls. He'd had blow jobs before—plenty of them—but none made him feel the way this one did. He had iron self-discipline, but many more strokes of her sweet tongue and he was going to explode.

Jace pulled her up and into his arms, kissing her as he took her down to the bed. The condoms were there, a strip spilling from the box, and he fumbled for them. Then he sat back and tore one off while she propped herself on her elbows and watched.

"You're so sexy, Jace."

"I was thinking the same thing about you."

She dropped her gaze to where his cock jutted thick and proud. "I really wanted to make you come that way," she said.

His balls tightened. "And I wanted to let you. But I want to be inside you even more." He rolled on the condom, then stalked her backward on the bed, tugging her beneath him, letting his gaze drop over her delightful body. The firm, high tits. Narrow waist, dark pubic hair. She parted her legs, revealing slick pink flesh that he wanted to spend hours exploring.

Jace stroked his fingers down her body, between her legs, skimming over her clit before pushing two into her body. She bit her lower lip, arched up to him as he fucked her slowly. He added his thumb to the mix, swirling it over her tender flesh until she gasped.

"Jace—please."

"Please what, Maddy?"

"Stop teasing and fuck me already."

God he loved it when she said that word. "Say that again."

"What?"

"Fuck me, Jace."

She blushed. "I didn't say that."

"You did."

"Not exactly like that."

"Baby, I want you to say fuck. Better yet, say it in my ear while I'm deep inside you, okay?"

She smiled. "Okay."

He replaced his fingers with his cock, pushing slowly inside her while she sucked in her breath and then let it out again in a moan. "Oh. Oh my."

He held himself on his elbows so he could watch her take him. Between the sight of his cock disappearing into her body and her eyes dilating as her mouth fell open, he was in the best heaven he could imagine.

He held still for a long moment, trying to capture this feeling in his mind so he could take it out and examine it later, when she was gone from his life. But how would he ever remember it all? The way the soft light of her bedroom lamp spilled across her skin, the peaches and vanilla scent of her, the way his chest felt tight and his heart full, the sound of a car driving by on the street outside. Even the sound of her cat crunching food somewhere nearby.

This moment was everything. Intimate, important, overwhelming in ways he couldn't quite understand. To lose it was going to cost him more than he wanted to pay.

He started to move, pumping slowly into her, stoking the pleasure between them like a small fire he intended to turn into a raging inferno. It didn't take long. Flame raced along his skin, through his bones, his blood, and into his heart. He fucked her faster, harder, driving them both toward a cliff that he wanted to stand on the edge of before falling into oblivion with her.

He took her mouth, kissed her while he drove into her. She wrapped her legs around him, holding on tight—and then she ripped her mouth from his and put it against his ear. "Fuck me, Jace. Harder—oh God, so good."

He couldn't help but respond to that command. He did as she asked, and when she plunged over the side of the cliff, gasping his name, he followed her into the languid pool below, pouring himself into the condom and wishing there was nothing between them but skin.

He saw stars. His body quivered with the force of what he was feeling. He didn't understand it, but he understood it was unique. That he'd never experienced this with a woman before.

He rolled to the side, taking Maddy with him. She clung to him, her body damp, her eyes closed, a groan on her lips.

"That. Was. *Spectacular,*" she breathed.

He ran his fingers down her side, around to cup her ass. He was still inside her, but he'd have to move soon. If he didn't take care of the condom, they'd have a mess. "It was," he told her.

She sighed and pressed her mouth to his neck. Her tongue teased him for a second, then she pulled back and pushed herself away. He wanted to grab her to him, but he let her go. Her hair was messy, her eyes sleepy and satisfied. She smiled down at him. "I think you delivered on your promise."

"What promise was that?"

"Not just one, but *two* secret weapons licensed to give the best orgasms ever."

He almost snorted. "I'm glad to hear I lived up to expectations." He sat up and grabbed the base of the condom so nothing leaked out. "Let me take care of this and I'll be happy to do it all again. In case you need another demonstration."

She yawned and stretched as she lay back on the pillows. "Yes, maybe you'd better show me again. I need to test for quality control. You can't keep your license if you don't prove you can provide a quality experience each and every time."

Jace bent and kissed her. Then he walked away, chuckling. "Hold that thought, babe. I'm going to rock your world so hard you'll never forget this night."

He thought her smile faltered for a second, but maybe he imagined it because she spread her legs open, enticing him with a view of glistening flesh. "Come and get it, honey."

MADDY JERKED AWAKE, confused. She'd been having the most delicious dream where she was warm and satisfied and happy. And then it hit her that it wasn't a dream. She was in her bed, in the dark, and a warm body lay beside her. They'd had sex three times before falling asleep in a tangle of arms and legs. She didn't even remember falling asleep it had happened so fast.

She pushed a hand through her hair and scooted away from Jace as carefully as she could. He reached for her anyway, coming awake as he did so, his hand closing around her wrist.

"Babe, what's wrong?"

She pushed her hair behind an ear as she leaned over to kiss him. "Nothing. I need to pee and check on Kitty."

"Hey, think we can heat up some pizza?"

She laughed. "You want pizza?"

"In case you weren't aware, I burned a lot of calories pleasing you."

Maddy laughed. "Did you now?"

"Hell yes. It's work making you come so many times."

Maddy pinched him. Lightly. He sat up, the sheet falling down his torso, and her mouth went dry. The light from the living room snaked down the hallway and through her open door. They hadn't exactly turned everything off before hitting the bedroom, though Jace had gone back at one point to shove the remaining pizza in the fridge. The man had priorities.

"I could have a snack too, I think."

"Meet you in the kitchen?"

"Sure."

Maddy went to the restroom while Jace got up and dragged on clothes. It wasn't until she joined him in the kitchen that she realized all he'd put on were a pair of gray boxer briefs that accentuated his firm ass—and whoa, the impressive outline of his package when he turned to face her. Had she really been underneath him just a few hours ago, enjoying that gorgeous body?

She had. She wanted to again. Liquid heat flooded between her legs. She was already slightly sore since it'd been so long, but she still wanted more. She wanted to feel the imprint of Jace on her. Inside her. For all time.

Jeez, Maddy, way to go getting all sentimental about the first guy to make you come in over three years.

Kitty did figure-eights around his legs and Maddy made herself focus on that instead of the chaotic emotion swelling in her chest. "Kitty-girl, are you hungry?"

"I heard her eating crunchy food earlier. Does she need more?"

Maddy went over to a cabinet. "She gets moist food too." She pulled out a tin and opened it, dumped it into a fresh bowl. Then she went over and set it on the floor while Kitty meowed for it. Then Kitty dove in, purring, and it was quiet again.

"She's cute," he said, getting a plate out and putting pizza on it. "You want some?"

"A slice."

He added to the plate.

"She is cute," Maddy said, suddenly feeling awkward. She'd put on her robe in the restroom, but it was short and she felt more exposed than she liked. Which was crazy because he'd seen her naked. Done things to her body that she'd never forget for the rest of her life.

"How long have you had her?"

"She was Mimi's cat. Mimi got her when she was a kitten, which was only six years ago now. Seems like a lifetime." Maddy shook her head. "Anyway, I think she made Mimi feel like everything was all right, you know? I'm pretty sure Mimi was starting to slip, but it was only three years ago that she had to go to the facility. So Kitty was her rock until then."

"Where were you?"

"New York. I'm fortunate enough to be able to base myself here now, but when I first started with Barrington's, I had to be in New York. I did a lot of museum work, a lot of private collector work in the city. I wasn't sent on a remote job until I'd been there for two years. Then I had a lot of jobs, and when I realized what was happening with Mimi, I had to come home. They were very understanding at Barrington's. I tried to be here for Mimi but it was clear she couldn't live without help. I'd get calls that she was found wandering down the street in her bathrobe. She made it over to the City Dock a couple of times." Maddy tried not to let the sadness choke her, but it was there in the back of her throat anyway.

Jace tugged her into his arms and rubbed his hands up and down her back. She loved the closeness, the way she felt at ease with him. She could love him. She really could.

No, it's too risky.

It was too risky. He led a dangerous life of intrigue that she didn't understand. And she didn't think he was going to give it up to get a desk job in DC so he could get married, buy a house, and raise two point five kids—with her or anyone.

"I'm sorry, honey. That had to be difficult."

"It was. I finally realized she needed around the clock care when I came home one day and she'd set the kitchen curtains on fire." Maddy shuddered. "I was just lucky I walked in when I did. Mimi had lit a candle, and she'd put it too close—"

"It's okay."

She swallowed. "It wasn't just that she'd made a mistake. It was that she didn't know me, or where she was. She kept insisting she wanted to go home, that her mother would be looking for her. I knew I needed professional help." She sniffled and pushed away again. "Anyway, that's how I got Kitty. I wasn't going to rehome her. I loved her because she was Mimi's, but then I loved her because she's herself. Such a sweet girl. She means the world to me."

The microwave dinged but he didn't move. He was still watching her. Waiting for a meltdown maybe. Well, she wasn't going to do it. "Thought you were hungry."

"I am. You okay?"

"I'm fine. I've been living with this reality for three years now. I won't fall apart over it tonight."

He nodded before he turned and got the pizza. They perched at the kitchen counter and ate together in silence. For all the intimacy of the bedroom, it suddenly felt awkward between them. Maddy didn't know what to say. She thought of and discarded fifty questions, none of which she figured he'd answer anyway.

"I wasn't close to my parents," he said, not looking at her. Shocking her.

Maddy stilled. He'd never said anything so personal. "I'm not close to my mother. At all." He looked up. "She's a bitch," Maddy added. "She left my dad for another man. A richer man."

"I'm sorry."

She waved a hand. "It's okay. I'm over it. Have been for a long time."

He nodded. "I don't think I am," he said softly. "I don't think I ever will be. Which is funny in a way because my parents were monsters."

Chapter Eighteen

Her eyes glistened as she reached for his hand. She held it tight. "Oh Jace. I don't know what to say."

He shrugged. Why the fuck had he said that? He didn't know, but it had felt right when he did it. "Lots of kids have shitty parents. Or no parents. I didn't have it any worse than a lot of kids."

"It doesn't matter—if they were terrible to you, then you have every right to hate them."

"They weren't terrible. Not in the sense you're thinking." He sucked in a breath. He didn't know why he was saying these things to her, but something in him needed to get it out. And yet he had to be careful, too. There were things he couldn't say. Things he *shouldn't* say.

"So they didn't beat you, I take it. Mental abuse is just as bad."

He stared at their joined hands. He wanted to unburden himself. He'd carried this around for so damned long. "I was born in Virginia and raised there until I was ten years old. My parents uprooted me and my baby sister and moved us to Moscow first, then St. Petersburg. We didn't speak a word of Russian. Didn't even know our parents were Russian until we moved. It was a difficult transition."

"I'm so sorry." She didn't mention the fact he'd just admitted that both his parents were Russian. He'd told her before that he had one of each. He knew she hadn't forgotten it.

"I was bullied for not speaking the language. And then speaking it with an American accent."

She rubbed her thumb back and forth over his hand. Comforting him. As if he could be comforted, but he appreciated the gesture. Sweet Maddy.

He tugged her toward him and kissed her. She melted into him, her hand coming up to cup his jaw. He could get used to this. Coming home to Maddy, feeling her passion and her tenderness. Losing himself in her.

"You said your parents were dead," she said when he let her go again. "Is that when you left Russia? And what about your sister? Where is she?"

Jace's gut tightened. "They are all dead." He'd never seen bodies, but he'd been told they'd been targeted for crimes against the state. It was all too common, unfortunately. His parents he didn't care much about—but Natasha, well, she'd been so young when they'd been deported. He'd hoped her life would be unaffected by his parents' crimes, but that had been a vain hope apparently. He still held out a sliver of hope she was alive, but he didn't expect it was true. He hadn't been there when the authorities came for her and his parents and he didn't really know what had happened. But people didn't reappear once they'd been arrested for treason.

Spying for the Americans, they'd said. Wasn't that just fucking ironic?

Maddy climbed off her bar stool and came over to hug him tight. "I'm sorry. It sounds so lame, but it's true. I'm sorry."

He threaded his fingers into her wild mane of hair. "I didn't want to make you sad. It's in the past. I hated them for what they did to us. And I know that doesn't make a lot of sense to you since it seems their only crime was uprooting us and not telling us our heritage—but there's more to it than that. I wish I could tell you, but I can't."

Her green eyes searched his. "Jace Kaiser. Why did you pick that name?"

He slipped his thumb over her lower lip, caressing it. "Jace is short for Jason—like Jason Bourne in the movies. Kaiser comes from another movie."

"Which movie is that?"

"*The Usual Suspects.* Keyser Söze. He's a total badass who hides in plain sight for much of the movie. He's right in front of the police and they don't even know it. I changed the spelling to the German for emperor."

Jason Bourne and Keyser Söze. Two utter

badasses in his opinion. Men who didn't let anything stop them.

"I like it. It suits you."

"I can't tell you my birth name, Maddy. I know you want to know. But that name—there's a lot of baggage that comes with it."

She dropped her gaze. "I understand."

He tipped her chin up. "Do you?"

She swallowed. "Yes. I mean I wish you trusted me enough to tell me more, but I understand why you don't."

"I don't think you do," he murmured, searching her gaze.

"That's not fair. I haven't pushed you."

"No, you haven't. But Maddy—I don't tell you because it could mean the difference between life and death. That name—my name—is death. Better you don't know."

She shivered as she burrowed into the circle of his arm. "I wish you wouldn't say stuff like that."

"I'm only telling the truth."

"So you say your real name and I drop dead? It's silly."

"No, you won't drop dead. But if anyone comes looking for me, and you know the truth, you're vulnerable. I won't put you in that position."

He could tell he was scaring her with this kind of cryptic talk because she shivered in his arms. "It's three a.m., Jace. Take me back to bed, please."

He searched her gaze. "Back to bed to sleep? Or back to bed for something else?"

She ghosted her thumb over his lower lip. Heat flared in his groin at that tender gesture. "I want to scream your name. Loudly. Often."

He growled as he kissed her. "I can make that happen."

THEY FUCKED HARD. Harder than she might have expected, but considering what he'd revealed to her over early morning pizza, maybe she shouldn't be surprised. There was an edge of desperation to Jace as he licked her into a screaming orgasm and then rolled over and let her ride him hard and fast until they both exploded.

Yet it still wasn't enough. He'd disappeared to take care of the condom, then returned with his hand wrapped around his still-hard cock. When he'd rolled on another condom, she'd been amazed—and turned on beyond belief.

He'd flipped her over and lifted her ass in the air. Maddy had clutched the pillow in her arms as he slid into her from behind. They'd both groaned at the incredible sensitivity of their joining. Then Jace bent over her and bit her shoulder while pumping into her. His fingers found her clit, working it as he fucked her from behind.

Maddy shoved backward onto his cock, taking

him deep, moaning with the rightness of it. She'd never been wild in bed—until Jace. Now, she wanted everything he could give her. Because she feared their time was limited.

"Jace," she gasped as he lifted her hips, holding her hard to him and thrusting deep and fast. When he swatted her cheek, she thought for the briefest of moments that she might be angry with him. But then he swatted her again and her ass stung—and it turned her on. "Again," she cried.

He spanked her harder, hitting both cheeks, and Maddy writhed and moaned and thought she was crazy. Who liked being spanked during sex? She did, apparently. Who knew?

He spanked her once more, harder than before, and she gasped—then he reached around and pinched her clit in a quick rhythm while pumping into her faster. Maddy came unglued, straightening until her back was pressed to his chest, until she could turn her head and kiss him while he thrust upwards into her body. He didn't stop stroking into her, stroking her clit, and her orgasm steamrolled over her with incredible force and turned her into a begging, gyrating mess.

When it was done, she slowly collapsed, sliding down his body and panting into the pillow. He was still hard inside her. Still throbbing. He hadn't come yet. Which meant more deliciousness was about to happen.

He flipped her over, hooked his arms behind her

knees and spread her wide. Then he rode her until she exploded again. This time he went too, groaning brokenly as he poured himself into her, his body twitching as his balls emptied into the condom.

They were sweating as they lay side by side. Breathing hard. Jace reached for her hand, twined his fingers into hers. He didn't say anything for several minutes and neither did she. Then he broke the companionable silence by getting up and disappearing for a few moments. When he returned, he lay down and gathered her close, wrapping his arms around her as he tugged her into the circle of his embrace.

"You're beautiful," he murmured sleepily.

"So are you." And then her heart tossed up a new thought. She didn't speak this one aloud though.

I love you.

Maddy shuddered. How could you love a man you hardly knew? How could you know he was the one when you didn't have much experience of men and relationships?

He just is. He's the one.

He'd taken care of her, even when he'd thought she was someone else. He'd broken his orders to talk to her because she was sad over Mimi, and he'd guarded her fiercely like she was a priceless treasure. Bad men didn't do things like that. Bad men didn't care about others.

Maddy fell asleep with strong arms around her, troubled by uncertainty. She'd fallen for him and she wanted more time with him—but the way he talked, he wasn't staying.

JACE WOKE, showered, and pulled clothing from the bag Ty had brought over from the other house last night. When he stepped back into the bedroom, Maddy was still asleep. She wasn't a big woman, but she sprawled. Her bed was queen-sized, but she'd nearly pushed him out of it with her spread-eagled way of sleeping. She was still sprawling on her belly, one knee bent, the other leg shoved over onto his side of the bed. Her arms were above her head, hugging the pillow, and her hair spread down her naked back where the covers had slipped free and across onto his pillow.

He thought about waking her, just so he could spend a little more time with her, but it was better if she slept. He strode out into the living room. Kitty looked up from her position on one of the couch pillows and meowed at him. Then she jumped down and followed him into the kitchen while he repeated Maddy's actions of last night and got out a can of moist cat food for her.

She was purring when he set it on the floor. He gave her a stroke from head to tail and she arched her back in pleasure.

"Hope you forgive me for keeping your mama all to myself last night."

Kitty continued purring and ignored him. She'd been indignant last night though. She was accustomed to sleeping with Maddy and she didn't like that someone else was in her bed with her person. She'd crawled all over him while he was trying to sleep. Sniffed him. Then swatted him awake with her paw on his head. He'd had to gently remove her and set her outside the bedroom door. She'd meowed indignantly a couple of times and then left.

Jace rose and searched for coffee. There was a coffee maker on the counter, so surely Maddy had some coffee somewhere. He found the bag of grounds and the filters. Soon, he had a pot going. His phone dinged with the sound of someone approaching the house. He viewed the camera feed and saw that it was Colt.

Jace opened the door for his teammate. Colt looked him up and down, eyebrows lifting knowingly. "Looks like you had a great night."

"Careful, asshole." He stepped back and Colt followed him inside. "If you jerks were listening to anything over here last night, I'll disembowel you myself."

Colt held up a hand. "Nope, not me. Not Ty and not Brett either."

"Then why the comment?" Jace asked as he went into the kitchen to wait for the coffee.

Colt leaned against the counter and folded his arms. "Because you've been an uptight jackass ever since we grabbed Maddy Cole in Sokolov's house.

And today you're not. You look remarkably relaxed. I know how that kind of relaxation happens so don't even try to tell me it didn't. You've been mixed up over that girl from the moment we caught her."

Mixed up? Was he? He thought of it more like obsessed. In a good way, not a *I'm going to follow you everywhere until you love me* kind of way. Not that love was even an issue here. They were having a mutually good time.

Except, when he imagined himself leaving Maddy and never seeing her again, his gut twisted tight and pain emanated from that deep place inside that he thought he'd walled off years ago.

"Maddy's special," he said. "And I'm not talking about this with you. Whatever I did or didn't do last night is none of your business."

Colt raised both hands. "Just an observation, dude."

"Did you find anything on Tom Walls?"

Colt's expression hardened. "Oh yeah. Asshole has a history of assaulting women. And getting away with it. He chooses women who're working for him, or working for someone he's hired, like Angie's accounting firm, and he leans hard on their vulnerabilities. *Who will your boss believe?* kind of stuff. If they work for him directly, then he leans on the fact he can fire them. This isn't his first time trying to force a woman to have sex with him. No woman has ever filed charges against him though."

Jace was angry. "Motherfuckers like that need

their balls cut off and fed to them."

"I'd be happy to take care of that."

Jace studied his friend. Colt looked angry, like he could break a steel beam in half with his bare hands and never break a sweat. "You like her."

Colt's brows drew tighter, the frown lines in his forehead making him look meaner than an angry bull. Toddlers would scream if they were treated to that expression. Old ladies would clutch their pearls as they scurried away.

"I don't know what that means," he said. "She's pretty, sure. But I'm pissed that someone hurt her."

Jace wisely didn't pursue it. But he'd seen the way Colt looked at Angie Turner last night. And the way Angie very carefully didn't look at him. Jace couldn't figure out if it was because she wasn't attracted to him —or because she was.

"So where does Walls hang out? Or should we pay him a visit at his garage?"

"He likes titty clubs. Lately he's been hanging out at the Pink Palace, pretending to be a nice guy to the girls there. Tips big, doesn't touch inappropriately."

"Give him time," Jace said.

"I'd love to have a talk with him soon," Colt said. "The sooner the better."

Jace poured a cup of coffee and offered it to Colt. He accepted, so Jace poured another for himself. "I'm with you on that, but first we have to get Maddy settled."

"Get me settled where?"

Chapter Nineteen

MADDY HAD FOLLOWED THE SMELL OF COFFEE TO THE kitchen. Colt leaned against the counter with a cup to his lips and Jace stood nearby, also holding a cup. Her gaze darted between them. She didn't miss the shuttering of Jace's gaze or the way Colt looked down like he'd been caught doing something he wasn't supposed to be doing.

"Baby, you want some coffee?"

Maddy frowned. "Sure."

Jace got her a cup and poured. "Cream? Sugar?"

"Cream."

He got the cream from the fridge like he'd lived there his whole life and poured in a healthy splash. Maddy pushed a stray lock of hair from her face as she accepted the cup. Jace's gaze dropped down her body and she heated beneath the look he gave her. She hadn't gotten dressed. She'd simply dragged on yoga pants and a sports bra with a light jacket. Her hair was a mess, but she'd twisted it into a high bun and secured most of it. Some of it fell free anyway.

Maddy arched an eyebrow as she stared up at him. "Mind telling me what you were talking about and where you plan to settle me?"

"Uh, maybe I should get moving," Colt said, setting his cup on the counter. "Great seeing you, Maddy."

She threw up a hand, palm out in the universal *talk to the hand* signal. "Wait just a minute. Don't you go anywhere. And you," she said, turning back to Jace. "Start talking."

Jace leaned back against the counter. Sipped his coffee. Her heart tripped and flipped as she watched the slide of his throat, the way his eyes crinkled as he decided what to tell her. So damned handsome. So amazing. Had she really thought she hated him only a week ago?

She'd been so furious when he'd handcuffed her to the airplane seat. Now she could imagine using those handcuffs in much more interesting ways.

"Baby, you need to move to a safe house. It's for your protection."

Maddy drew in a breath. Let it out. "Okay. But I have to take Kitty with me. I also have to be on call. If Barrington's gives me an assignment, I have to go."

Jace and Colt exchanged a glance. "That was easy," Jace said.

Maddy popped a hand on her hip. "I'm not stupid

and I don't have a death wish. If you think I need to go to a safe house, I'll go. But not without my cat."

"She can go with you."

As if Kitty knew they were talking about her, she sauntered over to Jace and rubbed herself on his legs. He reached down to pet her. "Good kitty," he crooned. "So reasonable. Tell Mommy she's reasonable too."

Maddy gave him a look. "Well thanks. I'm glad I'm reasonable. And you, missy," she said to the cat, "way to suck up to the man."

"Reasonable *and* beautiful. Can't forget that one."

Maddy grinned. Colt cleared his throat and she hurriedly sipped coffee. "So when do we go?" she asked after the hot liquid scalded its way over her tongue.

"Sometime this morning, I hope. Just need you to pack a few things, get Kitty ready. We'll load everything in your car because we don't want anyone to see you packing for a trip. Then when we get the word we'll go to the new location."

"Do you really think somebody is watching me?"

Colt cleared his throat. "We have to consider every possibility."

Maddy studied them both. "Sounds reasonable. So why the secrecy?"

Jace jerked his head toward Colt. "It wasn't about you. He wants to go beat up the man who upset Angie last night."

Maddy gaped at Colt. "Really? You would do that for her?"

"I would."

She was still processing it. "Wait—you guys looked him up, didn't you?" She already knew that Angie had gotten home safely because her friend texted last night to tell her so. And Jace had confirmed that Colt watched her walk inside her townhouse, unbeknownst to Angie. "You know everything there is to know about him."

"We do. And we're going to kick his fucking ass," Colt said.

Maddy was furious for her friend, but she couldn't help smiling. "You're sweet, Colt. Angie could use a guy like you in her corner."

"I'm in her corner. I'm going to make sure Tom Walls never bothers her again."

Maddy studied him closely. Did he like Angie? But then she thought of the way Angie had avoided his gaze last night, even though Colt was very much her type. Tall, blond, and handsome? Alpha male to his core? Muscular and intense? A week ago, Angie would have taken this guy home and rocked his world without a second thought. Last night, she'd pretended he didn't exist.

Which bothered Maddy a lot. What had Tom Walls done to her friend to dampen her vibrant spirit?

She cleared her throat. "Do you think he did more than she said? She told me he grabbed her…"

Colt's brows drew down. "I don't know—but I

know he's got a reputation. Believe me, Maddy, it's my mission right now to shut him down so hard he won't be able to breathe without coughing up blood for days. Weeks if I'm lucky."

She wanted to be horrified. Instead she was cheering deep inside. She reached out and squeezed his arm. He was just as solid as Jace. Where did men like this come from? "Thanks, Colt. I appreciate that you want to protect her."

"He won't hurt her again. I promise you that."

Maddy was sick that he'd hurt her at all. Still, she smiled, though her smile shook at the corners. "Thank you."

Colt drained his coffee. "I'd better get back. Talk to you both later." He gave Jace a look. Jace didn't so much as lift an eyebrow in return. Then Colt walked out and she heard the front door close behind him.

"What was that all about?" she asked. "I know it was more than just Angie."

Jace drank his coffee, totally unperturbed. Then he sighed. "I'm not going with you to the safe house, Maddy. Colt will be with you though. You can trust him."

She concentrated on breathing slowly and deeply. Panic flared inside. She tamped it down hard. "Okay. Why aren't you going?"

His sky blue eyes met hers. "I'm too dangerous, baby. I can do a better job elsewhere."

"I don't know what that means."

"It means that I'm best equipped to search for Calypso before she strikes."

"That doesn't address the danger part. Why are you too dangerous? What does that mean?"

His gaze settled on her. Hard. "I told you last night. Or I told you part of it anyway. I can't escape who I am, Maddy. And I won't endanger you by staying close. I said that last night too."

Her throat was lined with razor blades. Panic dripped into her soul. "So last night was goodbye?"

"I didn't say that."

She stared at him. Hard. "Maybe not in words. But I think you said it just the same."

He looked suddenly fierce, like he'd ripped off the veil hiding his emotions. What she saw in his eyes shocked her. "What you don't understand is this—I'd do anything to keep you safe, Maddy. I'd cut off my own goddamn arm. And maybe that's what I'm doing. Did you think of that?"

Her coffee tasted like mud. She couldn't drink it. She set it on the counter and crossed her arms. Anger bubbled swift and hot. "Yeah, well I didn't ask you to do that, did I? Don't sacrifice yourself for me, Jace Kaiser. I don't want it."

He slammed his cup down and grabbed her shoulders. Squeezed them as he bent his head to hers. "Baby, it's *not* what I want. But until you're safe, I have to do whatever it takes."

She drew in a sharp breath. "Why? Why do you care, Jace? I'm nothing to you—"

His grip on her tightened so much it cut off her words. "You're not nothing, Maddy. You're far more than that."

Her breath hitched in. "I don't know what that means."

He let her go. Pushed her away suddenly but gently, as if she was too hot to touch. "It means I care about you."

She waited. He didn't say anything else, and she backed away, her gaze blurring. "But not enough, apparently."

"Maddy," he said, catching her arm when she turned away.

She faced him again, letting her anger and despair spill over along with her tears. "If you aren't willing to fight for me, Jace, then I'm not enough. You can't have it both ways."

"It's not that, baby. It's me. It's who I am."

She couldn't stop herself from slapping her palms against his chest. Breaking his hold on her. "But I don't know who you are because you won't tell me! How fair is that? You know who I am—you know about Mimi and my dad, about my mother. And I know that you lost your family, that they moved you to Russia when you were a child, and you resent them for it."

"I can't tell you more." He stood there, looking so remote and untouchable, and her heart cracked in two.

Maddy took a step backward, hooked her thumb

over her shoulder. "I'm just going to go get my stuff together. Pretend last night didn't happen."

"Maddy—"

"Nope. No." She held her hand up. "You don't get to say that to me. You don't get to tell me to be calm and reasonable because this is best. No, sir. You damned sure don't."

HE'D FUCKED THAT UP. Royally. Jace stood in the kitchen long after she'd left him there and worked on calming the inner turmoil raging inside. Wasn't he being noble? Letting Maddy go rather than endangering her because he was too selfish to say goodbye was the *right* damned thing to do.

So why did it hurt so fucking much?

His phone rang and he snatched it up. "Yeah?"

"Good morning to you too, Sunshine," Ian said. "You ready to turn over Dr. Cole's security?"

"Yes."

"I've got someone who can do the job of impersonating her. Jamie Hayes is similar in size and build. She's a brunette though so she'll be wearing a wig. She'll meet you at the safe house and go back with you after she talks with Dr. Cole."

"Sounds like a plan." Jace stared at the wall opposite, dying a little bit inside.

"You okay?"

"Fine."

"Man, don't do that. Don't impersonate every ex-girlfriend I've ever had."

Jace would have laughed if he weren't so pissed at the world in general. "I don't know what you want me to say, Ian. I'm going to execute the plan. I refuse to be happy about it."

"Yeah, I know. You're doing the right thing though. We both know it."

"I know." He put a hand on his neck, rubbed at the tension gathering there. "But I don't want to do it. What's that say about me?"

"It says you're human."

He could hear Maddy banging around in the bedroom. He wanted to go to her, strip her, and make love to her one more time. But she wasn't going to let him. Not after he'd as much as told her this was good-bye. He remembered her telling him last night that she'd lost her family and how much it hurt. He hated to be one more person leaving her.

"Maybe I'd rather be a robot then."

Ian didn't say anything for a long moment. "No, I don't think you do."

There was a world of meaning in those words, but Jace didn't ask what the bossman meant. It was none of his business anyway.

They ended the call and Jace went to check on Maddy. She glared at him as he entered the bedroom. She had a suitcase open on the bed and she'd thrown a bunch of stuff into it, none of it folded. "Are you really trying to tell me that you don't date anyone?

That your entire existence consists of one-night stands? That you don't want connection with *any*one?"

"I want what's best for you."

She threw her arms wide, clothes hanging from her hands. "Have you ever thought that maybe you're what's best for me? That I'm the one who gets to decide, not you?"

He didn't know what to say. He just stared at her. She dropped her arms to her sides, the fight leeching out of her.

"You know what? It's okay. What if we'd dated for a month and you broke up with me? Would I have the right to be crazy over it? Sure, but that wouldn't be your problem. So this isn't your problem either." She started taking clothes out of the suitcase and folding them properly. Whatever had happened inside her head, she'd found her calm place.

"Maddy—"

"No," she said firmly. "Don't tell me you care, Jace. Don't tell me you want to be with me *but*. It's much better if you just treat it like it was a one-night stand, you got what you wanted, and I'm the idiot for thinking there was more between us. Because I am an idiot, that's for sure. We've known each other for days. That's it. I slept with you once —well, technically a few more times than that—but one night together. People don't commit to each other after a single night. So I'm going to stop being the psycho who can't take rejection and you're going to act like you got what you wanted and we're done."

He ground his teeth together. "If that's what you want."

"Yep, it's what I want."

"Soon as you're ready, we're leaving."

"Fine." She flicked her fingers at him. "I don't need help. Please go away."

Jace left without replying. If this is how she needed to deal with it, then he had no right to interfere.

But holy hell, it hurt more than he expected it would.

MADDY DIDN'T KNOW what she'd expected a safe house to look like, but this one looked like a normal house. It was a small clapboard house on an acre of land on the Eastern Shore, tucked back inside some trees. There was a stream that ran behind it not too far away, and nothing but marshy wetlands beyond that.

They weren't far from the nearest town, but to look at the view, it felt like they were a million miles from civilization. Maddy frowned at the stream and marsh like she could make it turn into the streets of New York City if only she concentrated hard enough. Kitty was off exploring the house, and Jace was on the phone with someone.

They'd driven her car out here, but he'd told her that her stand-in would be driving it back. He'd helped her unload everything and then called someone. Colt, from the sounds of it. A few minutes later, Jace had stopped talking and a car made its way up the long gravel drive. Two people got out—one was Colt and the other was a woman who walked like she dared anyone to give her any shit. They came up the steps and knocked on the door.

Maddy started to open it, but Jace was there first. "I've got it."

She rolled her eyes. "It's Colt and the woman I presume is my double."

"Doesn't matter. Never answer the door, Maddy. Let me do it."

"You're leaving, remember?"

"Then let Colt do it."

She didn't get to reply because Colt and the woman were stepping inside then. The woman's gaze swept over her. Maddy automatically didn't like her. She didn't have a good reason for it. It was simply that this woman was driving out of here with Jace, pretending to be her, while Maddy wasn't going to see him again.

"Hi, I'm Jamie," she said, coming over and holding out her hand.

Maddy took it. "Hi." She had a firm grip and a nice smile and Maddy felt like a jerk for not liking her on sight.

"Maddy, we'll need your clothes," Jace said. "Like I told you."

"Yes, of course. I'll just go and change." Jace had explained that this woman would wear the clothing she was wearing right now back to her house. So it looked like Maddy had left for a while and returned.

Maddy swallowed angry tears as she jerked her clothes off and put on a pair of jeans and a baggy hooded top. "Stop it," she hissed to herself. "You aren't upset with Jamie. You're upset with Jace. She's a perfectly lovely person and doesn't deserve your anger."

Maddy sniffed and gathered her clothing, then returned to the living room with a smile on her face, determined to be pleasant to everyone. "Here you go," she said to Jamie.

"Thanks. I'll just run into the bathroom and change."

Maddy drifted over to the back windows again while Jace and Colt talked quietly. A few minutes later and Jamie was back. Maddy's clothes fit her just fine. With her hair, which was the same color as Maddy's, she could be Maddy if you didn't look closely enough. Unlike the woman in the airport photo, this one didn't have the same facial features though.

Jamie must have sensed something in the way Maddy looked at her because she smiled. "It's a wig. My hair is brown, and a bit shorter than yours actually. But this is enough to fool anyone who doesn't get face to face with me."

"It's a little odd seeing you in my clothes, I have to admit."

"Hopefully it won't last long, Dr. Cole."

"Maddy."

"Maddy. Do you mind if we talk for a few minutes? I've seen your file, but I need to know some particulars about your routine. I don't want to do anything that would arouse suspicion."

"Of course."

They went out onto the back deck and Jamie asked her a few questions. Maddy only half paid attention. Her heart was throbbing and asking her how she'd gotten into this mess, and her gaze kept drifting over Jamie's shoulder to where Jace stood with arms folded as he discussed something with Colt. They both looked intense, but only Jace made her blood sizzle.

When Jamie was done talking, she went back inside. Maddy did not. She turned away and kept her gaze on the stream and a blue heron that picked its way along the edges, seeking a meal.

It didn't take long before she felt another person's presence behind her. She didn't need to turn around to know it was Jace. She could feel him in her bones. Her pulse quickened at his nearness, and arousal began to pool low in her belly.

"We're going now, Maddy."

"So go."

"I didn't want to go without saying goodbye."

"I thought you already said it."

She felt a hand on her arm and then he turned her to face him. She jerked her arm away.

"Look at me. Please."

She folded her arms. "I'm looking."

He huffed a breath. "I'm sorry if I've hurt you. I didn't intend to. Last night…" He closed his eyes. Shook his head. "It meant a lot to me, Maddy. That's all."

He turned and walked away and she stood there, not seeing anything, until Colt stepped out on the deck. "Hey, Maddy. It's best if you come back inside. You don't want to stand out here for too long. You're a bit exposed."

"Right now, I don't care if Calypso shoots me," she muttered. "It can't hurt any worse."

Chapter Twenty

THE HOURS WITH COLT PASSED A LOT SLOWER THAN the hours with Jace had. Maddy fired up her computer and did some paperwork. It'd been over a week since she'd left Russia and no assignment from Barrington's yet. She had little doubt that Ian and Jace were responsible for that. Under Colt's watchful eye, she made a call to her supervisor and asked when she could expect to be sent somewhere.

He hemmed and hawed and told her soon, he was sure, but the business was slow right now. Even Leonid Sokolov was in no rush to continue the process. She'd finished the paperwork on his icons, thanks to Ian getting her computer back, and so Barrington's had issued a policy for those pieces. The rest were already insured, though the appraised values weren't current. Still, Sokolov was rich enough that it wasn't going to kill him if he had a loss and didn't get the full value for a piece.

Maddy ended the call feeling more frustrated than ever. Colt had briefed her when she'd gone back inside about the things she could and couldn't do. She could use her cellphone and her computer. He had technology to mask her location, so if by chance anyone was looking for her that way, they wouldn't be able to track her.

She couldn't leave the house unless he went with her. Not even outside, unless she cleared it with him first and he told her it was safe. She couldn't tell anyone where she was. There would be no visiting Mimi while she was under protection, either. That last had bothered her quite a bit, but she understood. She could only hope that Jace and his teammates found Calypso quickly so she could get back to her life.

"Heating up a pizza, Maddy. You want some?" Colt called from the kitchen.

Maddy closed her eyes. Why did it have to be pizza? Did these guys eat anything else? "Not hungry, thank you," she called back.

The day went much like that. Maddy frustrated and sad, Colt being nice and asking her if she needed anything. He was a decent guy, really. She learned that his name was Colton. His mom only called him by his full name and hated when friends shortened it to Colt. He said he didn't mind it either way, but it sure did annoy his mother.

He was as cagey with information as Jace, but she learned that he was prior military and had been with BDI for three years now. He was single, never been married—or at least she didn't think he had—and if he wasn't a freaking mercenary soldier/spy, he'd be perfect for Angie.

Maddy had tried to call Angie but her friend's voicemail came on. She hated that Angie was hiding, but she understood her friend's desire to be alone. Angie was an introvert at her core, same as Maddy. She just did a better job of pretending to be an extrovert than Maddy did. So Maddy totally understood the craving for alone time. She just wished that Angie didn't want that time now, after Tom Walls had attacked her. It made it hard for Maddy to know if it was just Angie being an introvert or Angie being more traumatized than she'd let on.

Eventually, however, Angie called her back. It was dark by that time and Maddy was watching Chip and Joanna, wishing she could move to Waco and forget everything.

"Hey, Mads," Angie said.

The hair on Maddy's neck stood up. "Ang, what's wrong?"

"Wrong? Nothing's wrong. Why would you ask that?"

Maddy blinked. Colt was sitting nearby, reading something on his phone, but he'd lifted his head the instant he heard Angie's name. His gaze sharpened as he watched her.

"You sound upset. Is everything okay?"

Angie sniffed. "Oh sure, everything's fine. I just…

Maddy, I don't want to be alone right now. Can I come over?"

Maddy closed her eyes. *Fuck.* "Honey, I'm not home. I'm, uh, staying somewhere."

Angie's voice broke. "Oh, okay. It's just… I don't feel safe here. Tom called me… he says he's not finished with me yet."

Maddy's gut twisted. She saw red. "Angie, no. No way in hell is that bastard touching you again." She glared at Colt, furious. *Help me,* she mouthed.

He was frowning hard. "What do you want me to do?" he said in a low, angry voice.

"Pick her up. Or let me tell her where I am."

"I can't do that, Maddy."

"You damn well *can,* Colt," she hissed, hand covering the mouthpiece.

"I'll go to a hotel," Angie was saying. "I'll be fine."

"No, honey. No. Do you feel like driving? I'm staying on the Eastern Shore—"

Colt was waving his hands at her, his expression furious. She ignored him.

"I can't tell you exactly where, but I can tell you the town. Drive there and I'll come get you."

"Okay," Angie said, sniffing. "I love you, Mads. I hope you know that."

"Of course I do! I'll see you soon, Angie. I won't let anybody hurt you, swear to God."

"I know."

Despite Colt's frowning and growling, Maddy told Angie to drive to the grocery store on the main drag in town and to call her when she arrived. Then Angie ended the call and Maddy prepared for Colt's fury.

"You shouldn't have done that, Maddy."

His expression should have made her cringe, but she was too worried for Angie. They'd been together through thick and thin. Angie was there for her when Mimi started slipping, and Angie had helped her make the decision to move Mimi to the Oaks. She'd even helped Maddy figure out how to afford it.

"I couldn't leave her. She's scared. You saw her yesterday. You know how upset she was."

Colt shoved a hand through his hair. "Still. I know she's your friend, but you can't compromise your location. Once she gets here, she can't leave. You realize that? She's as stuck here as you are, and I don't care how much she wants to go—or even if her work demands it. She's stuck."

Maddy shot him a grin. "Oh hush. You like her, Colt. It's not going to bother you to have her in the same house for a few days."

He growled. "Doesn't matter. It's risky."

"So call Ian or Jace and tell them I did it. But when she gets to that parking lot, I'm going to go get her. With or without you."

"I've got the car keys, Maddy. You think about that?"

"Then I'll walk—which I don't think you'll let happen. So we go together. You can check out her car and everything, then she can follow us back. Or if you don't want her to do that, make her leave the car and ride with us."

Colt shoved a hand through his hair and swore. "Jace will kill me if anything happens to you. Do you realize that?"

Frost encased her heart. "I think if he cared that much, he'd still be here."

Colt shook his head. "I guess you don't know much about Jace if you believe that. He's actively hunting for Calypso. For *you*, Maddy. Not for Ian or for BDI. For you. So you can go home again and forget you ever met us."

That last bit made her heart hurt. "What if I don't want to forget?"

"You may not want to," Colt said. "But you probably should."

IT WAS weird as fuck watching Maddy's house and knowing she wasn't in it. Jamie Hayes did a credible job of looking like Maddy from a distance, but up close there was no way they were the same woman. She somehow managed to imitate Maddy's walk and her mannerisms, which meant she'd probably fool a casual observer.

She didn't fool him. If anything, watching her from a distance made his heart ache more, not less. He'd sent Maddy away today. Left her with Colt and told himself he was doing the right thing in saying goodbye.

So why didn't he feel any better about it? Why did his chest feel hollow and his soul empty? And why did he have this deep unrest that he needed to be with her because she wasn't really safe without him there to protect her?

"Son of a bitch," he growled when his thoughts didn't subside. They just kept turning, kept accusing him of shutting her out when he should have held her close.

Dammit, she was *safe*. He'd been on too many ops with Colton Duchaine not to trust the man. Colt was a lethal warrior with a wicked aim. He wasn't going to fall down on the job.

Jace stood and paced inside the house across the street from Maddy's. There was nothing suspicious on the cameras. Nobody who stopped where they shouldn't or crept around Maddy's backyard or peered in her windows or anything.

Maybe they were wrong about Calypso's priorities. What was one woman who could possibly identify her in the scheme of things? Especially when she changed her look so frequently? The only immutable part of the description was the tattoo—and that's assuming it had been real in the first place. A good operative would fake that as well. Hell, a good operative wouldn't even have a readily identifiable tattoo in such an obvious place—unless she'd come to the business later, in which case she should really be getting the tattoo removed.

He thought of the phoenix on his shoulder. It was identifiable, yes. It was not in an obvious place. He should probably have it lasered off, but it reminded him that he was the one in control. He could leave his old life in ashes and rise again. He'd done it twice so far, even if he hadn't wanted to the first time. He could do it again if he had to.

Ty strolled into the room. "Anything interesting?"

"Did I yell for you?"

"Whoa, whoa, whoa, man," Ty said, hands up and palms out. "Just making small talk."

"Well, don't."

"Copy that, brother."

Jace pinched the bridge of his nose and concentrated on breathing for a few seconds. "Sorry, Ty. I'm on edge."

Ty picked up a bag of chips from the coffee table and grabbed a couple. "So I gathered. The pretty doc?"

"Yeah." No use denying it. Everybody who'd spent time in this house over the past few days knew better anyway.

"So wrap this up and date her. It's obvious she likes you too."

"I wish it was that easy."

"Why isn't it? Sure, we travel a lot, but so does she according to her file. It's not like she'll be sitting home alone."

"You know what we do here, right?" Jace asked, only half jokingly. "You didn't just show up at BDI with no expectations of secrecy or danger—or has Ian been lying on the recruitment poster again?"

Ty shrugged. "Just saying. Been in the game a while myself. But I'll tell you what—if people in our line of work couldn't date or marry or even fuck the same person on a regular basis, then I'd wager that all the spy and law enforcement agencies in Washington would have a lot fewer employees. But they don't, do they? Because soldiers and spies and cops have lives—they may not tell the truth to their partner, or only some of the truth, but they still have lives outside this job, man. No reason why you can't too."

What he said made sense—if Jace were anybody else. "Trust me, there are reasons."

"Whatever you say. But just remember that even if you aren't going to date Maddy, some other guy will. And there's no guarantee he'll be the regular guy you think she needs. This town is full of people pretending to be something they aren't."

"You know what? You aren't helping. In fact, you're pissing me off."

Ty laughed. "Sorry, dude. Just thought you should know that while you're planning to be noble and give her up, that doesn't meant somebody else will feel the same way. In fact, I'd wager that any man she dates won't meet the standards you set for her."

"You sure are full of unsolicited advice," Jace growled.

Ty finished the handful of chips. "Just a service I provide. No charge."

Jace rolled his eyes. The guy was annoying but funny.

"You want to know something?" Ty asked as Jace turned away.

"What?"

"My dad says that the first moment he saw my mom, he knew she was the one. It wasn't lightning or magic or anything. Just a feeling he got right here." Ty pressed a fist to his gut. "I always thought that sounded like a bunch of bullshit, to tell the truth. But he saw her at a high school baseball game. Rival schools. He swears he turned to his friend and said 'that's the girl I'm going to marry.' Four years later, he did. They've been together ever since."

"That's a sweet story, but what does it have to do with me?"

"Don't know. Just like to tell it when a guy's having girl trouble."

Jace shook his head as he went back to the computers to study the camera feed. Nothing stood out from the ordinary. Nothing at all. Where the hell was Calypso?

MADDY WAS STARTING to get worried. Angie hadn't called yet and she wasn't answering her phone. Had she gotten lost? It was more than two hours since they'd talked, and Maddy couldn't stop imagining Angie's car in a ditch somewhere.

"Something happened to her," Maddy said. "I just know it."

"She might have been delayed," Colt said. "Or she stopped somewhere for a restroom break. Chances are she's not getting a good signal, or her phone died. Both things happen to people, you know."

Maddy chewed a fingernail and paced back and forth. "I know, I know. But she sounded upset, and I just don't know what she's thinking."

Colt came over and put a hand on her shoulder. "Calm down, Maddy. I'll make some calls."

"Thank you."

He dropped his hand and retrieved his phone from his pocket. When he started talking to someone on the other end, she went into the kitchen to get a bottle of water. Maddy opened the bottle and took a cool sip. Where the hell was Angie? No way would Angie do anything drastic to herself. She wasn't that sort of person, and one groping wasn't going to make her be so.

Maddy was still pondering when her phone buzzed in her back pocket. She snatched it up, glancing at the screen. "Angie," she cried. "I was getting worried."

"Hello, Madeline Cole," a female voice that wasn't Angie's said. "Listen to me carefully and do *not* warn the man there with you about anything I say. If you do, your friend will die. Are we clear?"

Maddy's heart was in her throat. Sweat broke out on her brow, her chest, as heat flashed through her. Ice followed on its heels, leaving her shivering. In the movies, they always asked for proof before answering. But if this woman was calling on Angie's phone, then she had Angie. But was her friend already dead?

"Who are you? What do you want?" She whispered the words so Colt wouldn't hear her. But he was still talking, so she didn't think he'd notice she was on the phone too. There was a wall between them and he couldn't see her anyway.

"Oh, I think you know who I am," the woman said. "We have met before."

"Calypso."

"Ah yes, you do know. Now here is what you will do. You will step outside onto your back deck. You will not inform your bodyguard and you will leave the door open. Understand?"

Calypso knew where she was. Knew and was waiting for her. Oh God. "Are you going to kill me?"

What a stupid question to ask. If Calypso was going to kill her, would she really say so?

"I haven't decided. But if you wonder if I plan to assassinate you when you are exposed and walk away, the answer is no. I have use of you."

"What about Angie?"

"She is alive."

"I want to talk to her."

"Ah, Dr. Cole, you are in no position to make demands. Walk outside in the next three seconds or I will put a bullet in Angie Turner and dump her in this godforsaken marshland."

The deck ran along the back of the house. There were doors leading from the kitchen, the living room, and the master bedroom. They were all covered in blinds and the blinds were closed. Maddy went to the kitchen door and lifted a trembling hand to the knob. If she walked out there, Calypso could kill her. But if she didn't walk out there, Angie might die.

"Prove to me she's alive," Maddy said on a rush.

"She won't be if you don't open the door. But I will tell you this—I'm a professional, Dr. Cole. I don't kill people simply to kill them. I kill with purpose and reason. I have no reason to kill Angie—unless you give me a reason and then I will do so. But here you go," Calypso said. "Now put the phone in your pocket and walk outside."

A second later a text pinged Maddy's phone. She pulled it away to see a picture of Angie with duct tape over her mouth and tears running down her face. She was in her car, a cute little BMW 1 Series convertible, that she adored. The dash clock said 11:18 p.m. That was eight minutes ago. It could be staged, of course. But Maddy didn't have time to figure it out.

She twisted the door knob and pulled the door open. Two things happened at once. First, an ear-splitting alarm cut through the night. And second, Calypso appeared out of seemingly nowhere and yanked Maddy out the door, spinning her around and putting her head behind Maddy's. The barrel of Calypso's gun jammed into Maddy's throat.

Colt appeared a moment later, yelling, "What the fuck, Maddy? I told you not to—"

He didn't say anything else because Calypso fired.

Maddy screamed as he dropped.

Chapter Twenty-One

CALYPSO DRAGGED MADDY DOWN THE STAIRS AND into the woods, turning her and shoving the pistol into her back. "Go," she said harshly, yanking Maddy's phone from her pocket and stuffing it into her own.

Maddy put one foot in front of the other, unseeing. She sobbed brokenly, the tears coming fast and hard, blurring her vision.

"Shut up," Calpyso ordered.

But Maddy couldn't stop. It was all her fault. She'd told Angie where to find her. Not precisely where to find her, but somehow Calypso had figured it out. Colt was shot—probably dead—and Kitty was in that house with the blaring alarm and a wide-open door.

Maddy stumbled and dropped to her knees. Calypso jerked her harshly to her feet. "Move."

Maddy thought, for the briefest of moments, that it was over. That it needed to be over. She should just fall and refuse to get up. Then Calypso would kill her and the misery would be over. Because she'd lost Jace, she'd lost her dad and her grandmother, her cat was probably terrified—and Colt. Oh God, Colt. He'd been nice to her. She'd liked him. And she'd caused this to happen.

His mom, who hated that he let people call him Colt instead of Colton, would never see him again.

She stumbled again but didn't fall. Calypso kept pushing her through the woods. And somewhere during the dark journey, instead of giving up, she started to get mad. This woman—this horrible woman—killed people. She'd killed two people at Sokolov's birthday party. She'd kidnapped Angie, she'd shot Colt, and she was going to shoot Maddy eventually.

Unless Jace found her. A surge of strength roared through Maddy's blood, into her brain, her heart and lungs. Jace had promised to protect her. He'd sworn he'd keep her alive. And she believed him. He *would* find her. Somehow.

She stumbled again, only this time she reached for the vegetation, ripping some of it out and dropping it. Calypso kept pushing and Maddy kept stomping along like an elephant, hoping to leave a trail of some kind that Jace could follow.

It was probably hopeless, but she had to focus on that idea. On the idea of him finding her and making Calypso pay.

They emerged from the woods onto a dirt track

where Angie's car sat with the engine running and the lights off. Calypso yanked open the door and reached for a bag. Maddy's heart tripped as she spied shoes—but there were feet in those shoes, and Angie moved. She was lying against the driver's side door in the backseat, her hands and feet bound, her mouth taped.

"Oh my God, Angie!"

"Shut up," Calypso growled, jamming the gun in Maddy's ribs. For the barest of seconds, she considered trying to take the gun. But her courage failed her. She hadn't succeeded with Jace back in Russia and she was too uncertain of her skill to try now. What was one self-defense course a couple of years ago against a trained assassin? She hated herself for it, but she also knew it wasn't just her life at risk. If she failed, Calypso might kill Angie in revenge.

Angie moaned and Maddy bit her lower lip to keep from sobbing again. "What do you want from me?" she asked.

Calypso took plastic zip ties from her bag and zipped Maddy's wrists tightly together. "Get in the car. Front seat."

Maddy did as she was told. Then Calypso pulled out Maddy's phone. She hit the button to wake it up, then shoved it into Maddy's face until the phone recognized her and unlocked itself.

Calypso scrolled for a moment. Maddy studied her face in the glow of the light. She was fine-boned, strikingly pretty. She wasn't as heavy as the maid, nor did she have the short hair the maid had. But a wig could have fixed that, as Jamie had proven today when she'd dressed to impersonate Maddy.

Calypso's eyes, when she raised them, were piercingly blue. She smiled. It was familiar somehow. "Ah, here we go. Jace is what he calls himself now. Interesting."

Maddy's blood chilled. This woman knew Jace? He hadn't said he knew her. Then again, he'd claimed not to know Calypso's identity at all. "What do you want with him?"

Calypso's gaze was hot, wicked. "What do I want? Nothing less than his soul, sweetheart."

"Good luck with that," Maddy said, deciding to pretend like she couldn't care less about Jace. Wasn't that the smart thing to do? "He's a player. One-night stand kind of guy. You might get his attention, but it won't last."

Calypso laughed. "Oh, Maddy, you are delightful. I'm not interested in making him my lover. I'm interested in selling him to the highest bidder. And you're going to help me do it."

"Me?" she croaked.

Calypso bent close. Then she snapped a picture of Maddy. "Oh yes, you. You're the bait. The thing he can't resist. I owe you, Maddy. When I took the job at Sokolov's party, I had no idea what gift you'd bring me. I've been searching for years. I knew he was out there. Hiding. But I could never quite find him. Until you brought him to me."

Maddy knew that it wasn't a good thing Calypso

was telling her these things. Talking to her like it didn't matter, because it meant Maddy would never get a chance to repeat any of it to anyone. But she also wanted answers. "How could you know I'd bring him to you?"

Calypso was busy tapping on Maddy's phone. "I didn't." She pressed send because Maddy heard the whoosh. "There. Any second now."

She slammed the door on Maddy, then walked around and got behind the wheel. She flicked on the lights, popped the car into gear, and started driving. A moment later, Maddy's ringtone blared.

JACE'S PHONE RANG. "A door's been breached at the safe house," Ian said. "The alarm hasn't been shut down yet."

Which meant the breach wasn't accidental. Jace's guts twisted tight as panic shot down his spine. "How far away is the response team?"

"Five minutes. I'm sending them by air."

Ian didn't have to say it, but Jace knew why. In case there were casualties. They'd need to be med-flighted out, if they were lucky. If they weren't then the site had to be cleaned before the locals figured out what had happened.

"Jesus H. Christ," Jace growled.

"I put her in a safe house because you wanted it. She wasn't supposed to be in danger there."

"What the fuck happened?" The panic was twisting higher inside him, threatening to erupt in rash action and bad decisions. He couldn't let that happen. He had to be cool and methodical. For Maddy. If he stood a chance in hell of getting her back, he had to think this through.

But what if she's dead?

Jesus, no. Please no. He'd said goodbye to her today, fully intending to walk away and never see her again. But if that was a reality? If she was gone and he never *could* see her again? Never bump into her accidentally on purpose, never see her smile?

If he couldn't simply know she was alive in this world so he could continue doing what he did, then he didn't see the point in existing.

"Maddy told Angie Turner what town she was in. Not the address, but the town. Angie was upset about something and wanted to come stay with her."

"Goddammit."

"But Angie never made it to the rendezvous point. Colt called to see if we could track Angie because Maddy was having a fit over it. Brett was on the line with him—the alarm went off and Colt yelled at Maddy. There was a single gunshot—and we've heard nothing from Colt since."

"Jesus, Ian—" His phone dinged and he pulled it away to glance at the text. Everything inside him went still at the picture of Maddy squinting into the flash.

Then he read the words. *Your life for hers, Nikolai.*

Jace hit the speaker as rage engulfed him. He

didn't mind the rage. It centered him. Made him calm. Determined. "I just got a text from Maddy's phone. She's alive. Calypso wants to make a trade."

"A trade for what?"

He didn't need to read it again to know. "Me. She knows who I am, Ian."

"Fuck."

"It was inevitable, don't you think? How long could I run from the truth? Hiding in plain sight was always risky. Time's up."

"We'll figure this out, Jace. Don't do anything stupid." Ian's voice was steel. Jace didn't care. Nothing mattered to him anymore. Nothing but Maddy.

"I'm making the deal," Jace said. "I have to."

"We'll get Dr. Cole out alive. You need to work with me on this and not go off half-cocked."

Jace shoved a hand through his hair. "I'm hanging up and calling her. I'll let you know."

"You'd fucking better. You owe me, Jace. I'm calling in the marker."

Jace's jaw worked. "I'll do the best I can—but Maddy comes first."

Ian swore. "Do what you have to do. But you have the full force of BDI behind you, so don't do anything stupid. Let me do what I do best."

"Thanks, boss." Jace cut the call and dialed Maddy's number.

"Hello, Nikolai," a smooth voice said. It tickled his memory but he couldn't quite place it. "It's been a long time."

"You'll have to remind me."

She snorted. "No, I think not. Such a bastard, aren't you? So smug. Traitorous."

"If you say so." He ground his jaw tight. "Maddy had better be okay."

"What, no concern for her friend too?"

Fuck. "Yes, Angie too. Both of them, Calypso."

She laughed.

"I fucking mean it."

"Yes, yes. I get it. They are both alive. For now."

"What do you want?"

"You, Nikolai. You're worth a lot of money. Did you know that?"

"How much?"

"More than you can afford, if that's what you're thinking."

"How do you know what I can afford?"

"I don't. But I know that even if it was sixty million dollars, you still wouldn't have enough."

Jace frowned. Calypso hated him. And he didn't know why. Who the fuck was she? He searched his memory, trying to conjure up a face or a name of some woman he might have jilted. Someone who had been in the same business he'd been in.

He came up with nothing.

"So we've established you hate me. Why?"

"I'll let you figure that out. Here's what's going to happen, Nikolai. You are going to drive to the address I text to you. There, you will find a change of clothes. Put them on and leave yours behind. Follow the instructions you find in the pants pocket. I'll be in touch."

"Let me talk to Maddy."

"Why should I?"

"Because if I know she's alive, I'll be more than willing to do as you ask. Everything you ask."

"Maddy, say hello to Nikolai," Calypso said.

"Jace?" she asked in a small voice.

"It's me, baby. You okay?"

"Yes—she shot Colt. I think he's dead. It's all my fault—"

"Baby, it's not." He sucked in a breath, her quiet tears ripping his heart in two. She should be scared—probably was scared—but the first thing she thought about was Colt. That said a lot about her. About her loyalties and strength. "I need you to know something," he began.

"Enough," Calypso said, coming back on the line. "Do as I say, Nikolai. It's the only way she lives."

Chapter Twenty-Two

THEY WERE IN A WAREHOUSE. MADDY KNEW THAT much. After Calypso had talked to Jace, she'd driven them to a dark spot in the road where someone in a van was waiting for them. A man who spoke Russian jerked her from the car while Calypso dragged Angie out.

"Kill that one," the man said coldly. "We don't need both of them."

Of course Angie had no idea what they were saying. As Maddy opened her mouth to protest, Calypso calmly pulled her pistol and pointed it at the man instead. The mermaid tattoo on her arm stood out in stark relief in the light from the headlights. "Don't tell me what to do, asshole. Give me one more order, look at me cross-eyed—and I'll blow your balls off. And if you think you can bide your time and eliminate me when you see a chance, you'll have to answer to the Syndicate for it—and they will turn you inside out while you're still alive if you do anything to me. Are we clear?"

The man's eyes widened. Maddy's heart thumped, wondering what was about to happen. But then he gulped. "Of course. I meant no disrespect."

Calypso tucked the weapon away. "Let's go then."

Maddy and Angie were thrown into the back of the van and chained to the floor. The van had no windows, other than the one in front, so it had been no use trying to figure out where they were going. Instead, they'd huddled together while the man drove and Calypso sat in the passenger seat with her feet propped on the dash and her phone in her hands.

"Are they going to kill us?" Angie had whispered.

"I don't know," Maddy said softly.

Angie had trembled. They didn't say anything more to each other because Calypso had turned and glared at them. "No talking. Keep talking and I'll start removing fingers."

Now they were in the warehouse, chained together inside a metal cage that was about twelve by twelve. A spotlight shone down on them. All around them were crates, stacked high and with a logo on the side.

ATHENA ARMS COMPANY

Guns, she supposed. Or mortars and rocket launchers. Not that it mattered all that much to her. Calypso shut the door to the cage and locked it. Then she stalked away. As soon as she was gone, Angie let out a quiet wail.

“I’m so sorry, Maddy. I don’t know who she is or how she found me, but she came to my house. I answered the bell because I thought she was soliciting —but then she pulled a gun and came inside. She made me call you, made me tell you that story about wanting to stay with you. I didn’t know what else to do, and I was so scared that if you didn’t tell me where you were, she’d kill me. But I’m sorry. Really, truly sorry.”

She started to cry. Maddy tried to hush her. “Angie, honey, it’s not your fault. How could you know? It’s *my* fault for not telling you what really happened in Russia. Who Jace was. Colt. All of them. They’re spies… I think so anyway—and I got into the middle of their operation when they were trying to capture her. It’s a long story, but anyway, they were protecting me. I should have told you. I should have insisted they protect you too—but I didn’t know she’d go after you.”

“Who is she?”

“Honestly, I don’t know. I just know she’s killed people, and they wanted to capture her.” Maddy drew in a sharp breath that hurt going down. “She killed Colt. It’s all my fault.”

Angie started to cry. “No, it’s mine. If I hadn’t asked where you were…”

“But I didn’t tell you the address. How did she find it?”

“I don’t know. She talked to someone, but it was in Russian. Or I think it was anyway. She made me drive until we got there, then she tied me up and put me in the back seat. She left me, but I couldn't get free. Then she was back and you were there."

Maddy gritted her teeth. "We're getting out of here, Angie. Jace won't let this happen. He's coming for us."

She didn't know if it was true, but she hoped it was. She was so confused right now. Calypso had called him Nikolai. Was that his real name? The one he wouldn't tell her? It had to be. Calypso had said he was worth was a lot of money. She didn't know what that meant, but she feared for him. And she knew what he was about to do. He was going to come for her, but he would give himself up in exchange if he couldn't get her out any other way.

But she didn't think it would matter if he did because she didn't believe Calypso was going to let her live. She'd seen and heard too much. So had Angie.

Maddy didn't know how long they were there before she heard the scrape of metal. A key in the lock on the outer door. She sat up, jiggling Angie as she did so. Angie came awake, stiffening when she heard it too.

There were voices, but she couldn't hear what they said. They came closer, the voices coalescing into Russian. "Do you really think he's going to give himself up? For these women?"

It was a voice she hadn't heard before. But then Calypso answered. "Not for both of them, no. For Dr.

Cole, yes. He's fascinated with her. He believes he can save her—save them both and himself too—or he wouldn't be coming. But he won't succeed."

"You hate him, don't you?"

"That's none of your business."

"It is when my money's on the line. I expect you to turn him over, not kill him out of spite."

"I'm a professional. I won't kill him. But he will wish I had."

Maddy's gut churned. She wished she could see Jace one more time. She wished she could tell him what was in her heart. What she'd known last night when he'd made love to her so intensely.

She loved him. He was so much more than the man who'd tackled her that first night at Sokolov's party. He'd been protective, tender, understanding. He'd listened to her cry over Mimi, and he'd promised to keep her safe. She trusted him. Believed him.

Loved him.

Wildly.

What if she never got to tell him that?

Maddy gritted her teeth together tight, determination sinking into her bones. She had to tell him. She had to live long enough to do so.

No, even more than that, she had to *believe* that Jace was going to save her. And she had to do whatever she could to save him. Even if she had to sacrifice herself.

She couldn't do anything less for him than he was

willing to do for her. Knowing that made a strange kind of calm settle over her. She would stop being so scared and start paying attention to everything. She didn't think she'd get an opportunity to escape, but she was no longer blindly accepting that she was a prisoner and there was nothing she could do. There had to be *something*. She just had to think of it. Then she had to act.

JACE HAD DONE everything she'd told him to do. He'd driven from one location to the next, changing clothes, changing cars, circling back on himself and changing again. He knew why she'd done it. To prevent him from bringing BDI along with him. If he'd had any conventional trackers, they were long ago discarded. By the time he arrived on the wharf in Baltimore, he was alone and unarmed. At one point, he'd had to discard his phone. He'd wrestled with that one, but Calypso was tracking his phone through Maddy's. If he used it, she would know. So he'd discarded it when told. Calypso and her people had cameras at each location, and they would have known if he kept anything.

So he hadn't. He hadn't stopped either because they'd know that too. He was using their cars and they tracked everything.

He was literally arriving with nothing. No weapons. No Ian. No BDI. Nothing but his fucking name and the fact somebody wanted him alive. He could work with that. He *would* work with that until he couldn't anymore.

Jace put the car in park and threw the door open as he arrived at the next location. Since this one was the wharf, he had a feeling it was the final checkpoint. He'd already grabbed the tire iron from the trunk and he dragged it with him as he climbed from the car. They hadn't thought to take that away. He got out and stood there, tire iron hanging at his side, waiting.

If they were watching, they'd see him.

A phone rang nearby. Jace turned his head, looking for it. It kept ringing. He walked in the direction of the sound—and found a cell phone taped to the back of a pole. He ripped the tape off and answered.

"Very good, Nikolai," she said. "You found us."

"Where's Maddy and Angie?"

"They're alive."

"Going to need proof of that."

"Warehouse sixteen. Be there in five minutes—or you'll be too late."

The phone went dead. Jace turned to get his bearings. Then he took off at a run, heading for the warehouse, counting them desperately as he passed, scanning for the numbers before heading for the next one.

He finally found number sixteen and skidded to a halt. His blood pounded in his ears. The sounds of heavy loading equipment and voices came to him in the darkness. The wharf was busy around the clock with containers being loaded and unloaded. The noise was in the distance though. Here, it was quieter.

He still clutched the tire iron as he walked up to the door. He tugged it quietly open and slipped into the blackness of the interior. Straining to hear any sound, he moved as stealthily as he could. He knew this was a game to Calypso, knew the likelihood of finding Maddy and Angie and freeing them so they could escape was a shot in the dark. But he had to try.

He moved between floor-to-ceiling shelves and shipping crates, making his way across the warehouse, listening for any signs of life.

And then he heard it. Someone was crying. His heart skipped a beat as anger crashed into him. But he forced himself to breathe more slowly, to find the calm he'd need to act. Jace moved toward the sound, always listening for any other noise that might indicate ambush.

A single bulb illuminated a large cage in the middle of all the shipping crates. Inside the cage, two women sat on the floor, their hands bound in front of them. Only one of them was crying. The other looked furious. *Maddy.* His Maddy. She sat up tall like a queen, frowning hard, her jaw set in a determined expression.

"Ang, honey, stop crying. Jace is coming. I promise you he's coming. We aren't dying here."

"It's a bomb, Maddy. A *bomb.* Aren't you terrified?"

"Of course I am."

Jace's gaze dropped frantically over them both and then over the cage until he spotted the bomb. It looked like a simple steel pipe bomb, but it was located inside the cage, lying in one corner of the structure. He dropped all pretense of stealth and rushed the door. Maddy cried out and dragged herself up with her hands on the cage's bars.

"Jace! Oh God, Jace."

"Hang on, Maddy. I'll get you."

He tugged on the door but it was locked. He dropped the tire iron and spun around, looking for something to pick the lock. A nail, maybe.

A set of picks lay on a crate nearby. He grabbed them.

Calypso was one sick fuck.

Jace went to work on the lock, freeing it within seconds, then rushed inside. He needed to get Maddy and Angie out of there before the bomb went off. Defusing a bomb wasn't typically done by one guy rushing in and cutting wires. That was a Hollywood solution performed for effect, and Jace knew his chances of setting the thing off were greater if he tried to yank a wire or disturbed the device in any way.

Maddy was already up. Her friend was trying, but her legs were bound. Jace went over and scooped her up. Maddy leaned into his side, her body shivering. He wanted nothing more than to kiss her, but there was no time.

"I knew you would come," she said.

"Come on, baby. There's no time to talk." He started toward the cage door.

Feminine laughter rained down on them. The door slammed shut and the tumblers slipped into place. Calypso walked out from among the crates, shaking her head as she tapped something on her phone screen. "Well, well. Here we are."

Jace put Angie down and then pushed her and Maddy behind him. He peered at Calypso. She was still in shadow, but he could see she was small boned, with medium length gold hair and fine features. She did not look like Maddy, which was both a relief and a frustration. She'd played them all back in Russia for reasons of her own.

Her tattoo was noticeable, and much the way Maddy had described it. Clearly a vanity she hadn't been willing to give up.

Jace threw a desperate glance at the bomb. She'd said he was worth money, but maybe she'd decided to kill him instead. She followed his gaze.

"Oh, it's a fake. I just wanted to see what you'd do. If you'd do the work to save Maddy and Angie or if you'd turn your back and walk away. You're good at abandoning people who need you, aren't you?"

Jace frowned. *What the fuck?*

"I don't know what you're talking about."

"Of course you don't, Nikolai Alexandrovich. You're not only a traitor, you're also a soulless bastard."

She stepped into the light then and tilted her chin up. The truth of who she was staggered him. Knocked the breath out of him. He hadn't seen in her so long now, and she'd grown up a lot. Equal measures of surprise, wonderment, and confusion rocked through him. Behind him, Maddy nudged a little closer, curling her fingers into his shirt as if offering her support. He appreciated that more than he could say.

"Natasha?" he asked in disbelief. "Are you really alive?"

She frowned. "Please don't pretend like you care. You didn't care about me then, or about Mama and Papa. The gulag was brutal, Nikolai. Brutal. And you did not come."

His guts turned to ice. "I didn't know. They told me you were dead. All of you."

"We were, big brother. We *were*."

"Natasha—my God, what happened? Are they still alive?"

She tossed her hair. Looked at him with icy disdain. "No, they are not. I survived because I was young and pretty. And because I could be used. They were executed."

He'd known his parents had been executed. He'd thought she had been too, and he'd mourned her. Natasha was little when they'd been thrown out of the US and returned to Russia. She hadn't grown up with the stigma he had, the doubts. She'd been so bright and pretty and filled with ambition. He hadn't seen her very much once he'd joined the army. She'd matured without him to look out for her like a big brother should.

And she hated him for what had happened to her.

"What happens now?" he asked.

"Many things, Nikolai. First, I'm going to make you regret you were ever born. Then I plan to collect the bounty on you."

It didn't surprise him there was a bounty. He'd always figured he was on a black list of wanted criminals. It had made the trips into Russia heady, but there'd been things to do for Ian and BDI, and he'd been the one who could do them. He knew how to hide in plain sight and he'd done it well.

"I'm sorry, Natasha. I didn't know you were in that place. I would have torn it apart to get you out if I had known."

She snorted. "Such pretty things you say for Dr. Cole's benefit. Please don't bother. She won't live to remember any of it."

Ice water filled his veins. "You said you'd trade her for me. And now you have me. So let them go, Natasha. Let them go and I won't fight you."

She laughed. "Do you think you're in a position to fight? Really, Nikolai—even you, my big bad *Spetznatz* brother, cannot fight your way free of this. You're in a cage, and I'm out here. I see no incentive to do as you ask."

Overhead, the rumble of a helicopter approached. Jace cocked an ear, but he didn't take his gaze off his sister. She was unpredictable, angry, and he didn't know what she might do. The helicopter reached them, but it didn't keep going. He didn't know if it was his Bandit brothers up there, or if Natasha was planning to take them away by helicopter.

She looked up, as if realizing the aircraft wasn't moving away, and frowned. Two seconds later, the windows shattered as commandos infiltrated the building. Natasha jumped at the sounds of shattering glass, but she recovered quickly, pulling her pistol and hurrying around the side of the cage until she had a clear shot—at Maddy.

"Too bad, brother. Now you can feel some measure of what I've felt. *Dosvedanya*, Dr. Cole."

Jace twisted his body—and threw himself at the woman he loved just as his sister pulled the trigger.

Chapter Twenty-Three

MADDY LAY ON THE FLOOR BENEATH A HEAVY BODY while someone screamed. She thought she might have blacked out for a moment, but she shook her head and stared up at the bars of the cage overhead. The screaming turned to sobs.

"Angie? Is that you?"

The sobs turned to hiccups and then Angie was there, bending over her. "You're alive! Oh God, I thought—and now Jace—" Angie shook her head. No more words came out.

The body lying on top of Maddy didn't move. She remembered Calypso with her pistol, and then Jace had leapt in front of her…

Maddy's blood froze solid. "Jace? Jace!"

She struggled to push him, but her hands were bound and trapped between their bodies. Angie was no help because she was bound too. "Jace, oh please. Jace," she pleaded.

There was movement on the perimeter, black-clad bodies approaching with weapons drawn. The cage door rattled as they worked to open it. She couldn't even care any longer. Jace was still and unresponsive. And something warm and wet seeped into her clothing.

Suddenly, the weight of his body was gone. A grease-painted face peered down at her. She recognized the eyes and she clutched the man's shirt. "Ian! She's his sister, Ian. Calypso is Natasha. Oh God, please tell me he's okay."

She started to cry. Ian helped her sit up and sliced away the band around her wrists. She hadn't realized how much it hurt until the band was no longer there. Feeling began to come back with sharp pricks and tingles, shooting pain into her scalp and down her spine.

Her gaze strayed to where two men bent over Jace. There was blood. Too much blood. She felt light-headed, but she swallowed it down and refused to swoon.

"We're going to do everything we can," Ian was saying. She had to jerk her gaze back to his. Had to try and focus on the words.

"I'm going with him," she growled as the men put Jace on a stretcher.

Ian helped her up. "Of course you are. We all are."

"Did you get that bitch?" she asked as Ian helped her to the exit. Angie was just ahead of her, being helped by one of Ian's men as she hobbled along. She'd been cut free too, but her limbs were probably stiff and aching from all the time she'd been bound.

They emerged into night air that smelled of petroleum and fish. There was a van sitting nearby, cargo doors thrown wide open. Inside, a blond-haired woman was chained to a ring on the floor. She turned her head and met Maddy's gaze.

"There's your answer, Dr. Cole," Ian said.

Maddy drew in a deep breath. Then she marched over to the van and stopped, glaring at Natasha. "There's no way in *hell* your brother knew you were alive. He's a decent man with more honor in his pinky finger than you have in your entire body. If he'd known, he'd have done whatever it took to get you out of there."

For the briefest of moments, a flash of anguish crossed Natasha's features. But then her expression hardened again. "You do not know this, Maddy Cole. You only wish it. I, however, have to live with the reality of what was done to me—and the fact my own brother abandoned me to it."

"He didn't. You will never convince me."

Natasha snorted. "You have known him for how long? Please. You will never convince *me*."

Ian slid the door closed, effectively ending the conversation. "Come on, Dr. Cole. You need to concentrate on Jace right now. Forget his sister."

He took her arm and moved her toward another van. "She called him Nikolai."

"Yes."

"You knew?"

"Of course. Who do you think rescued him from that life?"

Maddy blinked as she stared up at this mysterious man with so many secrets.

"The authorities were coming for him too. It wasn't just his parents and Natasha. It was all of them. He got out. They didn't. And believe me, I have regretted that for years."

"But he said his parents were monsters."

Ian sighed. "Relationships with parents are complicated."

She thought of her mother. "Yes, they certainly are. What aren't you telling me?"

"Get in there with Jace. You should be with him at the hospital."

Maddy knew she'd get nothing else from him right then. She climbed inside the van that had been turned into a private ambulance. The men with Jace were still working on him, but his eyes were open. Maddy cried out as she got as close to his face as she could. He reached out and she took his fingers in hers. His grip was good, though not as strong as she might have hoped.

"Maddy."

"I'm here, Jace. I'm fine. She didn't get me." Tears dripped down her cheeks and she dashed them away with her free hand. "She got you, you stupid man. I was supposed to save *you* this time. I'd planned on it and everything, and you had to go and get in the way."

One corner of his mouth lifted. "Always… protect you… Maddy. Told you that."

"I know you did." Her heart thundered in her ears. "And I love you for it," she said in a rush, because she had to say it to him even though she had no idea if he felt the same. Heck, he probably didn't. It was too soon, and most people didn't fall in love in a matter of days. He was going to think she was a crazy stalker and then it would all be over.

He squeezed her hand again. "I love… you… too."

IAN STALKED down the hallway of his secure building and into the waiting cell where he'd had them stash the prisoner. She sat on a chair, secured to the table by chains. Her eyes flashed with anger and hatred. He should be sending her to Guantanamo, but something stopped him from turning her over. For now.

"Natasha Orlova. We thought you were dead," he said by way of greeting.

She frowned. "I was dead. Who are you?"

He sat across from her, studying her features. She was a master of disguise, that much was clear. All the photos of a potential Calypso looked different from the woman in front of him. She wasn't heavy-set.

She was lean and willowy, about five foot five, and fine-boned. She'd worn wigs, padding, platform shoes—whatever it took. Prosthetics too, he'd imagine.

But the mermaid tattoo on her forearm was prominent. She could have covered it, and probably did. But Maddy seeing that had been a bigger break than he could have imagined.

"Ian Black," he said in answer to her question.

Her eyes narrowed. "I've heard of you." She jerked her head toward the door. "Nikolai works for you?"

"Yes. I got him out seven years ago. They were planning to arrest him too."

She snorted. "I don't believe you. You'd say anything right now. Anything to get me to share information. I won't."

He sat back against the seat. Shrugged. She was lovely. Fiery. And evil. He couldn't forget that.

But was she really? He could imagine what she'd been through. They'd broken her, and then they'd built her up in the mold they'd wanted her to be. She was an instrument. A weapon. She'd been indoctrinated. Did he have what it took to undo the damage? Or was he fooling himself out of misplaced guilt?

"Fine. You don't have to tell me anything you don't want to. But yes, Nikolai—Jace now—works for me. I got him out and I gave him a new identity. I could do that for you, too."

For a split second, her expression crumbled. And

then it hardened again. "You have nothing to offer me."

"So tell me what it would take. Tell me, and I'll get it done."

She looked away. Struggled with herself. He could see it happening. She speared him with a glare once more, her steely facade intact. "If what you say is true, why didn't you help us all? Why only him?"

Regret flooded him. He'd fucked it up badly. He'd recruited the Orlovs when they were disillusioned with their lives in Russia and then he'd failed them. They weren't saints, but that didn't matter. "I didn't know there was an arrest order. I didn't know until you and your parents were taken."

"But you got Nikolai out."

"I did."

Her nostrils flared. "So they were right. My parents betrayed us to the Americans."

Ian leaned forward, elbows on the table as he made eye contact. She didn't look away. *Such pretty eyes. Blue.* "You *are* an American, Natasha."

She jerked the chain binding her. "I'm not. That was taken away from me when I was four years old. I am Russian. Russia is a culture. America is simply a place."

Ian leaned back. It was time for a different approach. "You were in the gulag for two years. They weren't kind to you there."

Her eyes flashed. "Do you wish a medal, Ian Black? Your powers of deduction amaze me."

"Would you like to kill those people who hurt you?"

She reared back on her chair. He'd wondered if maybe she was just crazy. Soulless. That she'd killed all the people she'd killed because she liked it. But he had doubts. She wasn't unaffected by emotion. He'd thought she was a psychopath, but now he wasn't so sure.

"Don't promise me that, Ian Black. You can't promise me that." Her nostrils flared, her cheeks reddening.

"And if I can?"

She jerked the chains. "Fuck you. And fuck Nikolai too. Did I kill him? I hope I killed him." She gritted her teeth as she said the words. As if she were hiding great emotion.

"He's alive. You shot wide, Natasha. The bullet went through his arm. Oddly enough, you did the same thing to my other operative. Oh, but you hit an artery there. We almost didn't get to him in time, except that he managed to tourniquet his arm and slow the bleeding. He'll recover, but it'll take longer. You weren't using defensive rounds either, which would have certainly caused more damage. Did you do it on purpose?"

Her cheeks were red. "I was unnerved."

"I doubt anything unnerves you."

She turned her head, her jaw working. He had the strangest urge to put his fingers under her chin and force her to look at him. He didn't do it, though.

"If I accept your offer," she began, "what makes you think I would honor it and not return to… my employers?"

"You mean the Gemini Syndicate? You could. Probably should, in fact. But what if you returned to them—and really worked for me?"

"So you would not give me a new identity. That was a ruse. I see."

"I can. Or you can return to the Syndicate and take down those who hurt you from within. It's up to you."

She didn't say anything for a long moment. "I want to make them pay. But they have something of mine. If I don't return…"

"What do they have, Natasha?"

She looked at him with wide blue eyes that shimmered with tears. Then she shook her head and closed her eyes as she bowed her head. "No. No, I will not risk it. I can't trust you. I can't trust anyone."

Ian reached for her hand. Her fingers were cold, but the arc of sensation that rocked through him at the simple touch was shocking. He didn't know if she felt it too, but she jerked her head up, their eyes clashing. "No, you can't trust anyone," he told her. "You never can. None of us can. But I swear to you that I will help you as I helped Nikolai. Whatever it takes. You just have to give me a little trust. And if I betray your trust, you can shoot me yourself."

She dropped her gaze to their linked hands. She

didn't try to jerk away. She simply stared. "I will think about your offer, Ian Black. It's all I can do."

"Why did you use Dr. Cole? She's innocent."

She lifted her head. Withdrew her hand. He thought that was it. The end of her cooperation, however tenuous. But then she spoke. "I have seen her before. At another collector's home. And while she speaks good Russian, she is American. If the assassination could be blamed on her..." She shrugged.

He understood the subtext. An American scapegoat would play well with the media. And then there was the prospect of worsening relations between the US and Russia, which was certainly the goal of the Gemini Syndicate.

"Was Sokolov really the target that night?"

"If I tell you what you want to know, do I get to leave?"

"Depends on what you tell me."

"I will say anything to get you to let me go. Don't you know that?"

"Yes. But Natasha, I'm the only one who will help you escape. Think of that. The Syndicate doesn't care. I do."

"Fuck you."

He stood. There was nothing more he could do. He'd go away and let her think. If he was right, she'd be an asset. If he was wrong, well, Guantanamo was still a possibility.

"Colonel Isaev," she said as he walked to the door. "Look him up."

He gazed at her for a long moment. She was an enigma. Hard, cold, beautiful. And strangely vulnerable too. Lost. Like him in some ways.

"I will. You have twenty-four hours. I'll need a decision then."

She snorted. "A decision. As if there is a choice. Yes, and you might help me. No, and you will keep me imprisoned. What do you think I will say?"

He grinned. "You'll say yes regardless. But what I want is for you to mean it." He turned to the door, then turned back. "Did you break into Dr. Cole's house?"

"Of course."

"Why? It was rather obvious. I don't think that's your style."

"I wanted to flush Nikolai out. See if he'd respond. He did. They all did. You should really talk to your people."

"The camera?"

"Easy enough to drain the battery with the right equipment."

"And then you found them at the new location."

"Child's play. I tagged her car. Once I had confirmation on the town, I looked to see where they stopped the longest before driving back."

"Care to tell me who you were planning to sell your brother to?"

"Not really."

He didn't think she'd share that one, but he'd had to try. "All right. See you soon, Natasha."

"I'll be counting the minutes."

He almost laughed at her sarcasm. Instead, he stepped through the door. The guard locked it behind him.

Ian didn't stop thinking about Natasha Orlova the entire way back to his office.

Chapter Twenty-Four

JACE'S ARM HURT LIKE FUCKING HELL. IT WOKE HIM from a drugged sleep and he rolled his head on the pillow, trying to focus his attention. Memories crashed in on him. Maddy. The cage. Natasha.

His stomach flipped and his heart squeezed tight. Natasha was alive. His baby sister. He'd thought she was long dead, but she'd emerged from the darkness filled with hatred. And she'd shot him.

Well, she'd shot at Maddy, but he'd intervened.

Natasha was Calypso. He could hardly wrap his mind around it. He'd never gotten even a hint of it from the few grainy photos they'd had. She was clever with her disguises.

He was angry at her for what she'd done to Maddy and Angie, but he couldn't quite hate her. Not yet. Not until he knew she was irredeemable. Because he could still see her little blond head, her sleepy eyes when she'd been four and clinging to him while there were men in their house arresting their parents. She'd cried, and he'd rubbed her back and held her close. What had happened to that baby girl to make her do the things she did now?

Jace didn't know what time it was, but he shifted in the bed and tried to sit up. The room was dark and his arm throbbed.

"Jace?"

He turned toward the voice. "Maddy?"

"Yes. Oh God, you're okay." She flung herself at him, hugging him hard, and he fell back on the bed. The pain he felt was negligible compared to the joy. She was here. Alive.

"Why are you still here?"

She sat up again and sniffed. "Like anyone could make me leave. I've been here since they brought you in."

"When was that?"

"About six hours ago? They gave you painkillers and knocked you out. But you aren't hurt badly. In case you were wondering."

"How long have you been here?"

"Since they brought you in. Where else would I go?"

He dragged her onto the bed with him, even though his arm screamed in pain and she squeaked a protest. "Jace, your arm!"

"Baby, I'll live. We both will." He hugged her tightly. She threaded her arms around him and hugged back.

"I was so scared," she said against his neck. "I thought she'd killed you."

"She didn't." But he didn't know if it was on purpose or because she'd simply missed. Natasha. Baby Natasha. *Fuck.*

"Will you tell me who you are now?"

He held her close, taking strength from her warm body next to his. He loved this woman. Loved her with all his dark heart. And even if it was dangerous for her, how could he keep the truth from her? She'd already endured enough danger because of him. She deserved the truth. Then she could decide for herself.

"You can look it up, *solnishka.* Alex and Susan Oliver were deported for treason against the United States. It's public record. They would have been imprisoned, but when the US offered to trade them for American spies, the deal was accepted. So there was an exchange. It wasn't exciting like in the movies. No bridges were involved. But Alex and Susan, with their children Nicholas and Natasha, flew to Russia and left behind their lives in the US. My parents were citizens. Naturalized, not born. Natasha and I were born citizens. But we were stripped of it when we were deported. I hated my parents for years over that. Natasha was much younger and it didn't affect her as much."

He hated thinking about it, but he needed to. "I became Nikolai Orlov. I was angry and lost, but I eventually embraced him—and my country. I joined the army. The *Spetznatz*, which is like Delta Force or the Navy SEALs, and I did whatever I could for Mother Russia. Then my parents were arrested again, this time for conspiring with the United States, and thrown into prison. So was Natasha. I was next, but Ian helped me escape."

"So you became Jace Kaiser," she said.

"Yes." He hugged her tight, taking comfort in her warmth. "I'm sorry I couldn't tell you the truth."

"I understand, Jace. Your entire existence depended on secrecy. How could you tell someone you'd recently met?"

He tipped her chin toward him so he could meet her eyes. "I could tell you anything, Maddy. I know that now. I just didn't want to endanger you. The less you knew, the better."

"Except that's not true anymore."

"No, apparently not." Ice crackled through him. "Colt—what happened? Do you know anything?"

Maddy stroked his temple, his cheek. Ran her fingers into his hair and over his scalp. It was soothing. Sweet. "He's going to recover. He lost a lot of blood, but he'll make it."

Relief left him weak. Or maybe that was the drugs. *Thank God.*

"Kitty is fine too. The door was open when Calypso—Natasha—shot Colt, but Ian's response team found her under the bed."

"I'm glad." He hadn't known Kitty was in trouble, but he was glad she was okay. Because Maddy loved her. And he loved Maddy.

Jace squeezed her harder. He needed out of here. He needed to go home with her so he could make love to her immediately. "Let's get out of here," he whispered. "So long as you still want to be with me after what I just told you."

"I think you have to wait until morning," she told him. "They want to be sure everything is fine. And of course I want to be with you! Did you think I spent all this time here in an uncomfortable chair just so I could say good bye when you woke up? No. No way. You're stuck with me."

"Fuck this," he growled as he reached for the call button. "We're going home."

MADDY DIDN'T THINK they'd let Jace go, but they did. The hospital they'd been in was private, exclusive, a place apparently set up to receive the kind of clients who might get shot in the line of duty but couldn't actually report it. It was called Riverstone, and the doctor in charge was a lady named Dr. Puckett.

Dr. Puckett didn't take any crap, and she also didn't let Jace go just because he wanted to. She said she'd speak with Ian. Thirty minutes later she was back, and Jace was free.

A car arrived to take them back to her place. When they arrived, Kitty was waiting. So was Ty. He stood and stretched from his position on the couch, smiling at them.

"Hey, there," he said.

Maddy snatched up Kitty and hugged her tight, burying her face in the cat's fur while she tried not to shake apart and sob. Kitty purred, completely nonplussed by her adventures. Jace talked to Ty and then there was silence. Maddy turned to see that Ty had departed.

Kitty began to struggle and Maddy set her down. Jace looked strong and whole, though a big white bandage wrapped around his arm.

"Come here," he said, opening his arms.

Maddy did as he asked, rushing into them and hugging him tight. "You took a bullet for me," she said on a rush. "You shouldn't have done that. Don't ever do that again."

He chuckled and kissed her hair. "Maddy, baby, I'd do it again. And again. I promised you I'd protect you. That's non-negotiable."

She sniffed and tipped her head back so she could meet his eyes. "I don't want you taking any bullets. Not again. Not for me."

He squeezed her ass, and desire flared to life inside her. "I don't intend to, but if I have to I will. You're it for me, Maddy Cole. My reason for being. I'll protect you with my dying breath if I have to."

"Stop," she said, and then she kissed him.

It didn't take long for things to escalate. She worried about his arm, but he said he had no problem being the bottom to her top. And he didn't. He kissed her from head to toe, licked her into a shattering orgasm while she put her knees on either side of his face and gripped the headboard, and then she rolled on a condom and lowered herself onto his hard cock.

She sank down until he was deep inside her, then drew in a breath and let herself just feel everything that bombarded her at that moment. He gazed up at her, hands on her hips, eyes bright.

"I love you, Maddy Cole. I want you to know that."

"I know it. I love you too. It's so crazy, but I do."

"Then fuck me, baby."

Maddy swirled her hips and gasped at the sensation streaking through her. "All night long, honey. Or until one of us is comatose."

He snorted. And then he gripped her hips and drove up into her and Maddy forgot to breathe.

Chapter Twenty-Five

It was a long while later when Maddy woke and went to make coffee. The night was fresh on her mind. The intensity of Jace's lovemaking. The way she felt fierce and happy and determined all at once. He was hers, and she wasn't giving him up without a fight. If he tried to leave again, she was going to knock some sense into him however she could.

Maddy fed the cat, then poured coffee and carried it to the bedroom. Jace was sitting up in bed, looking sleepy and gorgeous at the same time. She climbed into bed with him, handed him coffee, and sipped hers. And then, because she didn't plan to wait, she said what was on her mind.

"If you're thinking about telling me you have to leave me so you can keep me safe, I hope you realize that's a bullshit excuse and I won't accept it this time."

His eyes widened. "I wasn't thinking it, actually."

"Good. Why not?"

"You already know the worst. You know my name. You know my sister is Calypso—hell, I'm still wrapping my head around that one myself. I can't promise it's safe for you now that she's caught but I hope it is."

"You aren't leaving BDI, are you?" She knew he wouldn't, but she had to ask.

"No. It's my job. It's what I do. And I'm probably still a hunted man, Maddy. You need to consider that before you make any plans for the future with me."

She frowned as she remembered her dad and how he'd always been traveling to Russia. He'd spent so much time away, and she'd missed him. There were other things, little things, that hadn't added up at the time. She thought about them now, and she wondered.

"Jace…"

"Yeah, baby?"

"I think my dad might have been a spy."

He took her hand in his, rubbed his thumb in her palm. "I think that's a good guess, Maddy."

She snapped her gaze to his. "Do you know something?"

He sighed. "I know what was in his file. He did some work for the CIA. It wasn't uncommon. Still isn't. As a linguist, he'd have been recruited."

Maddy processed that. Her gut churned but it wasn't a surprise. Not really. Was that what drove her mother away in the end?

"He died under mysterious circumstances. A heart attack, they said. In Moscow."

Jace squeezed her hand. "That's what the file says."

"But nobody knows for sure, do they?"

He kissed her palm and she shivered. "No, I don't think they do."

Maddy withdrew her hand and wrapped her arm around her body. The other still held the coffee. Her heart ached. Her eyes stung.

Jace flipped the sheet back and swung his legs over the bed. He went into the bathroom and when he came back, he was wearing the clothes he'd had on last night.

"Where are you going?" she asked.

He looked at her. "I don't know. But I don't want to hurt you, Maddy. You're upset and I get it. So I'm going to leave so you can process this alone."

Maddy set her coffee down and stood. She'd slipped on one of his T-shirts that he'd forgotten when they'd left for the safe house. It came to mid-thigh, but she was naked beneath it. She popped her hands on her hips and glared. "You're going to abandon me? After everything?"

He looked confused. "Abandon you? I thought you'd want me gone. Your dad was a spy. I knew it and didn't tell you. I didn't tell you a lot of things—I figured you'd had enough of my chaotic existence."

She walked over and poked a finger in his chest. "In case you forgot, mister, I was willing to take a bullet for you—though you beat me to it. I love you, you thick-headed man! I'm going to get mad at you—

I may even yell at you—but you don't need to abandon me every time I look at you cross-eyed. Not ever. I know what I'm getting into, and I want it. I want *you.*"

He just stared at her and she thought he might finally be getting it. He was so used to people failing him, to being on his own and never knowing love and belonging. He'd been running since he was ten years old. But he could stop now because she wasn't leaving him.

He swore and then he swept her up hard against his body and kissed the living daylights out of her. Then he ripped the T-shirt off and worshipped her nipples while she clutched his shoulders and begged him for more.

By the time he tossed her on the bed and came down on top of her, she was wet and ready and hungry for him. He growled as he entered her, his hard cock gliding deep and touching all the sensitive spaces within.

"I love you, Maddy," he groaned against her neck as he exploded a short while later. "I'm never leaving you. Never."

She wrapped her arms and legs around him and held him tight while they trembled and floated back down to earth. "We're in this together," she whispered. "Always."

"Always," he repeated.

JACE STARED at the door to the room Ian had led him to and hesitated. "I'm not sure about this."

"Neither am I. But you need to see her," Ian said. "For your own peace of mind."

"Did she say who's hunting me?"

"She won't share the name, no. But you don't have to worry about it anymore. Nikolai Orlov is dead. He died in that warehouse and nobody's resurrecting him. I've paid people to forget he ever existed."

Jace could only gape at his friend and mentor. "How do you know it's going to work? They didn't forget me before, and I was nobody in the scheme of things."

Ian squeezed his shoulder. "Because I paid a lot of money, that's why. You're clear."

"Natasha knows."

"She does. But she won't talk. It's her skin if she does. The famous Calypso murdered you, Jace. If she goes back on that, she'll endanger her own life with those who will no longer trust her."

"She's going back to the Syndicate."

"I think she is, yes."

"You're risking a lot with her."

Ian's gaze was hooded. "I know."

He gestured and the guard opened the door. Natasha sat in a chair on the far side of the table. She wasn't restrained. Jace's heart squeezed at the sight of her. His pretty baby sister. She'd been so young when he'd been conscripted into the army. When she'd been arrested, she'd barely been nineteen.

He walked inside and the door closed behind him. "Hello, Natasha."

"Nikolai."

"I prefer Jace," he said. He had mixed emotions about her. She was still a blond-haired baby girl in his mind, but she'd also terrified Maddy and Angie and shot Colt. He had a hard time forgiving her for that even if he didn't hate her for it.

She nodded. "Jace then. How are you?"

He went over and dragged out a chair. Sat. "Do you care?"

"I don't know. I'm trying."

He gestured to his arm. "It hurts but I'll live. So will Colt. Either you're a lousy shot or you're beyond amazing."

She grinned and it shocked him. "I like the second one. Let's go with that one."

He put his hands on the table. She didn't reciprocate. "What happened to you, baby girl? What did they do?"

Her grin faded. Her expression hardened. "Nothing I care to share with you."

He reached for her hand. She resisted but ultimately gave up. He stared at her, trying to communicate his heartbreak and sadness for what had happened. There was a human inside that shell. He knew it and he wanted to reach her. "You're my sister.

I love you. If I'd known you were alive I'd have broken down those walls, I swear to you."

"You could not have done so. They would have tortured you too."

He dropped his gaze, furious, hurt, lost. It landed on the mermaid on her arm. It took him a moment, but he realized that mermaid was covering scar tissue. Fury ate at him like acid. He wanted Maddy here with him. She would help him process this. But she was in another room, waiting.

She'd understood that he needed to see his sister. She'd encouraged it. But he knew she was worried. And he knew she didn't much care for Natasha after what she'd done.

But Maddy was still there, waiting with her sunny smile and her warm hugs. Her sweet, sweet beauty that grounded him. He would do anything for her. Anything.

"I'm sorry," he said.

"Yes, well, sorry is such a pretty word. It does nothing though, does it?"

He looked up, speared his gaze into hers. "I swear to you, Natasha—I did not know. I did *not.* I was told you were all executed. There was nothing I could do. If I had known, I would have worked ceaselessly to get you out."

She withdrew her hand. Folded her arms over her chest. "Well, we will never know, will we?"

He didn't know what to do. He wanted her to understand. Wanted to convince her. And then he thought of something. He reached for the pistol tucked into his waistband and withdrew it. Natasha flinched. But he grabbed her hand, put the pistol in it, wrapped her fingers around it. She was deadly with a weapon and he knew it. His baby sister.

"I swear to you on my life, Natasha. If you don't believe me, shoot me." He pulled her hand up, placed the barrel against his chest. His heart thumped and Maddy filled his head. *What the hell are you doing?*

But he knew. He had to do it. If he had any chance at a normal life, a life where he wasn't being hunted, he had to convince this woman right here that he was in her corner. That he'd never abandoned her or forgotten her.

A tear leaked down her cheek. Her lips trembled. He dropped his hand away and she shoved the pistol harder against his chest. For a moment he thought he'd made a mistake.

But then she dropped the weapon on the table and shook her head. "I don't know what I believe, Nikolai—Jace. But my will to kill you is gone."

He holstered the weapon, shaking a little as he did so. Then he got up and went around the table, bent down and wrapped his arms around her. She didn't reciprocate, but she shook.

"You're my sister and I love you. In spite of what you did to Maddy. But Natasha, if you ever come for her again—if you ever harm a hair on her head, I swear to you that I will end you. There will be no place you can hide, no sanctuary that will protect you. I'll kill you without a second thought."

She started to laugh. Then she pushed him away. He dropped his arms and stood. "You are weak over that woman. That's how I found you. Your weakness. Are you sure she's worth it?"

"I'm sure."

She stared straight ahead. "I won't see you again," she said. "When I am free, I'm returning to Russia."

"You don't have to. You can stay. Ian will fix everything."

Her gaze was hot. "There are some things even he cannot fix." She shook her head. "I'm going. But you don't have to fear me anymore. I won't be back. Not for you, not for Maddy Cole. I have other things to take care of."

Jace sucked in a breath. Then he bent and kissed her forehead. Swiftly, before she could react. "Take care of yourself, baby sister. If you ever need me, I'm here. All you have to do is ask."

He walked out of the room without a backward glance. He couldn't walk the path with her. But he hoped she'd find her way again.

He strode down the hall and into the waiting area where Maddy sat on a chair. She jumped up as he entered. Then she rushed over and threw her arms around him, squeezing him tight. He squeezed back.

Love flooded him, crowding out the unhappiness and hurt. This woman. She was everything. He tipped her head back and kissed her. She clung to him. She'd filled all the empty spaces inside him, made him whole again.

"Are you okay?" she asked when he let her breathe.

He smiled down at her. "Yes, I'm fine. Natasha is who she is, but I don't think she's completely lost. There's hope for her."

"I pray you are right." She smiled a watery smile and he knew her tears were for him. For how his emotions might be in chaos right now. God, he loved her. No one else cared for him as she did.

"I love you, Maddy Cole."

She patted his chest. "I love you too, Jace Kaiser."

"Come on, babe. Let's go to lunch. Then we're going back to your place and doing what I should have done to you the first day we kissed."

She snorted. "You will never get over giving orders, will you?"

He laughed. "Okay, okay. Would you like to go to lunch and then go home and have an orgasm or several?"

She put her arm in his. "I thought you would never ask."

Epilogue

TWO WEEKS LATER...

MADDY WAS NERVOUS.

Jace squeezed her hand. "Baby, relax. It's going to be okay."

"She might not recognize me today. How can I introduce you to her if she doesn't recognize me?"

Jace stopped her. They were walking toward the entrance of the Oaks, and she was about to vibrate apart with anxiety. It was a gorgeous sunny day, with birds singing and a soft breeze, and Maddy wasn't enjoying any of it. She wanted Mimi to meet Jace, but she was having second thoughts. Not because she didn't want Jace to meet her grandmother, but because she couldn't predict what her grandmother would do or say.

He put his hands on her arms as if imparting

strength. "Maddy, it's okay. If she thinks I'm the janitor, I don't care. If she thinks I'm her long lost boyfriend from high school, it's okay. Doesn't matter. We're going to see her, you're going to love her like you always do, and we're going to leave again without you loving her any less. Don't worry about it. I'm fine."

"You're too good to be true, you know that?"

He grinned. "So you said this morning after that thing we did in the shower."

And there came the heat in her cheeks. She laughed. "Rotten man. Making me blush before we go inside."

He took her hand and kissed it. "Come on, let's go."

Mimi was in her room, sitting by the window with a book. She looked up as the nurse announced she had a visitor. Her whole face lit up with joy. "Hello, honey," she said as Maddy went over and gave her a kiss on the cheek. Her gaze drifted to Jace standing in the doorway. "Oh, you brought my son with you. Oh my goodness, Christopher, where have you been?"

Maddy panicked. "No, Mimi—"

"Hello, Mama," Jace said, walking over and taking the hand Mimi held out. He knelt beside her, holding her hand gently, and Maddy's heart filled with love and sorrow at the same time. "I've been working. I see you're looking beautiful as always."

"This is my son," Mimi said to the nurse. She said it so proudly. The nurse said all the appropriate things even though she knew Jace wasn't Mimi's son. Jace met Maddy's gaze over Mimi's head while Mimi held on to his hand tightly and started to talk about whatever popped into her head. He smiled to let her know it was okay.

And it was. They stayed for an hour, until Mimi began to drift off to sleep. She'd held Jace's hand the entire time. They walked back to the car and Maddy sucked in a breath so she wouldn't cry. Jace took her in his arms and held her beneath the shade of the tree he'd parked under.

"Baby. It's okay. She's happy."

She clutched him. But she didn't cry. Acceptance settled over her at last. "You're right, she is. And you were wonderful. I didn't know she'd think you were my dad. Thank you for playing along."

"Honey, if she thinks I'm him every time, I don't care. She might not ever know that I'm your husband, but that's okay."

Maddy blinked. Then she tipped her head back to gaze up at him. "Husband?"

He looked a little uncertain for the first time since she'd known him. Jace, uncertain? Her badass protector? Her warrior?

"Yeah. I was hoping maybe… Someday… When you're ready…"

"Yes."

His eyebrows lifted. "Yes? That's it, just yes?"

Maddy laughed as she stood on tiptoe to kiss him. "You looked like you needed a basic answer you could process before you died of embarrassment on the spot."

He laughed too. "I'm not embarrassed. But I've never asked anyone to marry me before."

"You still didn't. Not really. But that's okay. I like the side of you that gives me orders. It's a turn on."

"I didn't order you to marry me." He sounded indignant.

"Of course you didn't. But you would have it you'd thought it would work."

"Yeah, I would have. Marry me, Maddy Cole. Be my wife and have my children—assuming you want kids—and let's grow old together."

"I do want kids, and yes, I want to grow old with you."

"Then it's settled."

"It is. There's only one thing left that I still need to do to you."

His blue eyes sharpened. "What's that?"

"Hand cuffs, baby. Your turn to spend some time in them while I have all the control."

He shuddered, but she didn't think it was in a bad way. "I only cuffed you because I thought you'd kill us all if I didn't."

"I know. But I still get a turn. Maybe you'll like it."

"Maybe I will."

"Only one way to find out."

"That's true." He swatted her ass. "Get in the car, babe. We're going home. Now."

ONE MONTH LATER...

"YOU ARE JUST the picture of domestic bliss, my friend," Brett Wheeler said as Jace stood at the grill and flipped burgers.

Jace grinned. "You think?" He picked up his light beer and sipped it. His gaze sought out Maddy. She was sitting at the big table they'd put in the backyard, chatting with Angie.

"Yep, look at you. Living here in this cute little house with your pretty art historian, flipping burgers in the backyard, a cat inside. All that's left is a wedding ring and a baby."

"Yeah, maybe so."

"She domesticated you. Never thought I'd see the day."

"It happens, my friend. You better watch out."

Brett snorted. "Oh no, man. Not me. Been there, done that. Not doing it again. I married the mega bitch from hell. Barely escaped with my balls intact." He tipped his chin toward where Colt sat near Angie Turner. "Look at poor Colt. He wants that girl so bad and she won't give him the time of day."

Jace had yet to figure that situation out. When Colt was injured, Angie had visited him in the hospital a few times. Then she'd come around

Maddy's house a few times when Colt was hanging out, but lately she'd started freezing him out.

"Yeah, well maybe she's not the one for him."

"Somebody better tell Colt."

"I'm sure he'll figure it out."

Brett looked up and cheered. "The boss is here."

Ian swaggered into the yard, grinning. He held up two six packs of beer. "Brought the good stuff. How's it going, friends?"

Ian went over to the table to greet everyone. Brett peeled off and went to join them. After a few minutes, Ian got up and walked over to where Jace still stood at the grill, watching the burgers and enjoying the sheer American normalcy of having a cook out.

"How you doing, Jace?"

"Never better. You?"

Ian shrugged. Jace knew he'd never get the real story out of Ian. He was a man who held his emotions in check and played his cards close to the chest. He shot at look at the gathering around the table.

"I have to admit I didn't think this would work out for you, but damn if you don't look like a natural."

Jace laughed. "Even mercenaries get to have lives."

"Yep."

"You hear anything from the Syndicate?" What he meant was anything about Natasha, but he didn't have to say it. Ian knew.

"Nope. Nothing yet."

"I still don't know why you let her go." He was

somewhat upset about it, but Ian knew what he was doing. He hoped.

"She wanted to go. If she decides to help us, she'll be more effective there."

"Yeah, but what she must have went through—"

"Let it go, Jace. She's twenty-six. Old enough to make her own decisions. We can't change what happened to her, but we can be there when she needs us."

"If she needs us."

"She will."

He looked so certain that Jace just shook his head and flipped a burger.

"So let me get this straight," Ian said. "You and Colton and Ty and Brett paid Mr. Tom Walls a visit in his garage last week?"

"Would have done it sooner but Colt wanted to be involved."

"Did you break his balls for him?"

"He won't bother Angie again. I'm not sure he'll bother anybody. He has a very fine understanding of consent now."

Ian laughed and slapped him on the back. "You kids. So crazy. The things you do without telling Daddy."

Jace snorted. "You'd have gone with us if you knew we were going."

Ian's expression darkened. "No, I'd have gone alone—and they'd have never found the body."

Jace met Ian's gaze. He didn't know what was

behind those words, but he understood that Ian meant them. "I hear you, boss."

"Hurry up with those burgers, would you? I'm starved."

"Coming right up."

Ian wandered back to the table, beer in hand. Maddy got up and came over to put her arms around Jace. He kissed the top of her head. "Everything good?" she asked.

"Better than good," he told her. "Everything is perfect."

Who's HOT?

Alpha Squad

Matt "Richie Rich" Girard (Book 0 & 1)
Sam "Knight Rider" McKnight (Book 2)
Billy "the Kid" Blake (Book 3)
Kev "Big Mac" MacDonald (Book 4)
Jack "Hawk" Hunter (Book 5)
Nick "Brandy" Brandon (Book 6)
Garrett "Iceman" Spencer (Book 7)
Ryan "Flash" Gordon (Book 8)
Chase "Fiddler" Daniels (Book 9)
Dex "Double Dee" Davidson (Book 10)

Commander

John "Viper" Mendez (Book 11)

Deputy Commander

Alex "Ghost" Bishop

Echo Squad

Cade "Saint" Rodgers (Book 12)
Sky "Hacker" Kelley (Book 13)
Dean "Wolf" Garner (Book 14)
Malcom "Mal" McCoy (Book 15)
Jake "Harley" Ryan (HOT WITNESS)
Jax "Gem" Stone
Noah "Easy" Cross
Ryder "Muffin" Hanson

SEAL Team

Dane "Viking" Erikson (Book 1)
Remy "Cage" Marchand (Book 2)
Cody "Cowboy" McCormick (Book 3)
Cash "Money" McQuaid (Book 4)
Alexei "Camel" Kamarov (Book 5)
Adam "Blade" Garrison (Book 6)
Ryan "Dirty Harry" Callahan (Book 7)
Zach "Neo" Anderson

Black's Bandits

Ian Black
Brett Wheeler
Jace Kaiser
Colton Duchaine
Jared
Rascal
? Unnamed Team Members

Freelance Contractors

Lucinda "Lucky" San Ramos, now MacDonald (Book 4)
Victoria "Vee" Royal, now Brandon (Book 6)
Emily Royal, now Gordon (Book 8)
Miranda Lockwood, now McCormick (SEAL Team Book 3)
Bliss Bennett, (Book 13)

Also by Lynn Raye Harris

HOT Heroes for Hire: Mercenaries

Black's Bandits

Book 1: BLACK LIST - Jace & Maddy

Book 2: BLACK TIE - Coming Soon!

Book 3: BLACK OUT Coming Soon!

The Hostile Operations Team Books

Book 0: RECKLESS HEAT

Book 1: HOT PURSUIT - Matt & Evie

Book 2: HOT MESS - Sam & Georgie

Book 3: HOT PACKAGE - Billy & Olivia

Book 4: DANGEROUSLY HOT - Kev & Lucky

Book 5: HOT SHOT - Jack & Gina

Book 6: HOT REBEL - Nick & Victoria

Book 7: HOT ICE - Garrett & Grace

Book 8: HOT & BOTHERED - Ryan & Emily

Book 9: HOT PROTECTOR - Chase & Sophie

Book 10: HOT ADDICTION - Dex & Annabelle

Book 11: HOT VALOR - Mendez & Kat

Book 12: HOT ANGEL - Cade & Brooke

Book 13: HOT SECRETS - Sky & Bliss

Book 14: HOT JUSTICE - Wolf & Haylee

Book 15: HOT STORM - Mal ~ Coming Soon!

The HOT SEAL Team Books

Book 1: HOT SEAL - Dane & Ivy

Book 2: HOT SEAL Lover - Remy & Christina

Book 3: HOT SEAL Rescue - Cody & Miranda

Book 4: HOT SEAL BRIDE - Cash & Ella

Book 5: HOT SEAL REDEMPTION - Alex & Bailey

Book 6: HOT SEAL TARGET - Adam & Quinn

Book 7: HOT SEAL HERO - Ryan & ?? ~ Coming soon!

The HOT Novella in Liliana Hart's MacKenzie Family Series

HOT WITNESS - Jake & Eva

7 Brides for 7 Brothers

MAX (Book 5) - Max & Ellie

7 Brides for 7 Soldiers

WYATT (Book 4) - Max & Ellie

About the Author

Lynn Raye Harris is the *New York Times* and *USA Today* bestselling author of the HOSTILE OPERATIONS TEAM SERIES of military romances as well as twenty books for Harlequin Presents. A former finalist for the Romance Writers of America's Golden Heart Award and the National Readers Choice Award, Lynn lives in Alabama with her handsome former-military husband, two crazy cats, and one spoiled American Saddlebred horse. Lynn's books have been called "exceptional and emotional," "intense," and "sizzling." Lynn's books have sold over three million copies worldwide.

To connect with Lynn online:
www.LynnRayeHarris.com
Lynn@LynnRayeHarris.com

Made in the USA
Monee, IL
26 December 2022